D1527935

BATTLE MINER

A SLICE OF LIFE HAREM FANTASY

KIRK MASON

Need to contact me?

kirkmasonbooks@gmail.com

CHAPTER
ONE

I needed a change. The two-minute-slow clock above the boss's desk ticked its monotone song. I knew it'd be a bad day as soon as I noticed the ticking. It droned on in my skull, each second passing by painfully slowly.

I'd read somewhere that the brain is designed to detect the new, the exciting, the unknown.

Behold the civil servant, I thought, *bemoaning the sound of a clock.* One of the few things I was qualified to fix if it broke.

It shouldn't have been like that. I worked for the city government. It was far from glamorous, but I wanted to help people. Somebody had to punch in numbers, make sure that the infrastructure was up to code, and have access to every number of every department to respond to every possible need.

Instead of doing any of those things, I found ways to look busy. We played an endless game of *that's not my depart-ment,* pushing any poor sap who came looking on to the next person down the line. To do something—anything at all—required permits and signed authorization. Nobody wanted to be bothered, which meant that no one person could do anything.

Thus, I found myself staring blankly at my computer, half-heartedly hoping that the girl from *The Ring* would crawl through the monitor and take me away from the situation.

Nope.

I kept on double-checking memos and forms, but there was nothing for me to do.

The office around me was sparsely furnished, consisting of a couple of cubicles and a perpetually empty water cooler, because we were moving offices soon. Apparently, we needed a bigger staff. There weren't enough people spreading two hours of work over a much longer shift.

Suddenly, a tote of loose papers crashed onto my desk, and I nearly jumped out of my chair. It may as well have been Sadako clawing her way toward me, for how much it freaked me out.

"Ha! Careful, Jim," a voice said.

Misspeaking my name through an uncomfortably large grin of bleached white teeth was the boss, Nate Olson.

"The movers found some loose paperwork," he said, "while loading the old records into the vans. I'd like you to sort through them. See if there's anything worth keeping. Thanks."

He smacked my shoulder and moved back toward his desk without waiting for my reply. I blinked after him, unimpressed. *What does it say,* I thought, *that the boss knows none of us are too busy to take on a sudden task?*

I shrugged. *Whatever.* It was a change of pace. I took it.

I quickly realized that the papers were pointless. A couple receipts that'd likely fallen out of someone's pocket. Some faded to-do lists. A few voided memos.

Suddenly, something caught my eye: an envelope with my name, *Jack Calvinson*, on it. There was an unusual weight to the envelope, I shook it, and something jingled inside.

Confused, I opened it.

Three keys on a small keyring fell from the packet, clattering on top of my desk. I didn't recognize them, and I certainly hadn't lost any keys, so that was more than a little unusual. There was also a bundle of papers stapled together. An official letterhead greeted me when I unfolded it: Acanth Village Department of Industry and Agriculture.

Acanth? Why did that sound familiar?

My great grandfather.

He'd been a miner, delving into the earth in search of treasures like something out of a movie.

Well, he was actually after ore, but digging for lost treasure was a fun thought.

If memory served, he'd owned the mine and managed a whole team of workers, from miners to cooks to cleaning staff. They all worked together to keep the mine and its facilities in order, there was no passing the job on to the next person.

I hadn't seen him since I was seven years old, and that'd been the second of two occasions when I saw him. He'd fallen out with my parents over something or other.

Who was he? What was his work like? I didn't remember. There was such a vast difference in our work. His was back-breaking, mine was mind-numbing.

How far we've come, I thought with a roll of my eyes as I picked up the letter.

The message was bloated by legalese and technical terms, but the contents were as obvious as they were unbelievable. My great grandfather had given me the Antrum Estate, which included his house and the mine.

Wait, I thought. *The mine is, well...mine?*

I lost count of the times I read that paper before the contents broke through to me. The document had been given to the city office to bestow ownership of the mine to me, requiring only my signature. Somehow, it'd gotten lost in the endless flow of paperwork. A massive estate way out in rural nowhere sat waiting for me. With it came the mine and all the necessary equipment.

The biggest detail came in the next line. A caveat. The mine belonged exclusively to me, but the house, land, and money were split between me and three other people. It specifi-cally said that while I owned the place, I was not allowed to evict any of the three.

"What the hell?" I muttered to myself. I didn't have any cousins or other relatives that I knew of.

No matter how hard I tried, I couldn't remember the mine, or my distant relative. There was a fuzzy image of playing with a miner's daughter, but that was it.

I considered it for a moment. If nothing else, I had the strength for it. Sure, I was an office worker, but I hit the gym regularly, so I was in decent shape. *Medication through physical exertion,* I liked to call it. I had never lost the childhood need to move. Being sedentary brought frustration and even a little anxiety. I'd never been able to be comfortable unless I moved. So, I consumed my true crime trash through podcasts instead of TV, on the treadmill instead of the couch.

The only problem was that I didn't know a damn thing about mining.

"As if." I put down the letter. Exercising was a lot different from the back-breaking work of mining, and I had no idea how to actually run a mine or anything involved with it.

It did bring one resolution, though.

After work, I would call the number on the form. Even if it was ridiculous, it had to be sorted out. What about the three employees, too? Who were they? They ought to know that they wouldn't be getting a new boss any time soon.

The letter moved to the side of my desk, and the thought to the back of my mind. I worked through the rest of the tote. Nothing else of interest came up. The only remaining question was where to put the damn thing. Sadly, the only way to find out was to talk to Olson. I stood and picked it up. On impulse, I grabbed the envelope to ask about it.

Olson sat looking at his monitor, holding his chin with a look of obviously fake interest. When he looked up to me, the interest was equally fake. "How can I help you, Jim?" he asked.

"It's Jack," I deadpanned. "I sorted everything. Most of it's junk, but there are a few things that we're supposed to keep on record. Where should I put it?"

"Trash the trash and pass the rest to the moving crew."

It seemed like the only chance to ask about the letter, so I said, "Hey, Olson?"

"Please, call me Mr. No. I have the initials, why not use them. Too bad I'm not a doctor, eh? Dr. No. Get it?"

I got it. It was a James Bond reference. I got it the last hundred times he brought it up, too.

"Mr. No," he said, obviously satisfied with himself.

Everyone in the building refused to call him that.

I slid the envelope from my pocket and placed it on his desk. "I found this. It was addressed to me. Any idea why I never got it?"

"Must have been a misfiling." He opened the papers and looked at it like a hungover man reading the drunk texts of the previous night. After a few moments, he laughed. The sound was loud and booming, distracting more than a few people. Some of my co-workers winced at the sound.

"Oh, this is rich," he said. "I had no idea you came from a mining family. Do people still even do that?" He snorted a laugh that flared his nostrils. "Well, not in the civilized world, anyway. But I suppose you're right to ask. This sort of thing does require paperwork and signatures, if only to push it away. Take care of it over your lunch break, will you?"

He pushed the envelope across his desk, losing interest in me before he'd even fully turned to his monitor.

I bit my tongue, took the documents, and walked away. Taking the tote to the first floor, the office seemed bleaker than usual. Each department was a sad copy of the last. Sterile white walls. Old computers. Overstuffed filing cabinets. Hunched shoulders feeding an endless workload. How many of these people had come in with my naivete?

A movie shot came to mind. I imagined a lateral tracking shot, cutting between me with my pointless load and my great grandpa with ore. His shoulders stooped from labor, mine from excessive computer time. Him trapped from daylight by stone, me by fluorescent lights and curtains. I nodded curtly to an ever-revolving lineup of unfamiliar coworkers, while he spoke to the team members who respected and trusted him.

I hated my own uselessness.

This couldn't be it, right? There had to be some way to do real work, to help people. As always, the situation made no sense. The job had separated me from the community I wanted to help. Even at the gym, I was so bored and anxious from the day that I needed it as meditation. I closed off the world and forgot about my dream of helping others.

By the time I got back to my desk and lunch rolled around, I caught myself staring at the letter. I made my way to the breakroom.

Olson was there, waiting on the coffeemaker. When he saw me, he said, "I still can't imagine it. Hard to believe there are still mines in the world."

"It's kind of necessary work," I said in an even tone.

"I suppose, but who thinks about that sort of thing? The whole point is to move beyond all that, right?" He looked up at me and for once his smile seemed genuine. "You're doing well, by the way. I could imagine you getting a promotion once we move offices."

I blinked. "Seriously?" I asked. I should have felt happy, overjoyed even, but instead I felt...nothing.

No, worse than nothing, I felt dissatisfied.

"Oh yeah. I've never once seen you take a sick day. You hand in your work on time, volunteer to help with odd tasks, and work through lunch on the rare days we have serious assignments. I respect the long game you've played, Jack. We've noticed you. It's a thin line to toe, but you've got it, doing everything short of asking for a raise."

"I'm just doing my job." I shrugged. I didn't feel any pride in it—or in the praise from a guy like Olson.

He chuckled. "Sure." He nodded and winked at me.

I frowned. His words bit at me. The comments about my relative's livelihood, accusing me of brown-nosing when I barely felt competent, brushing off misplacing my letter for months.

"I mean it, Olson," I said firmly, "This is the job. We're trying to help the city," I said firmly.

"Oh, I'm glad you brought that up." He took the cup of coffee and poured in a spoonful after spoonful of sugar and what looked like a half a gallon of milk as he spoke. "This is more a personal suggestion than a professional one, but be mindful, alright? Sometimes when we have clients, you get some personal feelings involved. We have to take care of the office, alright? More than that, the most important thing is to look out for number one. It won't do you any good to get tangled in other people's lives."

I blinked. "Isn't it our job to be involved?" I asked, ire rising in my belly.

"A moving slogan, but no." He sipped his coffee, if it could even still be called that. "We make the paperwork look good and make sure that the numbers add up. We keep things functional. You're also missing the perk of this job. Yes, we work for the city, but with enough time and the right title, the city works for us."

My mind went blank and I stared at him. Slowly, it dawned on me, too slowly, considering all I'd seen while I worked here.

Olson didn't care about people. He didn't care about helping them. He didn't want to make the world a better place.

He was just out for himself.

"Don't look so down, Jack. Hang in there." He slapped me on the back with a broad grin. " If you'd like, I'll even put in a recommendation for your promotion. Imagine the PR," he said, and swept his hands apart like he saw a name in neon lights, "from a family of nothing you worked your way to civility. That story goes a long way in the right circles. People love a self-made man."

"Don't even go there," I warned.

Olson rolled his eyes. "What? Are you offended on behalf of a dead man? You can't get hung up on these things. You'll never get ahead if you try to hold hands with the people around you. They'll just hold you back."

There it was.

The straw that broke the camel's back.

My boss spat on my entire reason for taking this job. He insulted my family and told me to use my history as a puff piece. Olson didn't want to use this position to work for people, he wanted it to work for him. His words fuelled the frustration that'd been building all my adult life.

I spoke without thinking, but didn't regret the words one bit:

"I quit."

CHAPTER
TWO

I have not thought this through.

That thought absorbed all others from the moment I told off my boss. It remained when I signed the paperwork, when I handed in my notice of resignation, and it was definitely still there when I loaded the rental car.

Why was I doing this? Why had the thought possessed me to go to a city I hadn't seen since I was a child? No, it wasn't even a city. It had been a village, right?

Why was my memory about it so fuzzy?

The drive was long enough that I couldn't ignore the stupidity of the decision. Even my playlist mocked me. I skipped the track when Axl Rose's nasally croon asked, 'where do we go now?' I tried putting on the Johnny Cash cover of *Dark as a Dungeon*, hoping to find some solidarity in a song about going 'down in the mines.' No such luck. All it did was drive home how little experience I had with the actual work.

Eventually, after dozens of miles of forest, I broke through a green treeline to find my grandpa's estate. It seemed to sneak up on me. The forest ended in an unnaturally straight line, with the opening for the road carved like some gate to a separate world. The village lay further along the heavily cracked, two-lane road, around the curve of the forest.

The house itself was as I remembered. It looked like an optimist had refurbished Norman Bates's house. Three floors of red brickwork stood on a green hill of manicured grass. The late afternoon sun glinted off spotless windows. I thought I could see some motion behind one of them, but it was impossible to be sure.

I'd expected to find it looking like the abandoned place in *Fight Club*. Instead, I couldn't get over how clean it was. It must have been the other three who were mentioned in the will. Maybe, I thought, this would be easy. If they kept the property this nice, they might just have everything working better than I remembered. Maybe I could come in, contribute, and we'd all earn a fortune together.

Of course not. Even getting out of the rental car and pulling the key from the city office out of my pocket, I knew that. Still, it was nice to imagine. I held that optimism all the way to when I put my hand on the door handle.

Instantly, the door flew open and a strong hand grabbed me by the collar, yanking me inside.

A flash of bright blue eyes and ginger hair pinned me against the wall. Sharp points dug into the arm pinned against my back. A growling, feminine voice said, "You're awfully bold, thief."

"What? This is my—"

The points dug as a furred grip clamped down on my shoulder. "Nobody comes out here. You expect me to buy your excuses? Save your breath."

I didn't respond at first, but I swore from the glimpse of her she looked familiar. It was probably wishful thinking.

She shoved me back to the open door. "Get out of here before I change my mind! We don't need your trouble!"

I finally got a good look at her, and a spark of recognition lit my face.

I knew who this girl was.

"Tabitha?" I asked.

Her anger vanished as if doused with a bucket of icy water.

Glowing sapphire eyes gaped. Two pointed cat ears flew up in surprise—I'd thought them a fashion choice, but they seemed real, even as I told myself they couldn't be. She had short red hair that flared out under her ears. Her lips, only a second ago in a sneer, relaxed. The sharp teeth stayed in view, a silent warning.

"Who are you?" she demanded.

"It's me, Jack."

I couldn't believe it. I used to play with this girl in the field by this house when we were kids. She'd changed as much as I had. Toned, golden-tanned arms led to slender fingers tipped with sharp claws. The rough outline of abs stretched beneath a gray sports bra. I gawped just as hard as she did. I may have had the deed, but she *owned* the space around us. The confidence, the presence, and bluntly, the muscles, left me almost speechless.

Fluffy ears. A fluffier tail. Pointy canines? It was so unreal my brain took time to catch up, to really process what I saw, and when it did, it couldn't deny the sight before me.

With effort, I forced myself to think practically. This beautiful woman, my one-time childhood playmate, was a gorgeous creature of fantasy. Did that mean my yet-to-be-seen co-worker and roommates would be too?

I could fawn later. *Focus*, I thought. *Time to communicate.*

"I'm Jack Calvinson," I said, holding my hands up defensively, hoping she wouldn't see me as a threat. "My great grandpa owned the mines. It's in the letter in my jacket."

She searched for it, and I appreciated the lack of claws near my windpipe. Her hands moved quickly and roughly as they went through my pockets.

Once she found the papers, she stood back. Even this motion was unbelievable. Her head pulled back and up, and the rest of her followed in a fluid, full-body undulation. The pose was every bit as striking as the ears and the tail. She turned away, gripping the letter with both hands. She paced as she read it. The claws had retracted to look like human nails.

As she paced, I watched her, trying to fully register the existence of the person in front of me. Her full lips formed the words on the paperwork, quickly working through them. Her tail swayed back and forth in time with her steps. The sweatpants looked as if they were made just for her. A few buttons were on the upper part of the back side, and her tail poked out through the space of two undone center buttons. Tabitha's back was as hypnotically toned as the rest of her.

I got up, leaned on the rail of the porch, and waited for her.

The paper seemed to confuse her as much as it had confused me. She flipped back and forth through the pages, rattling them. "This doesn't make any sense."

"How do you think I feel?" I replied.

"What?" She turned to me.

I drew cat ears in the air above my head. "All this? And the tail? And...I have no idea what's going on."

Tabitha rubbed her eyes and muttered something I couldn't hear. "The ears get you, really? You remembered my name, but not that I have a tail?"

"Hey, I was seven, okay? I couldn't even remember what this place looked like. Hell, I can't remember what my great grandpa looked like."

Tabitha listened and nodded. Her thumb rose to her chin and a finger to her mouth. The tail spun inquisitively. "You don't remember this place vividly. That's what you said, right?"

"Yeah."

"Look, Jack. This is important, okay. Tell me, did your memories get any clearer when you drove through the treeline?"

"Maybe? It was mostly when I got a good look at your face."

She looked slightly taken aback at that, but she quickly recovered. "Okay. Visual connection. It may have just taken a moment for your memories to reset after you recrossed the border."

"I'm sorry, border?"

"Yes, the magical line separating Acanth from your world. Tell me, what exactly did you remember before you got here, and when exactly did the memories come back?"

Is she suggesting that there's a magic border in the trees that would affect people's memory? I wondered. That...might actually make sense. I would sooner believe in magic than in my phone's map not knowing about an entire village.

"Um, I had a vague memory of you," I said. "I knew that I had visited, and that I'd played with a miner's kid. I didn't remember your name until I saw the black spots in your ear fur."

Her tail and ears struck out straight. "Dammit," she muttered. "I'll need to dye that again." She scowled, then shook her head. "Okay...Huh. Memories influenced by magic usually take a second to come together. It might have just been awkward timing. She looked at the papers again. "This was sent out over a year ago. Why'd you only show up now?"

"The paper had gotten misfiled," I said. "I only found it when we were clearing out the office."

"Well, it came from a village that doesn't exist in your world. That might make it difficult for the mail." She read it again, a mix of frustration and curiosity playing on her face.

"Okay, it says you own part of the house and part of the mine."

"All the mine."

"What?"

"I own part of the house with you and two others, yeah. But the paper says that I'm the sole owner of the mine," I explained.

She checked again, then groaned. "Great. Just perfect. Wonderful. Shit." She tapped the paper several times, looking me over as she did so. "Well, I have no idea what to tell you. All I know about this is that I don't like it. Nobody's been in the mine in years, and no human has been here since, well, your great grandfather. You seem to be taking the whole magic and animal people thing well, by the way."

"I'm trying not to think about it too hard. My life is pretty messy at the moment."

"That much is obvious. Who the hell wants a mine in the middle of nowhere? I guess there's no chance I can get you to piss off back home, is there?" She shook her head. "No, never mind. You've already passed the barrier, and you even have a damn invitation. I guess that means we need to get you sorted out. You probably can't stay in Acanth, but we'll fix something for you."

She said it all as if everything made perfect sense. I found this more frustrating than the leg sweep or the scratches that burned on my arms. It was clear that she was used to answering her own questions. It made me feel like a spectator rather than a participant.

"What was your relationship with my grandpa anyway?" I asked.

"Oh, don't go getting jealous." She rolled her eyes toward the ceiling.

"I wasn't, just curious."

"I suppose it would be fair to tell you the whole story."

I nodded. *Finally, some answers.*

"We worked for him, and I guess he thought we were all dependent on the mine. He probably felt guilty that we all lost our jobs when the mine closed, so he put us in his will... Well, the three of us who remained in town. Honestly, the guy was a total recluse, nobody knew him. We thought he was a great boss because he never showed his face at the mine. These days, I feel bad about that, considering what he did for us after."

I mused on the words for a moment, trying to ignore the surge of guilt at wondering where the hell I was during all this.

I wouldn't get any answers from my great grandfather, but still I asked, "Where was he buried?"

Tabitha squinted at me. "His ashes were thrown off a cliff overlooking the village, as per his wishes. You're his relative and you don't know that?"

"Ouch," I said. "Fine. Tabitha. Forget that. What happens next?"

"Call me Tabby. And isn't it obvious?" She shoved the papers into my chest. Turning away, she added, "We're going to the civic center. Someone in Acanth invited you here, so we're going to them."

"Okay. Why are you going back into the house, then?"

"I need a shirt, obviously."

As she stepped into the house, it began to sink in. Regardless of magic or animal people or anything, it was *my* house.

And there was nothing left for me outside of this town.

I grabbed my backpack and approached the house.

Opening the door for the second time, I took my first good look at the house. The most striking thing was how clean everything was. It was beautiful, but just a little off.

As soon as I stepped inside, I saw a little entrance area with a stone floor. Several pairs of shoes and boots, mostly weathered and worn, cluttered the floor.

The floor changed to an oaky wood that'd been polished to the point of nearly being reflective. Because of the spotlessness of the wood, the carpet stood out more.

My options of where to explore were color-coded, like *Resident Evil* by way of early Rareware. Going left presented a jungle green carpet with smatterings of brown like an abstract art piece. To the right was a red carpet with intricate patterns of gold interlacing across. Going forward lay a sky-blue carpet with designs of clouds that seem to be a different material. Beside the hall going forward, almost facing the front door, was a staircase. The steps were black, with the sides a spotless white.

What I saw so far was beautiful, but a little off. Like something in a Guillermo Del Toro movie with how larger than life it all was.

Bags in tow, I stepped onto the stone.

Immediately, Tabby's voice rang out from above. "No shoes inside the house!"

"I didn't know cats had super hearing."

"It's the smell, obviously. I know every detail of this place. It's my house. I can practically *feel* whenever something wrong or dirty comes in here."

"It's my house, too!"

"Don't yell. Just a second!"

Frustrated, I put my bags on the wood, pulled off my shoes, and placed my sock-covered feet on the floor, feeling the cool of the wood against my soles.

Where are the other two? I wondered.

When I'd approached the house, I'd seen movement in a top-floor window, then the closing of a curtain. That person, I thought, might be a bit more reasonable, at least enough that they'd check the paperwork before they decided to attack me.

As I stepped toward the staircase, a picture caught my eye, and I froze in place. On the wall sat a picture of a group of miners standing at the entrance of a cave. They were all animal people. More interestingly, they were all women, no hint of my grandfather there.

Curiosity and disbelief guided my eyes from one picture to the next. Slit-eyed women scaled the walls of a cavern, setting the cables for lights. A bear of a woman—literally— with a shimmering black pelt hauled a cart of ore. An owl woman, two monkeys, and Tabby stood holding a giant ore of gold.

Together, the photos presented a collage of life and community around the mine. A team that set up the lights, laid the tracks, checked the maps, set to work, and relaxed once the sun had set.

Most of the pictures were black-and-white. Stepping back, I saw color further down the hall.

As I approached, a stern voice called from above, "Don't touch anything."

Tabby's ginger head poked from above the second-floor rail, cat eyes narrowed in a look that I could only consider cute. I held her gaze. Since she'd already knocked me down once, I wanted to show that I wouldn't be pushed around.

"I won't touch anything, Tabby," I said. "If you're busy, I'll go into town by myself."

She rolled her eyes. Then, she surprised me again.

Effortlessly, she hopped up, swung her legs over the railing and fell toward me. Her bare feet landed on the slanted stair railing, and she walked down without issue. The angle should've been impossible to walk on, and her weight should be more than the rail can handle, but it didn't even creak.

The steps had a graceful rhythm, her legs, hips, and tail swishing back and forth in a dangerously hypnotic pattern.

As she descended with that unnatural poise, I couldn't help but think she was beautiful. Her blue top matched her eyes, hanging loose over her breasts and flowing above her toned frame. The jeans, however, were tight around long legs and slender hips. Her tail stuck out from a custom-made hole in the back of her pants. Again, it was a series of buttons, two undone in the center so that the tail could fit through. Had she made those herself, or was there a place to buy tail-friendly clothes? There had to be a place, right? It seemed like all of Acanth was likely

21

made up of people like her, but I still struggled to believe it.

She hopped to the ground and nodded to the door. "You think you can go into the village by yourself? Please. You don't know anyone or anything. Best case scenario is that one of the traders rips you off for all you're worth."

"Point taken," I muttered, annoyed. "Is it sanitary for you to walk barefoot around the house?"

She snickered, moved to the stone, and put on sandals the color of her hair. "I'm the cleanest thing in this house. Don't worry about it." She turned to me. "Now, come on. You should be grateful I agreed to come along. You'd just get lost if you tried to explore the village on your own."

She paused, her expression darkening. "Plus, some of them would start getting ideas. They might think we can reopen the mine."

Wait. Did she just say re-open? "I'm sorry, what?"

She raised an eyebrow and cocked her head. "Didn't you hear what I said before?"

"I've been a bit shell-shocked trying to get over the whole catgirl thing," I said dryly.

"The mine's been out of operation for years. Nobody can go in."

THREE

Acanth, shit.

Even with the description of *village* and a faint memory of having been there once more, I expected something more than *this*. A road curved around the trees to a circular village of wood and stone buildings. The pavement abruptly turned to flattened dirt at the edge of them. A dozen or so buildings formed a ring around a large open area. Aside from the road from which we entered, two other dirt paths forked away, deeper into the forest. The largest building in the circle, a comparatively massive three-story structure with a metal sign, stood between these branching paths.

The building, however, did not hold my attention for long. I was too preoccupied with the inhabitants. Several people walked back and forth through the open area in the center of the village, and I couldn't help gawking at them.

As with the photos, they were all animal girls. Every type that I could imagine surrounded me. Tall ears, flat ears, hidden ears. Bright fur, dark fur. Shaggy and smooth.

Scales, quills, and feathers. They all looked at me as they walked by, staring like *I* was the strange one. Conversations ceased for a moment, but they resumed after a brief hiccup of surprise.

A bold, shrieking laugh sounded from a building to my side, and I craned my neck to look. Above a pair of swinging doors were the red, hand-painted letters *The Monkey's Paw Tavern*.

Of course they have a tavern.

My eyes moved to a window, where a small but thickset woman was smacking her table and laughing. From the hair covering the back of her hands and the cute round ears sticking through her black hair, I recognized her as a monkey woman. Her bombastic 'hehe' laugh sent her ample breasts heaving with each mirthful howl.

After a moment, she calmed enough to slam back a tankard of ale. Foamy gold liquid gushed down the corner of her full, smiling lips. As she smacked the tankard back down onto the table, she licked at the white foam running down her skin. The sight halted me for a moment.

A long, dextrous tongue slid out and cleaned away the ale. I didn't know if I was more impressed with the skill, or stunned by how sexy it was. The shimmering white teeth, including sharp canines, completed the image.

Then, she saw me.

An eyebrow rose. Her hand glided up the tankard. Instead of gripping it by the side, she traced the rim with her index finger in a tipsy sort of dance. A long tail popped up from behind her, wrapped around a second tankard on the table, and raised it to her lips. Every second of taking the drink, she maintained eye contact, raising a single eyebrow as she did so.

Hot damn. I swallowed hard.

I decided to meet her on her level and, not being the kind of guy to usually do this, threw caution to the wind and gave her a wink.

The monkey woman brought the tankard down onto the table and started that big, body-shaking laugh again, applauding me as I walked away.

Magical confusion or not, I thought, *this is the most fun I've had in years.*

The monkey woman's reaction also brought a question to mind. Why wasn't she surprised by me? Unlike Tabby, she hadn't seemed bothered.

I turned to Tabby, who had been making a point to not look at me as she led me into the village.

"If there haven't been men here in so long, and if it's impossible for mortals to enter, why aren't people freaking out?" I asked. "They just seem a bit surprised. My presence isn't breaking a treaty or defying a law of nature or something, is it?"

"Nothing like that, no. It's not impossible for mortals to come here. It's not even particularly rare. We may be magically disconnected from your world, but we are still connected to it, in a sense. Sometimes, we bring people in to deliver supplies or do odd jobs. The Amazon guys come in to do deliveries. There's a pizza place that delivers to the Antrum House. A spell is cast so they can't see the parts of

Acanth that aren't part of your world." She looked at me pointedly. "So, you're not special."

"You were awfully surprised when I showed up."

"That's different for two reasons. First, I thought you were a burglar. The delivery people always knock or ring, and they have logos on their vehicles. Second, this is the main village. Nobody gets past Antrum unless they're supposed to be here."

Then I'm supposed to be here, I thought, *and I'm not the first one, either.*

"At least the rental people are gonna be able to come and collect their car," I said. Then I paused. "So, my great-grandfather was invited here, too?"

"He must have been. I don't know the full story. Human men coming to live in the village is rare, but not impossible. There are only two cases that I know about." She turned and saw the growing smile on my face. "Hey, Jack, don't get too comfortable, okay. That's less than once-in-a-century. Sure, you've been invited, but we don't know what that means. I never agreed to share my house with you. Shouldn't you be more surprised or upset?"

All I could do was shrug. "Maybe I'm weird, but I feel calm. I can't remember the last time I breathed in this much fresh air or talked to someone this long about something other than work. The people here seem really friendly, too."

My response seemed to surprise her. Before she could react, though, someone yelled out, "Hey, Tabby! Who's the guy?"

I turned to the voice to see a tall, slim woman with rainy-day-gray curly hair. Curved black horns rose from her head.

26

She was standing in front of several tubs of fruit with prices listed in, of all things, American dollars. The goat woman said, "Any chance we can get that mine cleared out and running again?"

My guide's ears perked at the question. Suddenly, she was amiable, if a little exasperated. "I don't know, Hilda. Still figuring that out."

"Good luck! And tell Eo I said thanks. The smoothie machine has been working perfectly since she looked at it." She turned to me and waved. "Also, hi, new guy! Stop by later if you want any fruit. We also sell juice and smoothies if that's more your speed. In fact—"

Tabby's tail nudged my wrist. "She's doing an ad pitch. Don't get distracted. You'll spend your whole day with her, and she'll take all your money."

"She'd get all my money with *fruit*?" My disbelief was obvious in my tone.

She responded with dry seriousness. "You wouldn't be the first and no one would blame you. She once convinced a poor soul to spend their weeks wages on two crepes and a strawberry milkshake."

I blinked and walked onward, not daring to look back. I would not, I decided, make the same mistake as Orpheus.

What the hell is in that milkshake?

Sure enough, Hilda gave an impassioned, live performance commercial. She talked about a smoothie machine and magic soil and the lack of preservatives. A menu of fruit salad, yogurt dishes, and the infamous milkshakes filled the air.

To refocus myself, I tried to prioritize my many questions. We approached the building at the center of the town.

It stood out for more than its size. A black, metal sign with gold lettering said: *ACANTH VILLAGE CIVIC AND COMMUNITY CENTER.*

I had no idea what was going to happen inside. Everything that had occurred felt unreal and impossible. At the same time, that was exciting! I would have happily given up the conveniences of a city if it meant a real, genuine community.

It'd been a gamble to come out here, but I didn't regret it.

Whatever happens in that building, I thought, *I'm ready for it.*

CHAPTER

FOUR

I looked the clerk in the eye and said, "I'm not ready for this."

Tabby stood beside me, tail hanging limp and ears frozen in shock at their full height. She was stunned like a deer in the headlights.

Or a cat that saw a cucumber.

I was no better. I didn't sit down so much as my legs gave out and I collapsed onto the chair.

I read and reread the document. In front of us was a beautifully polished, dark wooden desk. The city clerk, a chameleon woman, sat across from us and had a similar job to what I used to have, except she seemed to enjoy what she did.

She looked back at me with the large bulb of her left eye. Meanwhile, her right eye focused on a computer while she typed. It was the most efficient and literal multitasking I'd ever seen. The spectacle pulled my attention away from the weight of my decision to enter Acanth.

She had human hands, with fingers slightly longer than normal, and she wore a navy blouse that could have fit into any office, or even a day out on the town. Above her collarbone, the skin of her slender neck changed into scales. They were a subdued orange that complimented the blouse. Earrings in a shape I didn't recognize hung from the curved crescents of scales on each side of her head. It seemed safe to say that these were her ears. She had no hair, but the scales grew into a short, brilliant fan that crowned her head from ear to ear. It gave her a dignified, almost regal appearance.

She was kind of freaky. I felt a little guilty to be happy that my roommate possessed more human features than her. *Fingers crossed about the other two.*

Suddenly, Tabby grabbed my wrist. Her claws subtly pressed my skin, not digging in this time.

That's a step in the right direction, I thought.

"Why the hell didn't you read the fine print?" Tabby asked.

I swallowed, sorted my thoughts, and replied, "To be fair, I did read the contract several times. Nothing in it led me to believe there was a separate document I had to worry about."

Whoever sent me that original notice of ownership had played a cruel joke. The most important sentence had been hidden among the rest of the terms: "In signing this contract, the signee agrees to follow the wishes of the previous owner."

Those wishes, it turned out, were not part of the contract. They were filed in a drawer in the Acanth office. The chameleon woman, whose name placard said *Karma Camilla*, had been patient as she explained it. Out of politeness, she'd even looked at us with both eyes for much of the conversation.

The short version was this: those wishes were located in the will and testament of my great grandfather. Due to a legal technicality regarding the boundary between the magical and non-magical world, that document had not been permitted to leave Acanth. If I'd had that, I would have known that by signing, I had agreed not only to accept partial ownership of the mine, but to become the manager and supervisor of all mining activity on the property.

I received nothing unless I accepted the workload and responsibility.

My lack of concern seemed to confuse Tabby. She looked at me, bright eyes pushing me to say something.

I decided to ask a practical question. "Is this a magically binding contract, in any way?"

Karma shrugged. "There is magic involved, but you aren't technically obligated to follow. By signing the document and crossing the border into Acanth, your belongings from your previous home were transported into a vacant room in Antrum Estate. Allow me a moment to check the specifics of your inquiry."

She tapped at her computer for a while. With both eyes on the monitor, the pace of her typing quickened to what seemed like double speed. After only a few seconds, she said, "Ah, I see. A request has already come in to terminate your previous lease. Should you so wish, it would require a signature. We could take care of all the details of your business, legal, and tax information from your home world."

I nodded slowly. Not from understanding, of course. After everything that had already happened, this didn't seem any stranger than anything else.

"Could you elaborate on that. How do you take care of it?" I asked.

Karma stopped typing. She allowed herself a gentle, patronizing smile as she said, "*Magic*." The professional monotone returned immediately after. "One consequence of this would be that you could not invite anyone to join you in Acanth. Brief visits are granted on rare, special occasions, but nothing permanent. You would not be permitted to have any communications or visitations to the human world."

It's not like there's anyone I want to communicate with, I thought.

I nodded again.

Why, I wondered, not for the first time, *am I not afraid?*

It should have horrified me, but I didn't feel scared. Nervous, yes. Confused, certainly. But scared? Not at all. In a weird way, it was a relief to know that I'd already bet all my chips, so to speak.

My belongings had been moved. I'd signed a contract for a job. I had a house, neighbors, and co-workers.

In a strange sense, I already belonged in Acanth.

Tabby was not so accepting of the situation.

"Don't act so calm!" my part-feline roommate said, "You... you're my boss now! That's not okay! The mine is closed. It's been closed for years." She shook her head vehemently. "Nobody can even enter it now. I can't believe this. You can't just wander in here and get everyone's hopes up about reviving Antrum! That house belongs to me, Eo, and Sunny. Not you!"

Stress and fear underlined the anger in her voice. I couldn't blame her. The situation was bizarre and unenviable. At the same time, I wanted to try. I'd tried and failed in the old world. Here, an amazing opportunity had fallen into my lap.

I would never forgive myself if I didn't at least *try* to make a good life here.

So, I turned back to Karma, "Does...Did the mine bring in a lot of money for the village?"

"Oh, yes. It was a major economic boon for us. Losing it was a blow." She shook her head sadly. "The town used to be so alive, so...together."

I remembered the pictures I'd seen back at the house. The mining community had certainly seemed to be a close knit one.

Tabby shook her head. "No. You can't be serious."

I looked her in the eye, willing her to feel the strength of my resolve. "I'm serious. I don't know if I'm smart, but I'm serious."

Her head shook harder, like she thought that would make all this disappear. "I don't believe this. I can't." Tabby got to her feet so fast that the chair she'd been sitting on went flying. She stormed away from the desk, but she moved with light steps. It looked like she ought to be stomping, but there was hardly a sound. Her sandaled feet barely made a sound as she left.

The slammed door was another matter entirely.

Karma raised a slight smile, the rest of her face maintaining its professional blandness. "For what it's worth, I'm glad you're choosing to stay. It's been a long time since there's been a permanent male resident of Acanth."

Oh yeah. That had been one of my questions, just at the bottom of my priorities.

"Why is that? I thought it was weird that I didn't see any men." I asked.

"Acanth is special in numerous ways, Mr. Calvinson. We're a historical and cultural heritage site. This village was established, built, and maintained by women. Men visit, of course, but part of the charm of the village is that we maintain the original concept."

I blinked stupidly, gawking at her. "So, it's a tourist spot?"

"I'd prefer you not be so crude. We have a long history for which we are quite proud." She raised her head, then dropped her chin. "Be that as it may, you're not entirely wrong. People visit through the gates further into town."

"Just a second, there are gates?"

Karma nodded. "They're located just past the inn. They are gates to various worlds." She arched an eyebrow. "You didn't suppose we were all born here, did you?"

"I figured it was magic," I mumbled. It hardly seemed like a stretch of the imagination after everything I'd seen.

She gave another slight smile. "You use airplanes. We use gates. Some of the people here actually commute to and from Acanth every day." She paused, shuffling some papers as though that would hide the frown on her face. "Tourists are somewhat rare these days, sadly. Part of the charm of Acanth had been in seeing a functioning mining village. The interest in our home left with the mine."

"Oh, I see..."

"Yes, I still remember when the village was alive." Her eyes lit with a nostalgic light. "Visitors would come from all over, they'd visit the mine, stop for something to eat, take in all the history of Acanth, bringing a much-needed stream of income into the town." She smiled, but it was forced. "Things were so much better in those days."

The information made me feel heavier. The task of reviving the mine hadn't become any harder, but it had become more significant. Revitalizing it would help the village. I could help the people here.

Without thinking, I looked down the hall where Tabby had left. She stood outside the office door, tapping her foot angrily. When I saw her, she opened her arms in a frustrated *what's-taking-so-long?* gesture.

One of Karma's eyes noticed. "Good luck. You have a long battle ahead of you," she said.

"I understand that. For now, I want all the information I can get about how the business operated. If you have any old contracts or bills or information on the equipment used, I'd appreciate that." I offered her a smile. I knew I was probably asking a lot, but it was necessary.

"Certainly. I'll see what I can do. I was referring, however, to the literal battle you'll have with the creatures inside the mine."

I blinked once. Then twice. By the third time, I finally processed what she said. "The *what*?"

"Goblins, mostly. Some assorted beasts. Rumor tells of a demon, but that may just be idle gossip." Her fingers stopped typing when she saw me turn pale. Slowly, her other eye looked at me. "You didn't know?"

I didn't have the energy to reply. After everything I'd learned in the span of less than a day, I didn't want to think, let alone speak.

Of all things, Johnny Cash came to my mind. I heard his warning as I came in, but I didn't listen. He told us young fellers not to go where the sun doesn't shine.

CHAPTER
FIVE

As we walked out of the civic center, Tabby kept her eyes down and her arms folded.

I had asked Karma to send the documents to the Antrum house. This had partially been a practical consideration, but more than anything, I had wanted fresh air. There was too much to think about. Not to mention, my guide needed to get away. Tabby seemed to become more frustrated by the minute, like a cat waiting for cream.

We stepped back into the sunlight, and Acanth once again entered view. A village of history and opportunity, magic and mining. Beautiful people, too.

Yes, I was in over my head, but it was hard not to be excited. It was beyond my wildest dreams.

And perhaps beyond my ability, a nagging voice in my head whispered.

I tried not to think about that. Instead, Tabby took my attention. Her being annoyed was more than understandable. To her credit, she didn't lash out at me. Not verbally, at least. The aura of hostility felt tangible. It was up to me to re-establish a connection between us. Silence felt wrong, but I had no idea what to say.

Thankfully, that great booming laugh sounded again. It pulled my focus to *The Monkey's Paw*.

"I need a drink," I said, finally cutting the silence.

Tabby's ears perked up slightly.

I continued, "The fruit place had prices in American dollars. I assume that the bar will take my cash, too?"

Tabby nodded. "I'm not taking care of you if you get drunk," she warned.

"I just want a drink. It's been a weird day." I sighed. That was the understatement of the century.

She pursed her lips in consideration. It was asymmetrical and, frankly, adorable. The left side of her face pouted, lips cutting off into cheek. After a moment, she sighed and said, "I suppose a hard cider would be nice."

With that, we walked to the tavern. As we stepped onto the wooden porch, the noise from within grew louder. The hum of conversation, the clack of billiard balls, and the din of a juke box added to the monkey woman's laugh.

I didn't care that I was the only human, and me being the only man didn't occur to me. This was just a visit to the local pub. I was grabbing my first drink at the watering hole in my new home, accompanied by my new roommate.

I almost laughed at how mundane that sounded.

My first thought when we entered The Monkey's Paw was that I should have expected it to look like it did. Pictures of the village from the past century filled the walls. Old mining equipment dotted some empty spots on the wall, making me feel like I'd just stepped out of a time machine. Lanterns hung from the ceiling, with the few electric lights swinging freely by their cables. Nothing in sight seemed younger than fifty years old—besides the patrons.

And, of course, the jukebox. The music barely fit this side of the half-century. Of all things, *Maneater* was playing.

We sat on cracked leather stools at a scratched wooden bar. The bartender walked up to us.

I had to do a double take. She looked like she belonged in a separate dimension from the rest of the building. Our hostess was a blond dog woman with hair cascading down to her hips. She wore a white blouse out of a musketeer movie; it flowed even more than her hair. The fabric danced over her body, swishing and bending with each movement. It must have been comfy. As loose as the fabric was, it clung to her chest. Those hypnotic, bountiful mounds seemed ready to slip free, but the fabric never dipped down.

The blouse was tucked into a crimson sash at her waist. Beneath that, she wore leather trousers that emphasized the magnitude of her figure and the brightness of her hair. A fluffy golden tail wagged softly, sticking out from beneath the sash. Two floppy ears poked through the hair, a golden earring through one of them.

"Hey, Fran," Tabby said. "Hard apple cider for me."

"Pint of whatever your most popular beer is, please," I said.

"Sure thing," Fran said with a friendly smile.

She turned to pour our drinks. That profile was damn near like a backward S, chest and rear filling the air before and behind with their gravity. The outfit, too. It was mind blowing.

She seemed curious about me. Fran's calmly smiling lips parted to say something, but she was cut off.

The monkey woman I'd seen earlier crashed onto the stool beside mine. She would have knocked the stool over if she hadn't collided with me.

As she drunkenly slammed into my side, my happy new friend stumbled through the chorus, "Watch out, boy. She'll chew you up!"

Her off-key singing broke into a fresh laughing fit. Evidently, she thought this was the funniest thing in the world.

Before she finished the line, she had to lean against me for balance, at one point throwing her arms around me like a long-lost friend. The deep laughter made her large breasts swell against me, then tremble and shake as her laughter broke into more gasps and heaves. I had to brace myself against the bar. The stool tipped beneath her, toward me. The monkey woman didn't seem to notice. Either that or she didn't care. The same must have been true about the soft, pleasant thwaps that fell against me with every breath.

This is strange, but I have no complaints.

From across the bar, Fran said, "Don't mind Sunny. She's always an energetic one." She shook her head, smiling. "I take it you'll be staying in Acanth for a while?"

I nodded. "Yeah. The name's Jack."

Fran placed a tankard before me. "House special. First one's free."

Again, it looked like she was about to say more, but the monkey woman—Sunny—stole my attention. She pulled herself up, sloppily climbing my shirt and sliding herself up my chest. On this frantic procession, I couldn't help but notice that she wasn't wearing a bra.

"Hey! Don't ignore meee!"

Sunny brought herself up, seeming to finally realize that her stool had tilted. With a swing of her hips, the stool clattered back to its normal spot. After all that, Sunny landed her elbow on the bar and the chub of her cheek against her palm. A tipsy smile and lazy glance landed on me. The woman radiated energy. She was short, vibrant, and vivacious. A well-worn *Mortal Kombat* tee shirt struggled to contain her. The words *FINISH HIM* stretched over, under, and across her chest. The curve-hugging fabric didn't quite make it to the waistline of her jeans. These, too, held snug against her, emphasizing the generous proportions of her thighs and hips.

"Hi," I said, accepting that she would continue to demand my attention. It was a request that I was happy to fulfill.

"Hi yourself."

From my other side, Tabby turned to Fran and asked, "How long has Sunny been here?"

"Since we opened. She bought breakfast and a beer, played darts for an hour, disappeared for two, came back, and has been drinking and playing pool since."

Sunny rolled her eyes and pointed at Tabby. "You're waaay too serious." Then she whipped around to look at me again. "So, new guy. What's your story?"

"I own the mine and live in Antrum," I said, deciding to keep it short and sweet.

Instantly, Sunny's demeanor turned oddly frantic. Her fingers tapped an excited percussion solo on the wood of the bar. She leaned forward toward Tabby, pressing her chest against the wood to show a valley of cleavage.

"Are we gonna reopen the mine?" she asked.

Tabby groaned and muttered under her breath, "I can't even have a drink in peace."

Sunny leaned further forward, dropping part of herself into my lap to get to the cat girl beside me. Her tail wrapped around the base of my stool and her hand clamped onto my shoulder for support.

"I didn't hear you," Sunny said. "Speak up!"

"We can't even enter the mine," Tabby said. "There's no sense in talking about reopening it. Besides, look at yourself." She gestured to the drunk, furry, adorable mess in my lap. "You wouldn't be able to work like this. You squander most of our budget here! If it wasn't for me and Eo, you wouldn't even be able to support yourself."

Oh no.

I looked to Fran. The golden bartender gave a serious nod, confirming my worry.

I've landed in the middle of a roommate crisis.

"Hey!" Sunny pulled herself up my body again, unintentionally holding me in place between them in the argument. "I earn my keep. There's nobody in this entire village better at swinging a pickaxe than me. Try to name someone. You can't! Also, I win most of the money back playing pool, anyway."

Tabby shook her head. "That's not the point! And stop pressing up against him like that. You look pathetic." She glared at the other woman, and I dared think there was a hint of something else besides anger there.

I cleared my throat. "Thanks for the beer."

"Happy to help," Fran said loudly.

Her smooth hands met the bar, bringing my neighbors to attention. Her smile and expression were relaxed, but it was clear that she maintained authority in her establishment. The golden frame of hair and the white billow of blouse complemented her skin beautifully. Her red-tinged lips and brilliant gold eyes seemed all the more vibrant.

Note to self: inquire about her fashion choices later. Also, ask why it's called The Monkey's Paw.

"I know you must be tired," Fran said, "but would you mind telling us what brings you to Acanth? I'm especially interested in why you might be Sunny's new roommate?"

Sunny chuckled, then squeezed my arm. "Hi, roomie." She giggled.

After a quick glance at Tabby, I gave the short version; *Sick of work. Found a paper. Signed it. Own a mine.*

Tabby had not shown interest nor sympathy since we'd last discussed it. Sunny and Fran, however, were on the edges of their seats—Sunny quite literally. They listened, Fran nodding and occasionally asking me to pause so she could fill orders for other customers. Sunny paid attention, keeping her wonky smile and holding my arm through most of it.

"And that's basically how I got here," I finished.

Tabby shook her head. Fran nodded. Sunny smiled and said, "So, we can go back into the mine."

"No. We can't." Tabby chugged the remnants of her cider and slammed the glass on the counter.

"It's worth trying," Fran said.

I'm getting real sick of this, I thought as I drank my beer. There was, sadly, nothing magical about the beer, but I enjoyed it nonetheless.

"A bunch of people have said that we *can't* go into the mine," I said. "Why is that? Is it just out of business? Is it because of the goblins or whatever else is inside?"

Tabby pushed herself away from the bar with a scowl. "I've had enough. There's more to clean at Antrum and someone needs to be near Eo. Sunny, you take care of him for a while. Jack..." She looked at me. Annoyance and frustration hit me, but her eyes softened instantly. The corners of her lips fell from their sneer. Tabby never finished her sentence. She knew that neither of us understood the situation. She wasn't ready to let me into her house, her business, or her life.

I couldn't blame her. Still, in that moment, with those strong, stressed, beautiful cat eyes focused on me, I found a new resolve.

I will do everything I can to make a place here.

As Tabby left, Sunny pulled at my arm. "I'll take good care of you, don't worry." She beamed, then cocked her head. "Have you tried to enter the mine yet?"

"Why do people keep saying it like that? It's always that people *can't* enter the mine. Is it closed down or what?"

Fran shook her head. "It's a barrier. Nothing alive has been able to go in or out for a couple years."

Sunny nodded. "It's suuuuch a bummer. Like, I get that they want to keep the demon inside and all that, but I'm starting to lose some of my muscle! I have the gym, but it's different." She raised her arm and flexed it. "Here, feel."

"Wait," I said as she grabbed my hand and clasped my fingers around her bicep, which was plump, yet firm. "Back up. Did you say demon?"

Fran smiled. A mischievous glint flickered off her canine. "Some believe there's a demon."

"There is!" Sunny said.

Dammit, everybody knows everything about the mine except for me!

It was still my first day, but I knew that there was only one thing I could do to take a definite step toward making a place in Acanth. The tankard went up. The beer went down.

And I said with resolve, "Sunny, take me to the mine."

CHAPTER
SIX

Antrum Mine was bigger than I expected. I didn't know what to expect, admittedly, but the sheer size of the great gray mountain made me whistle in surprise. Sure, the mass of rock had been visible from the house, but it looked larger and more imposing up close. The long connection of hills sat on the earth like an island on land.

Adding to the image was the large quarry. It wasn't clearly visible from the road, but it became impossible to ignore when you stood near the foot of the mountain. The ground opened into a dusty half-bowl with a flattened bottom. That gray expanse acted as the entrance hall to Antrum Mine.

If this place were operational, the extracted materials would be brought here, then lifted to the main level. From there, it'd be transported into town. On the way here, Sunny had explained the order of operations.

Hit rocks, get ore, smelt in the village, sell, and repeat.

The mental image was an appealing one. Bustling activity, loads of minerals, both practical and precious, put to good use after sitting in the bottom of the mine for who knew how long. With magical workers involved, I could see why it was a tourist pull, especially since I'd never seen an actual blacksmith in my entire life—like everything else here, it sounded fantastical.

Not sure how we're gonna bring that charm back, I thought as I drank it all in.

However great it may have been—or would be again—it was nothing but an empty pocket in the ground. A hole in a rock. How did I turn something so simple into an attraction that people came from all around to see?

"Heeere it is," Sunny said, throwing her arms wide open. The bottle of rum in her hand sloshed its contents about, spilling some down her hand.

I nodded. What else could I have done? There'd be no point to refute or ignore it. I nodded again, reminding myself that I had, in fact, signed up for this. From there, I descended into the quarry. The surface was uneven, grainy, and covered in dirt. Time and weather had begun to erode the border between the mine and estate. We'd need to change that.

One of many things on the list. I scratched the back of my neck in thought. That list was getting longer and tougher by the moment.

Soon, my feet planted themselves before the opening to the mine itself. I felt like Pinocchio, *intentionally* trying to get into the whale. Would it swallow me or lead me to my best life?

Probably some third, less dramatic option.

"Someone's not looking so confident anymore," Sunny said before taking another swig from the bottle of spiced rum.

Fran stood beside her, hands on her hips and that casual half-smile on her lips. The expression was carefully blank, a PR face if I ever saw one. Still, no matter how well her face hid emotions, the swishing of her tail gave away her interest in what was about to happen.

"Shouldn't you be running the bar?" I asked.

"I'm the boss," she replied. "Someone else can take care of it for an hour. I was too curious to miss out on seeing this."

"Heeey, new mine man," Sunny called out. "Do you know what you're looking at?"

"It's an artisanal mine, or ASM for short. Owned by myself. No company involvement. All the work and ore inside goes through me and whoever works it."

"You've done your homework." Fran nodded in approval.

Doesn't mean a damn thing if I can't enter the place.

My foot launched out before I could overthink it. The gravel crunched under my shoes. All of this would need to be cleaned and reorganized. The equipment...

No.

This was not the time for that. My first goal was to prove that I belonged here. Just inside the mouth of the mine, I saw a large lever connected to a thick black wire, which snaked up to the roof, where the ceiling was dotted with lamps. The lights. If nothing else, I could turn on the lights.

"Dooo it! Dooo it!" Sunny cheered, pumping her bottle in the air.

Easy to cheer from that distance.

I met the entrance. Instantly, the air changed. My body slowed as it hit an invisible pressure. It felt like trying to walk into a vertical wall of water. Except, of course, there was nothing there. The thick air began to push at me, a wave trying to regurgitate its victim back onto the shore. My muscles began to strain, but I continued forward.

My hand reached for the lever, trembling under the pressure of my exertion. Nothing mattered except that. The pressure came harder in the middle of my step, but I neither stopped nor went backward.

No more waiting on permits. No more serving a boss who doesn't care. This is my place, my team, my home.

I needed to do this. Not for the mine or for Acanth or the women behind me. For myself.

My next breath happened in slow motion, feeling like several minutes. Suddenly, I couldn't breathe. The strange, thick atmosphere left no air for my lungs. Beyond that was the weight of the invisible force. It pushed so hard that I wouldn't have been able to fill my lungs even if there had been air.

Suddenly, it pushed harder. My foot slipped back as a new, angrier wave slammed into me. By reflex, my hand flung out to the rock wall for support. That motion dragged on for what felt like minutes, and the hair on my arms stood on ends, my skin raised in tiny bumps. Every muscle involved felt strange. There was no pain, not even exhaustion. Just effort. It was like I was exercising the muscles for the first time.

Finally, my fingers found a purchase among the stone wall. I gripped, grit my teeth, and pushed onward.

The agonizingly long time was an illusion. That was obvious. The lack of breath was strange, but not painful. Something in the mine wanted me out, but I didn't listen to it even though every bone in me screamed to obey it.

The lever grew closer. At last, my hand wrapped around it. I had no proof or evidence that this would destroy the barrier. Somehow, it felt right. If I could pull that lever, the spell would vanish, I would be able to breathe, and nobody would have trouble entering the mine again.

That downward pull felt like it'd never end, but it did.

Clunk.

Immediately, the invisible tide vanished, sending me staggering against the wall for support. The machinery hummed to life and the lights flickered. Yellow lamplight blinked into existence, showing a long tunnel that never seemed to end.

I looked back at my audience. They remained in the same place I'd last seen them, confirming my suspicion that I'd only undergone that strange wave for a short while.

"Antrum Mine," I yelled, "is open!"

CHAPTER
SEVEN

I did it.

I yelled the message again, "Antrum Mine is open!" My voice aimed at the house, hoping that a certain set of cat ears might hear it. Maybe this would help her think better of me. Maybe she'd realize how serious I was about staying.

Fran nodded in approval, offering a clap of unknown sincerity. "I'm impressed," she said.

Sunny's jaw and eyes were open further than I would have thought possible unless she were part python. "The mine is open..." she said. Then, excitement replaced shock. Her feet began to stamp against the ground, throwing up a small cloud of dust. A wide, hyper smile rose as she jumped from one foot to the other. Her tail took her bottle so that she could pump her fists in the air. "The mine is ooopen!"

"You're welcome!" I yelled back.

"Yeeeah!" The excitement was too much for Sunny. She danced and jumped back and forth with more energy than

52

she could contain. Suddenly, she leapt from the top of the bowl and charged me. Those wide, joyful eyes took on a possessed, mildly horrifying look. As did her manic grin. My furred roommate-turned-wrecking ball charged me like she was going for a tackle. I dove to the right, barely dodging the happy attack.

It didn't matter to her. Sunny fell into a roll, sprung back to her feet, and whooped her way into the mine. She grabbed the bottle again from her tail, which began to whirl like a long-haired metalhead in a mosh pit.

If everyone was even half as excited as Sunny about the mine being open, then they'd still be pretty damn happy.

I looked back at Fran, tilting my head slightly toward the mine. "You coming too?" I asked.

Her expression didn't change, but her tail raised a bit. One ear cocked.

For now, that's enough.

I ran deeper into the mine, eager to keep up with someone who actually knew the layout of my new workspace. I had to sprint to keep up with Sunny, despite how much she'd drank. Along the way, I offered a silent prayer of thanks to the Eurobeat playlist which had motivated me through all those cardio sessions. Beside me, in the center of the tunnel, lay tracks for a minecart.

"Guess there's no demons or monsters after all," I whispered, though it did make me wonder why the mine shut down. Had my great grandfather just gotten too old to maintain it?

After a quick dash through a long tunnel, we arrived at a massive dome. The mouths of further tunnels stretched out in endless directions. The floor curved downward, with shelves of carved rock leading to further recesses. From the light cables and cart tracks, I guessed that a little over half of these had been explored.

More importantly, equipment was strewn all over the place. Carts lay on their sides. Picks and various tools sat at random places. Hardhats and chisels and hammers lay dropped and scattered about. Everything was covered in a layer of dust but seemed to be in working order despite that.

Sunny didn't seem to notice. She charged at a wall. Without slowing, her tail snatched a pickaxe from the ground and replaced it with her bottle. She leapt. That plump body became a model of strength as she scaled the wall. She made it look easy. She might as well have been, well, a monkey in a tree.

"Hi-hooooo!" she squealed like the long-lost eighth dwarf: Tipsy. "Hi-hoooo!"

Above her, I saw it. A patch of gold glittered near the ceiling. "Holy shit," I said, marveling.

No, this isn't the time to spectate.

Adrenaline ran high and hard through my veins, pushing me into action, and I was eager to put it to good use. I took a hardhat, gloves, and a pickaxe from the ground. Next, I began sorting the equipment and making mental notes of the things I'd need. A cart found its way back onto its wheels. Load by load, I moved everything I needed into it.

Soon, I was interrupted. "Oh yeees!" Sunny's voice boomed through the cavern, seeming to vibrate through the stone and up my body. With a yank of the pick, she tore a nugget of gold ore from the wall. From there, she leaned back, kicked her feet against the wall, and went for the ground.

It was beautiful, graceful in a way I'd never seen outside of the Discovery Channel. Her curvaceous form spun lithely through the air, twirling like a delicate ballerina. Her chest pressed outward, highlighted by the lamps. This was a master in her element, a goddess of the mine, a—

Sunny face-planted onto the stone with an undignified *plop*.

I gasped at the impact and dropped my stuff to hurry over to her.

"Sunny," Fran's matronly tone sounded from the cavern's opening. "What have Tabby and I told you about climbing while drunk? Even Eo thinks it's a bad idea."

I really gotta meet this Eo, I thought. *She can't be as crazy as the rest of them.*

In response, Sunny's tail stuck straight up like an antenna. Her ass went up with it. Her entire body folded inward to rise in an inverted sit-up, as if an invisible hand were pulling her up by the tail. Again, the grace was undercut. Her hands and feet found the ground beneath her, slipped, and sent her falling down again.

This time, the tail wrapped around Sunny's forehead and pulled. Her unbothered, drunken smile came into view as she literally pulled herself to her feet.

Perhaps I should have had some concern or criticism, but I felt a strange admiration for her. She was spirited, if nothing else. The full-body jiggle that accompanied her antics may have played a part in my judgments.

"Come ooon!" Sunny said to Fran. "I'm just excited! How can I not be?" She ran up to me, her entire body bouncing with each exuberant step. "Now, boss man. Let's seeeee. Can you swing a pickaxe?"

"Of course," I said.

"Show me! Show me!" Her hands disappeared in a flurry of quick claps.

"Um, okay. No problem. Does it matter where I hit?"

"No, no. Just swing. Let's see your form. Show me your muscles!"

I grabbed a pick.

YouTube tutorials, don't fail me now.

I'd done some research after signing the papers, but not much. I chose a specific point on the wall. My eyes focused on that point. My feet moved shoulder distance apart, with one foot slightly in front of the other. My left hand gripped the base of the pick while my right held it just beneath the head. I turned my upper body, raised the pick, and brought it down, transferring the force from my body to my shoulders and then to the pick. My eyes never left the target.

I did this a few times.

"Not bad. Nooot bad," Sunny said. "A bit stiff, but it's a start."

"Hey." Fran cut through our energy high with a serious tone. "Do you hear that?"

Sunny and I became still. I tried to listen. It took a few seconds, but I heard it. Something was skittering through a nearby tunnel.

"Goblins," Sunny said, narrowing her eyes.

The atmosphere changed. Fran raised her boot and pulled a dagger from it. Sunny spun her pick in her hand.

"We have a welcome party," Fran said. "They've had a few years to get used to owning this place."

"Weeell, how about we remind them who's in charge?" Sunny glanced at me.

"How many are in here?" I asked.

"Let me seeeee." Sunny spun the pick again. "When we closed the place, there weren't too many...that we knew about."

"That's not a number," I said.

"It's also optimistic," Fran added.

The skittering grew closer, the sound of scrapes and scratches of many claws against stone. Grunting and garbled sounds reached my ears, like a harsh, throaty language that I couldn't understand.

"We should leave," Fran said. "Entering the mine is already a miracle. We should be happy with that. Sunny, I don't want you getting hurt before you can pay your tab."

I nodded and began to back toward the entrance. Fran was nearly there, but she was still braced to strike. Sunny shook her head. "They must be surpriiised. They don't come to the light often. They uuusually hide in the dark corners we haven't explored yet."

Something's off.

The noise had been going on for too long. Our welcome wagon should've already arrived by that point. Clearly, Fran thought the same. Her gold eyes darted around the cavern, and her nose twitched with cautious sniffing. Her lip pulled back to show a defiant sneer.

"Sunny," I said, "we should go."

"You did your part, boss man! This part is for me!" She swung the pickaxe around like she was a ninja with nunchucks.

I give her points for confidence.

There was no question that she could hold herself in a fight. Still, this wasn't the situation to test her combat skills, not when there sounded like so many enemies, and definitely not when she had been drinking. Worst case scenario, I guessed she could have climbed away, but—

Climb.

My eyes shot up. The cavern's ceiling had a few cragged openings, barely more than cracks. From one of these crevices, a knobby, moss green body emerged, wearing brown rags. It held a knife clenched in its teeth. Two milk-white eyes, without irises, glared down at Sunny.

"Look up!" I yelled.

At that moment, several things happened at once. My body launched forward before I could think. The goblin dropped from the ceiling and brought the knife to its hand. Sunny turned to look at me.

My pick rose in a clumsy, awkward swing. The goblin never looked at me as it fell. Its milky eyes stayed fixed on its target. I wasn't worth its attention—or so it thought.

Recognition flashed in Sunny's eyes. She dove away as my swing connected. The heavy thwack knocked the goblin from the air. It fell onto its back, wounded and surprised but still moving. My pick rose and fell again. Just before I made contact, the murderous pest rolled away. Sunny fell on it with a single, decisive blow.

"Thaaaanks," she said, looking at me. "And fine. Let's go."

We ran out of the mine. As we went, I saw a cluster of the goblins standing in one of the tunnel entrances. They looked restless, raising spears and gnashing teeth.

During our escape, a ridiculous thought occurred to me.

I haven't even met all my roommates.

CHAPTER
EIGHT

The next few minutes were a blur of thought and activity.

When we emerged from the mine I asked, "Do we need to worry about them chasing us?"

"Noooo way." Sunny shook her head. "They've never set foot outside the mine. They usually don't even come as far as they did. They're waaay too comfortable."

"Well," Fran said. "They have possessed unchallenged control of the mines for a few years. Though that's about to change." Without paying attention to the motion, she raised her foot and slid the dagger into the tiny scabbard attached to her boot. With that finished, she looked at me. "Do you want me to keep this a secret? People here will want to know about the mine, but I understand if you want this to stay quiet for a while. You're not even settled in yet."

"Right." *I just helped kill a damn goblin! I'm clearing a damn dungeon and extracting gold! This is amazing!* "Thanks, Fran. Don't tell anyone just yet."

She nodded, then turned toward the village. It was hard not to watch the pull and stretch of the leather against her skin as she walked away. "Feel free to stop in at *The Monkey's Paw* anytime. I'll be there if you need me."

Was that an invitation, or am I just riding an adrenaline high?

Either way, there wasn't much time to think about it.

"Not bad for your first day." Sunny tossed a small yellow rock at me.

I caught it. Gold. Small, fragile, and lumpy. Still, it was gold. I held it up, smiling like an idiot as it shone in the sun.

"I'm going back to the bar. Tiiime to celebrate!"

"Don't tell anyone," I said absentmindedly. "Not until we have a plan."

"Riiight, right. Promise. Oh! Have you met Eo yet? You should see Eo. She can help you get a layout of the rocks and tunnels and everything."

"Where is she?"

"Probably in her room." She threw her thumb toward the Antrum house. Once again, the curtains were open on the top floor.

"On the top floor, I'm guessing."

"Yeeeah. It's her loft-slash-studio-slash-palace of introversion." Sunny wandered away before she finished speaking.

Once she was gone, and I was alone, the adrenaline ebbed away. Only the facts remained. I had a serious monster problem, help that didn't know me, and no idea how to use the equipment needed to run the mine.

The next obvious step was to learn the layout of the mine.

But maybe a nap, first.

It didn't take long for me to arrive at my destination.

"I'm back," I announced as I entered my strange new home. My voice went down the halls and up the stairs. Nobody responded.

Okay...where is my room, anyway?

At the civic center, Karma had told me that my stuff had been magically transported here. I just had to find that.

Rest, I told myself. *Just sit down. It's time to take a nap.*

Even as I reminded myself to relax, my body began to climb the steps. Tabby must have either been away or distracted by something. I didn't see or hear her. Eo, the third and final member of the house, was at the top of the house.

Talking to her was the final task on the checklist. There was no way I'd be able to relax until I met her. Not only did it feel polite to see my last housemate, it also felt wrong to leave such a simple item off the to-do list.

So, up the stairs I went. The second floor was a balcony filling the periphery of the main hall. Doors to other rooms stood closed at each corner of the square.

I feel like I should update my save file.

I half-expected one of the doors to have a zodiac sign above the lock. Thankfully, none of them had anything so suspicious. Each door did have a marker, however. The one by the stairs had an adorable, hand-knit image of a cartoon cat. It had a simple design, but it was still cute, with ginger fabric as the base and blue thread for the eyes.

I had to walk around the square to get to the next flight of stairs, so I passed the other doors. They had similar hand-knit inscriptions. One had the black face of a monkey with a big white smile. The next had a light brown bird's face with black eyes and beak. The final door had nothing on it.

Any chance this is it?

I knocked on the door. When no response came, I pushed it open.

Sure enough, all my stuff was in the room. From Karma's description, the image I'd gotten had been a pile of suit-cases in the center of the room that needed to be arranged and unpacked. Instead, everything was in place. The bed was made, my clothes hung in the open closet, and my TV sat in front of the bed.

They even transported my Zelda posters.

Seeing the bed, part of me wanted to sleep. It was a tempting idea, but it wasn't even late in the day. I still had to eat dinner and, more importantly, speak to my final housemate. Seeing my magically transported PC, I also got the idea that I might be up for a while yet.

Soon, my love.

With a sigh, I turned up the next flight of stairs.

The house became thinner the further up I went. At the top of the steps was a door. I paused when I saw it. The wood had been carved into an intricate, beautiful design. It showed an angelic, nude woman. Her arms were great wings, spread around her. The ring of feathers highlighted the gentle curve of her hips and the slight swell of her breasts. The dark hair on her head acted as a crown.

"Hello?" I knocked on the door.

No reaction.

"Hello?"

Again, nothing.

Unsure of what else to do, I pushed the door open.

The room held a huge loft. High ceilings opened into shrinking points. The light of the afternoon sun shone from two large windows. In the light, I saw a workshop. Massive shelves housed hundreds of small statues and figurines. The sheer range of color astounded me. They had costumes of all kinds, with hair of all colors and shapes. Body types, hairstyles, and fashion choices showed no influence from physics or modesty. There were breasts bigger than heads, abs that could have grated cheese, and hair that stood at impossible angles. These statues stood behind glass, filling most of the many cabinets on the walls.

Other cabinets had wooden doors. One of these was open. In it, I saw paints, brushes, carving knives, and all sorts of tools.

In the center of the organized chaos hunched a mass of chestnut brown. Her back was to me. A long ponytail fell onto her wings. A curtain of feathers covered and hung from her arms. I'd never thought that feathers looked cozy, but for a moment, that was all I could think.

The brown huddle was all I could see of her.

Nothing was visible even under the stool. She must have had her legs up on the lip of the seat.

"Eo?" I asked. "I'm the new guy in the house. Did you hear about me?"

No reaction. I stepped closer and said, "You might have seen me earlier. I went into the mine."

This time, I got a grunt reaction. It was a nasally, high-pitched sound.

"Okay..." I muttered. "I heard that you've got charts of the mine. I want to get to know the layout. Where would I find the maps?"

"Usual spot," a soft voice replied. "Why? Not like we can enter."

"I was just inside there," I said.

"That's nice."

Only a small part of me felt bad for invading her space.

The atmosphere was not dissimilar to my old work. Few things bothered me more than talking to someone who ignored me. The patronizing 'that's nice' and 'oh I see' were way worse than 'fuck you' could ever be. I didn't even need a lot of her time. All I wanted were a few papers. I decided to push.

"Eo, people can enter Antrum Mine again. I broke the barrier."

"Uh-huh."

For a moment, it looked like that was all I'd get, however, her posture changed.

"Wait." The arms began to move more slowly. The head lifted.

"Yeah?" I replied.

"We can go back inside?"

"Uh-huh."

"The barrier is gone?"

"That's right."

"You're a man, and a mortal?"

"Yes."

Suddenly, with her body entirely still, her head spun one-eighty to face me like Regan in *The Exorcist*. Unlike the possessed girl in that movie, thankfully, Eo was adorable. The quick-jerk turn was energetic, curious. Ink-black eyes looked at me, shockingly expressive despite the absence of visible iris or pupil. Maybe it was the eyebrows. They were raised up in inquisitive arches. Her small, soft mouth made a confused half-pout as an eyebrow rose.

"Who are you?" she asked.

Casually, her body spun to meet her face. Taloned, avian feet released the stool and moved to the floor. She wore a purple sweater which had had its sleeves and most of its sides cut off to make room for the hybrid arm-wings. I saw the opening of the fabric not covered by wings. The feathers covered her ribs and shoulders, but pale human skin showed in the gap between sweater and wing. The generous sleeve space added for her wings also revealed a fair bit of the curve of her breasts—not in a bra. She seemed unconcerned by it, not making any attempts to cover up.

Her wing feathers were striking, contrasted with the dark purple and highlighted by the brown. Her bird feet poked out through a pair of pink cargo shorts. This ensemble, clearly, was meant for range of motion rather than fashion.

"My name's Jack," I said. "It's complicated, but I live here now and I work in the mine. Technically, I own Antrum, but we can go over all that later. For now, all you need to know is that the mine is open. Whatever barrier was there, I got rid of it."

Poor girl. This must be a lot to take in.

I prepared to go into a long explanation. I had neither the energy nor the desire for it, but it seemed necessary. The sentences I'd just uttered definitely weren't enough.

Considering how important Antrum was to the people here, let alone to someone who lived in this house and prepared the charts, she must have been bursting with questions and varying emotions.

"Oh," she said. "Cool. Maps are in that chest by the door. I also uploaded them onto our shared cloud drive. Ask Tabby for the password. Is that all? I'd like to get back to what I was doing."

Just when I thought I was getting a read on the people around here, I thought, scratching the back of my head.

Eo turned back to her desk, reached up to a ring-light above it, and turned it on. Next, she took a pair of zooming goggles from the desk and fitted them to her head.

Overcome with interest, I moved to get a better look.

On the desk before her were two statues about eight inches tall. They were identical: a shirtless, muscular man with baggy blue pants, sandals, a pair of serrated swords, and a boar mask.

The statues may have started the same, but Eo had changed one. The smooth, Ken doll texture had been coarsened. The muscles were brought into fine detail. Instead of simply being part of the shape, they became their own distinct features. The fur of the mask had been darkened and carefully splotched with dirt and mud stains. The sandals had been worn to represent years of intense use.

I looked back at the shelf. On a closer look, each of them had an astounding level of detail. A specific one stole my attention. It was a green-haired, twin-tailed girl. This character, by far, was the most common on the shelves, in countless costumes and styles. This specific figurine had a long, flowing kimono. An intricate flower pattern had been painted from tail to neckline, spreading and flowing like a garden on the fabric. A subtle blush was added to her cheeks, with a eyelash-thin set of red over her lips.

"Wow," I said.

Eo didn't notice. She didn't seem to wish to talk about them.

"I'll just grab those charts and be on my way," I said.

Eo picked up a model. The feathers on her arms ended at her wrists, looking like a cute sweater.

"Hmm," she said.

I got the feeling it was about the model she was painting, and not me.

So I grabbed the charts, went to the door and hesitated. It felt awkward to leave without saying bye. At the same time, it seemed she was done with our interaction, and any further words would be a disturbance to her work.

Shaking my head, I left the room.

That settles it. Time for a nap.

CHAPTER
NINE

I opened my eyes.

"An unfamiliar ceiling," I muttered.

My first night in Antrum Estate had been surprisingly restful, all things considered. The exhaustion from the previous day likely played a part in that. I felt rested, but not quite calm. The single room that was now mine was bigger than the entire apartment I lived in just yesterday. High ceilings, clean walls, polished wood floors, two giant windows, blackout curtains, and a huge bed—all to myself. My stuff looked out of place on the handcrafted furniture that was likely older that I was.

As always when I felt confused or uncomfortable, I wanted to move. I got out of bed and opened the curtains, revealing the early morning sun. It was just beginning to crest over the hills.

Are the hills called Antrum or is it just the mine? I'll have to check that out.

The interplay of light and shadow, rock and grass, was beautiful. This was the sort of view that people dreamed about, the kind they put on postcards. If I stood there long enough, I could have seen the sun sweep its way up to the village.

Something distracted me, though. I wasn't the first one awake and moving. On the lawn below, stretched over a yoga mat and facing the rising sun, was Tabby. Her attire was similar to the first time we met: sports bra and sweatpants. These were a light blue, contrasting the ginger hair of her head and tail.

She went through a slow, exhausting-looking yoga routine. Her body twisted, torso almost turning backward. With each motion, I saw the lithe flow of skin and muscle. Long, deliberate breaths expanded her chest in time with the motions. Her back, shoulders, and core stretched, rolled, and pulled back.

The sunrise was beautiful, but in that moment, it was her spotlight. That magnificent vista may as well have served to highlight how mesmerizing she was.

Tabby's arms entwined above her as she stood to a wide-legged stance. With the smooth undulations of water, her hands dipped forward. Her body followed. The arms melted apart until her hands met the mat. Her hips continued to rise, then her legs. Soon, her bare feet swung upward in a slow, smooth arc. They came to a rest at the top of the arc, so she was doing a perfect handstand.

After a few seconds of this, her body did the same in reverse. Her feet came down in a smooth arc to the end of her mat. From there, her body descended in a line. Then, she rose hips first, sliding that tight, toned ass upward toward me.

I stood mesmerized for a while, then caught myself. This wouldn't do. Tabby, Sunny, and Eo were my housemates. I wanted to live and work with them, not ogle them.

But if things go well...

It wouldn't do to get ahead of myself, either.

I took a deep breath, then opened the window.

As expected, her ears twitched toward me. "You're up early," she said.

"Good morning to you, too."

"Don't get used to the view. I'll claw your eyes out if you make a habit of leering at me."

"How terrifying," I said, relaxing against the windowsill. "Though I do believe you're the one parked in front of my window."

"This spot has the best view of dawn," she said while doing a perfect split.

How can she hold a conversation while doing that? I wondered. I practically felt my thighs ache just looking at her.

I turned my eyes back to the morning sun. Suddenly, the realization hit me.

This was my home.

The sun could peek over and greet me like this every day. "It does look great," I said, drinking it in.

"Eyes on the mine, Jack."

"That's where I've been looking the whole time."

"Sure."

For a while, I was tempted to ask if she'd mind a partner. I'd done some simple yoga in the past. A life behind a desk brought back and joint issues. I'd been opposed to the idea at first, but yoga did help.

It seemed a little fast to ask her to share her spot, though.

"Do we have any coffee?" I asked instead.

"Kitchen," she answered, telling me which shelf to find it on. "We've got instant and a French press."

"French it is. You want a cup?"

Subtly, her head tilted to me. I couldn't see her face well from this distance, but the sapphire glow of her eyes were impossible to miss.

"Yeah," she said at last. "With milk and no sugar."

"I can do that. You want it brought to you or left in the kitchen?"

"Leave it. I'll be in soon."

Coffee, the universal icebreaker.

I went down to the kitchen. In the early morning, I heard neither Sunny nor Eo. The kitchen was down the hall with the green carpet, with its windows facing the road leading out of Acanth.

Unsurprisingly, the room was massive, old, and immaculate. The floors were polished to a ridiculous standard, as were the large counters, granite kitchen island, and forest green cabinets. The fridge had a magnetic calendar on the door, as well as a small marker board.

There was a message on the board: *"Remember to check on Eo. And Sunny: DO YOUR DAMN DISHES!!!"*

It didn't require Sherlock Holmes level intellect to figure out Tabby had written the message. By extension, the cleanliness of the house seemed to be thanks to her, our very own yoga cat.

The image of her rolling from her chest through her hips came back to mind, and my mouth went dry.

Careful, I warned myself. *She could scratch my eyes out.*

I found the mugs in the first cupboard I opened. From their shape and sturdiness, I guessed that they were handcrafted in the village. They were impressive, and, like the rest of the house, color-coded: red, green, and blue. I put my deductive powers to further use, using my little gray cells to surmise that the red mug belonged to Tabby.

Green for jungle equals monkey. Blue for sky equals bird. Red for...hair color? Temper?

Surprisingly, there was a fourth mug on the shelf. It was mine, the same one I'd used since college: a big brown one designed to look like a barrel, with the giant red letters 'DK' on the front.

Suddenly, another thought hit me. If the Acanth civic center magically transported my mug, what else might they have transported?

My hand flew to the fridge door.

"Yes!" I exclaimed.

My two leftover slices of pizza from my favorite pizza place remained.

Fancy bed, sexy catgirl yoga, and breakfast pizza? It was shaping up to be a damn good day.

I almost forgot about the coffee. I searched the cupboards for the grounds and the French press. Soon, I was enjoying my new slice-of-life with a slice of pizza and a cup of joe.

Tabby walked into the kitchen, brushing stray strands of hair from her face. There wasn't so much as a glisten of sweat on her body, which spoke to just how in shape she really was.

"Thanks," she muttered, taking her mug. She marched up to the cupboards and began to make a bowl of cereal.

I will not make a joke about a cat lapping at a bowl of milk. Must resist.

"So," I said, eager to make conversation. "Did you hear about the mine?"

"Sunny claimed that you broke the barrier," she said. Her voice carried a slight annoyance. "I checked it out." She shrugged. "We can enter. What's it like now?"

I explained as best as I could. About the wave, the thickness of the air. All the while, she nodded. Frustratingly, she didn't offer any information or gratification. Instead, she worked through her Cheerios like I was talking about something as mundane as the weather.

"So," I said. "What do you think?"

She took several more bites, then a long swig of the milk from the bowl. "Do you have any experience mining? Any at all?" she asked.

I tried not to focus on the milk-mustache that now graced her upper lip, even though it threatened to make me smirk.

"I'll learn," I said, my voice thick from trying not to laugh.

"Sure." She rolled her eyes. "I'll see what you can do. After breakfast, I want to see your capabilities." She finally ran the back of her hand over her upper lip, then licked the stray beads of milk off.

"Perfect." The word came out confidently. Unfortunately, I had to follow it up with uncertainty and a little fear. There was an important question that hadn't been answered yet. "So, Tabby, I keep hearing about a demon in the mine."

"Ugh," Tabby's tail dropped limp in exasperation. "It's an old rumor. Don't worry about it. Magic may be real, but that doesn't stop superstition. Some people think that there's a curse on the mine caused by a demon living inside it."

"Uh-huh," I nodded and took a swig from my comically oversized mug. "So, since I'm new to this, I need to ask an obvious question: are demons a thing?"

Tabby looked at me. A moment of judgment flashed through her eyes, followed by calm. It was a fair question for someone in my situation. Even she had to admit that.

"There are demons, yes," she said. "Just not the way you might imagine. It's difficult to explain."

"Nooo, it's not," a very loud, very hungover Sunny wandered into the room. She was wearing the same clothes as the day before, now just ruffled. Rubbing her temples, the monkey woman said, "Demons are easy to explain. Less Dante, more Gygax. They're well-dressed, melodramatic, and deadly."

"And," Tabby said decisively, "there aren't any in the mines."

"Ugh. Taaabby. Can we not right now? I'm dealing with a lot."

One is always angry, the other is impulsive and impatient. That's a volatile combo if I've ever seen one.

"So," I interrupted, "do you usually wake up this early, Sunny?"

"Ha!" Both of my roommates laughed.

Sunny continued, "I'm not awake. I'll down some water, shower, and pass out for a few more hours. Then, back to the Paw."

Seriously?

My eyes moved to Tabby, who shrugged and held out her coffee mug in a gesture which read, *Yeah, what did you expect?*

I nodded. "Okay. And Eo?"

Instantly, the air in the room changed.

Sunny moved to the sink, filled her mug from the tap, and downed the water.

Tabby looked to the stairs with obvious concern on her

face. As angry as she was with, well, *everything*, she obviously cared deeply for her friends. "I hope she slept, even a little. The girl's obsessive."

"Heh," Sunny chuckled darkly. "Her statuettes make most of our money these days."

"That doesn't make it okay, Sunny."

"You have a better idea?"

"Yeah." The blue of Tabby's eyes began to simmer with an angry fire. "You could stop drinking away our profits, for starters!"

I cleared my throat.

Tabby glared at me and Sunny groaned, clutching her head.

"How about," I said carefully, "I bring up a cup to Eo. Does she prefer coffee or tea?"

Again, the women hesitated.

After a few seconds, Tabby said, "There's a thermos on the fridge. Fill that with coffee. It may be a while before she notices." She sighed and gave a slight, sad shake of her head. "There are some granola bars beside it. Please take some of those to her as well. She may not notice you, but it's important that she has the stuff there. Don't worry if she doesn't acknowledge you."

Tabby pushed herself to her feet, planting her hands firmly on the counter. "Now, if you'll excuse me, I need to clean the kitchen. The mess is bugging me."

What mess? I looked around—the place was as pristine as when I entered.

No, there was a single drop of coffee next to my mug.

Seriously? I sighed, but I couldn't help smiling.

I recognized a sisterly care in Tabby's tone that made her seem softer somehow. There was a lot more going on in this household than I initially thought. This, I hoped, would be a start to understanding and building a bridge.

Also, I need these people to help me figure out the mine! I reminded myself. We needed to get along for all of our sakes, especially since there seemed to be money issues.

The gold nugget we'd found came to mind, and I hoped it would be enough to help, at least until we dug up more.

Sunny and Tabby began to bicker, but I decided not to push my luck. Instead, I filled the thermos, took some granola bars, and marched up to the third floor. Once again, there was no response to my knock. I entered without trying a second.

Eo was passed out at her desk, slumped against it, and snoring gently.

I walked up to her and put the thermos and granola bars in front of her, so she'd hopefully see them when she woke. As my hand stretched to check on her, I saw her work. The boar-headed dolls had been transformed. These were not simply dolls; they were statues. Detailed, intentionally dirtied, scarred, bruised, and *incredible*.

My eyes turned back to Eo. Perhaps because of the morning light filtering in, she seemed paler than the night before. Her soft lips gently breathed in and out.

She looked so frail, except for her hands. The hands were stained with paint. One of them still held a brush limply between two fingers. The statue-maker had fallen asleep with her arm under her cheek.

I looked again at the shelves. For the first time, I noticed that some of them had scraps of paper at their base. A closer look showed details of size, age, and asking price.

Fewer than half of the figures had a tag.

Hobby? Job? Obsession? All three? I couldn't decide.

That was a thought for another time. I returned to the kitchen. Sunny was gone by then, and Tabby was washing the dishes while grumbling to herself. I tried not to fixate on the fluffy tail that swished back and forth behind her. I failed.

Focus, man. It's time to work.

"What?" Tabby asked.

"I'm going into the mine today."

At first, she didn't react. The plate in her hands held all her attention. She washed it, scrubbed it, rinsed it, and dried it before replying, "What are you going to do?"

"There's a lot of work to do in there," I said honestly. "I figure it's best to get started early. You know the business way better than me. Help me figure it out."

"You have no idea what to do," she said.

I thought that was hardly fair.

Still, her next words filled me with hope, "But where better to test your abilities? I'll meet you there soon."

TEN

Heave, ho!

With a grunt, I hefted a mine cart off its side. Next, I began moving the spilled chunks of iron ore from the ground which surrounded it. It seemed whoever had abandoned it had done so in a hurry.

The main cavern, where we'd encountered that goblin attack, was even more of a mess than when I first saw it. It'd take a couple days just to sort everything out.

"Those goblins sure made a mess of things," I said.

"It's not just them," Tabby said.

She'd changed into a pair of thick, worn coveralls. I wore a pair also, and we both had on hard hats.

Tabby continued, "Most of it comes from what happened the day the barrier was made. For all we know, the miners in this area made the mess when they ran out of the mine. I hear that it all happened quickly."

Tabby didn't help as I worked. Instead, she stood in the center of the room, eyes and ears scanning all around. A sheath hung from her left hip. Inside was a shortsword. Before we entered the mine, I thought it seemed a bit small, but she'd explained that the caves demanded it. Nobody wanted to be caught in a small cave, lacking the room to pull out a bigger weapon.

I remembered a pretty brutal anime where that very thing happened.

"Goblins are easy to kill," she had said earlier that morning. "But it only takes one moment of stupidity or bad luck for them to overpower you."

I tried not to think about that too hard, but it kept coming back to me.

"What happened when the barrier was made?" I asked as I dusted off my hands. They were already dirty and covered with knicks and small bruises. I made a mental note to invest in some decent work gloves.

"I don't know the full story," Tabby said. "It was my day off when it happened. The miners had an encounter with something a lot worse than goblins. I've heard everything from bugbears to trolls to giant spiders."

"Shouldn't there have been witnesses?"

"Should..." Tabby grimaced at the word as if it were bad-tasting medicine. "It never should have happened. Most of the miners didn't see it. There was an attack of some kind, a lot of people got disoriented. Some people raised an evacuation alarm. Everyone ran out. Once everyone got outside, the barrier was erected. Since then, nobody's been able to enter."

"That's it then." I understood her frustration more and more. "Just like that, no more mine."

"That's the short version. Attack, evacuation, barrier. One ongoing theory—which I personally believe—is that someone had sabotaged the mine and placed a curse on it. Most people in Acanth aren't like us—the women in Antrum House, I mean. We grew up here, but a lot of women came here because they wanted to leave their old lives. A person doesn't live in an old-school village, working underground eight hours a day, without a good reason. I think that someone had an enemy who exacted some kind of revenge."

I shook my head. "That's vague, inconclusive, and disappointing."

"Well, that's what we have to work with. Attack, evacuation, barrier. The mining team was at a low point. The superstition was at a high. Some people were worried about that stupid demon rumor, and others thought we were going to exhaust the mine's resources. With tensions like they were, something a lot less dramatic could've ended the business. For me, at least, the idea that it's all because of someone's bitter ex with magical abilities gives me some closure. The whole thing is stupid." She shrugged. "Can't change it, so we might as well move on."

"That's still frustrating."

"Yeah? Most things in life are."

They don't need to be.

I bit my tongue. It wasn't the time to push back. Instead, my hands kept moving. I managed to organize most of the ore, equipment, and supplies into different carts. The cart on the tracks leading down the main entrance contained the ore, and the others were set and ready to go deeper into the mines.

The only equipment that surprised me was the weaponry. Throughout the cavern, and likely throughout the tunnels, there were weapons scattered about. It looked like there'd been a skirmish. That was one of the main reasons I couldn't believe Tabby's story of why the mine closed.

I'd press for details later, maybe with Karma. For now, we had pests to deal with. Because of that, I knew that I'd need a weapon for myself.

My weapon options were daggers, hammers, picks, and hand axes. I lacked experience with daggers. The hammer didn't feel right. The ax, I thought, was a happy medium. I took one.

The ax worked for Gimli, so why not.

My protector kept watching.

"Alright," Tabby said after a while. "We've got some movement from a tunnel. I'd guess two goblins from the sounds of it."

To my shock, she began walking toward a tunnel, one hand resting on the hilt of her short sword.

"Why," I dared to ask, "are you moving toward the sound of goblins?"

"Because this is not their home. They're an invasive species to Acanth and Antrum. It's time to start dealing with the pest control issue. Or are you scared?"

She spun on her feet to look at me, one hand resting on her hip. Even in the heavy coveralls, she moved smoothly. A smirk played on her lips.

The tunnel which she'd indicated was atop a short incline, and I looked over her shoulder at it. I didn't see or hear anything yet, but I had the vague sensation that I was being watched.

"Well," I said. "I've never used a sword or killed something that used weapons. I'll do it, but I'm not gonna pretend that I don't need practice."

"Honesty is good. In that case, let's get to practice. I'll take the attention from one, so you can fight solo. We need you to get used to it. Ready to put your ax to use?"

"No time like the present."

I thought I was doing a pretty good job at hiding my nerves, but I suspected Tabby could see right through it. If she did, she didn't comment on it.

With my first ever weapon in hand, we went down the tunnel.

"Remember, it's the same as dealing with any infestation. It's not difficult to deal with one at a time, but you can't underestimate them in groups. They won't form plans, but they have sharp instincts. Also, they can be vicious in numbers. Be quick and decisive."

Again, this didn't sit well with me. Tabby was telling the truth; there was no doubt of that. Still, the attack on Sunny yesterday seemed like more than instinct. A bunch of them had made noise in a tunnel while another climbed and attacked from above us. Perhaps their instincts had been honed through years of more intelligent enemies, but why would they have started with that? It seemed at least a little calculated.

Or am I overthinking it?

The thought soon left my mind. In a tunnel roughly eight feet tall, we saw them lit in the electric lights.

Instantly, Tabby pounced. I ran behind her.

As she'd guessed, there were two of the ugly things, draped in tattered brown rags. One of them raised a dagger at us and hissed. The other turned down the tunnel away from us and squealed.

"No you don't!" Tabby rushed for it.

The first goblin slashed at her, but it was like trying to hit a leaf in the wind. She dodged around the blade as if its own movements made her untouchable. Her blade flashed from her sheath and cut off the shrill note from the goblin that had attempted to flee—and probably get help.

I didn't wait. While the other goblin chased her, I rushed in. My first strike was a sweep at its knobbed legs. It fell to the ground, knocking up a cloud of dust. From there, I brought my ax up, careful not to hit the ceiling, and slammed it down onto the goblin with a wet thud.

My enemy stopped moving instantly.

"Congratulations," Tabby said. "You just got your first kill."

I smirked, more grateful for her smile than her words.

I expected to feel bad, to feel something, but it really was like killing pests—pests that were just as eager to kill us.

A slight movement behind Tabby cut off my excitement. Further down the mine shaft, barely noticeable, something moved from around a rock.

"Look out!" I lunged forward and pushed her aside.

Suddenly, sharp pain sliced across my arm. Stone and metal smacked and clattered off the tunnel wall behind us. We turned to the source. Four goblins appeared, snarling. They carried roughly made hatchets, bits of stone with jagged metal attached to one side.

They've turned mining equipment into weapons, I realized. *They created simple tools.*

As one wound up for another throw, Tabby's ears twitched back the way we came. "There are some behind us. We need to run!"

The bastards are trying to trap us! So much for being too dumb to form plans.

CHAPTER
ELEVEN

The creature snapped at me, saliva hanging in ropes from a mouth of cragged teeth. It stood only to my knees, but it used that to its advantage, slashing at my knees and ankles like a murderous toddler.

Still, it was small.

I jumped over its slash and kicked it square in the face, feeling its nose break under my shoe with a sickening crunch.

"Behind!" Tabby called, though the unthinking shriek from over my shoulder gave it away.

I spun, swinging the ax at full extension. *Dammit*, I thought mid-swing, *it's too high!* Luckily, my opponent had leaped, making my nearly doomed strike connect with its ribs.

That worked perfectly. It doesn't feel like an accident.

This wasn't the time to get lost in thought, so I pushed the idea away. With no enemies in my immediate area, I looked to my companion. Tabby used her short sword to bat away a club, rolled behind its wielder, and pushed her opponent into a deadly attack from its fellow. The fratricidal goblin did not hesitate. If anything, it seemed annoyed that it needed to push the body of its comrade aside so it could approach.

At that moment, while it was stalled pushing the body, Tabby surged forward. Her sword pierced through both chests with a quick pump of her arm, which she retracted with equal smoothness.

I'd expected to call out a warning to her, as she'd done for me. Now, that seemed unnecessary.

We'd managed to push our way back to the main cavern. Tabby had dodged and leaped through the goblins that had tried to catch us from behind. Our pincer had beaten theirs. Only one of that first group remained, but we could hear more coming.

The last of the attacking party lunged at me. I jumped backward and brought the ax down. The creature was fast, but I had more reach. Instinct guided the strike. The ax caught him mid-attack, splitting his skull open like a melon.

We'd beaten their ambush. The first part of it, at least.

As I pulled my weapon free and the goblin fell in a heap on the ground, a strange feeling grew in my chest. Energy surged through my body like an electric current, bursting from my chest and making my muscles sing.

"Oh, hell yes." I knew this feeling from the gym. It was similar to working out, that moment when I knew I'd pushed myself enough to try something heavier, more taxing. But it was way more intense. More immediate and rewarding.

The adrenaline wash took away the fatigue of cleaning and fighting.

Best not to get too excited, I told myself. *Overconfidence is more likely to kill than a goblin.*

My eyes turned back to the tunnel where they'd entrapped us. Several of them stood at the mouth, snapping their jaws and waving their makeshift weapons.

They're baiting us again.

I looked up. Sure enough, two goblins clung to the ceiling with daggers in their teeth. They hesitated when I met their eyes.

"Two above!" I called.

"I hear them. Follow my lead."

Instantly, Tabby screamed at the crowd in the tunnel, pretending that they held all of her interest.

The goblins stopped hesitating. They saw Tabby look away from them, and, like idiots, they leaped toward her. In the moment before their blades struck her, she dove to the side. They landed in ugly heaps on the uneven rock floor with wet *splats*.

We each took care of one, putting their broken bodies out of their misery, then flipped off the enraged, frightened attackers who snarled at us from the mouth of the cave.

"Push the cart," Tabby said. "We'll take some ore out. It'll piss them off."

She turned back to the group and raised her bloody sword at them like it was a middle finger. She hissed, "This is what you get!"

Still snarling, some of the goblins began to slither back, away from us, like they knew they were beaten.

Tabby and I pushed the cart down the track to the opening tunnel. It was easier than I'd imagined, and I found the sound of the wheels grinding against the metal rails to be oddly satisfying. Soon, we could see daylight.

"Damn," Tabby said. She released the cart and walked into the sun, hips swinging freely. A wide smile spread over her face. "I missed this."

"I didn't know you were such a fighter," I said as I stopped pushing the cart.

"Huh?" She turned to me. After a moment, she chuckled. "I guess this does look kinda messed up, doesn't it? It's not the bloodshed. It's the movement. I'm not happy unless I'm moving. This, the adrenaline, the rush, having to find the flow and work with someone, pushing ourselves. It doesn't even need to be fighting. I miss working with people. Pushing myself! It's so—"

She stopped. As Tabby had spoken, her hands had begun to move in energetic, joyful gestures. Her smile had widened into something bright and infectious. I couldn't help but feel happy at seeing her so excited.

Also, I understood exactly what she meant. I felt alive in a way I'd never known, like I'd not truly lived until that moment.

When Tabby saw me, probably grinning like an idiot, she caught herself. She cleared her throat. "Well, it's been a while. This was a nice throwback. I think I needed it. So, thank you, Jack."

"It's just the start," I said. "We'll be in there a lot."

Tabby's smile remained, but it changed. Her sapphire eyes glimmered. The joy turned bittersweet. She sighed, a heavy sound, and shook her head. "No, Jack. I appreciate your optimism. I really do, but it's not happening. This is only the first step. We'd need to sell the ore or smelt and forge it ourselves. There's no system for transporting the material to the village anymore." She shook her head. "We can't. And forgetting that, we don't have the team. Sunny is the one best with a pickaxe. Eo knows how to map and chart the tunnels. Neither of them are going to help. They're too stuck in their issues."

"I'm not giving up," I said. "I've only begun to try. I won't give up before I've had the chance to fail."

Tabby shook her head again. "I'm not getting my hopes up. Thanks for today, but no."

Come on!

I couldn't believe it. This was the happiest I'd ever seen her, and she didn't accept it. The opportunity was right there, and she didn't believe it was worth pursuing. My first instinct was to try to convince her otherwise. There was more than enough reason to try. Even today, we'd done so much. I'd never fought monsters in my life, but with the two of us alone, we'd cleared a small raiding party! We'd started the cleanup! Got some ore!

The simple, unbelievable fact was that Tabby didn't think it was possible.

I don't think I can blame her.

At that moment, she reminded me of myself and my co-workers when I worked at the city hall. People who did the same things day in and day out. When the chance came to do something, they—we—did nothing. On the few occasions we'd tried, we'd had our efforts ignored into submission. To care was to put in effort, to put in effort was to make oneself vulnerable to exhaustion and disappointment.

Her sense of defeat was frustrating and infuriating, but I couldn't blame her. That left only one option: prove her wrong.

"Where's the forge?" I asked.

She looked at me. "What?"

"Maybe I'll fail, but I still want to try. Where's the forge?"

"You have no idea how much work this will entail."

I shrugged. "If I fail, you'll get to say *I told you so*."

Once again, I had no idea what I was getting into. Unlike last time, though, I knew who to ask for help.

CHAPTER
TWELVE

Several days passed, and I found a comfortable routine.

As had become usual, I woke up a little after dawn and pulled back the curtains. Tabby was laying out her yoga mat, enjoying the pinkening skies beyond our hills. Every day, it was difficult to tell if I was more entranced by the dawn or the woman. As always, I ripped my eyes away from the scene to throw myself to the ground and do some push-ups, then a few stretches of my own. It helped me wake up and got rid of some of the soreness from the previous day's work.

After that, I made it downstairs in time to make coffee for both myself and Tabby. Breakfast was light, usually just toast for me, sometimes eggs. Tabby had cereal every day without variation.

After her routine, she entered.

"Good morning," I said, as had become usual.

"Good morning," she replied.

We ate in silence, but it was a peaceful silence, not an awkward one.

"You're still at it?" she eventually asked.

"That's right, and I'm not stopping, either," I said.

Tabby nodded, finished her coffee, and began to obsessively clean the house.

There was no crash from Sunny this morning, so I checked on Eo, lugging up the usual rations to her.

As had rarely happened, she was awake. Even more rarely, she wasn't working.

"Good morning," I said.

"Good morning to you, too." Her head spun to me before the rest of her body. She stood to take the thermos and granola bars I offered. Her fingers didn't have paint stains on them, yet another first. It was good to see that she was taking care of herself.

"You've been coming here at the same time every morning for a few days now," she said. "Who are you?"

Yes! Today might be the day to put my plans into motion.

So, not minding that I had already explained half of it to her before, I said, "My name's Jack. I live here now. I asked you about the charts for the Antrum tunnels a while back. I'm the guy who broke the barrier on the mine."

"Oh." Her eyebrows lifted. Considering the news, she wasn't all that surprised. "Oh yes, I remember."

How are you so unbothered about an unknown, mortal guy suddenly living in your house?

"I see. Um, you seem to be taking the news well."

"About Antrum Mine? Well, it's a surprise about the barrier being broken. But at the moment, I have too many orders to worry about. Besides, I'm behind schedule on my own projects." She stopped, tapping a finger on her bottom lip. "That reminds me, I ordered a new kit a few days ago. Have we gotten any packages?"

I cast my thumb at a box that I had put beside the ornate owl door. "One came in yesterday."

"Perfect."

"Um, Eo? I don't want to sound unappreciative, but you sure seem calm about a new housemate living here with you."

Her ebony eyes looked me up and down. The subtle change in the way light glinted off those black marbles gave away the movement. It was almost hypnotic to watch.

"If you were a problem," she said, "Tabby wouldn't have let you in. If you weren't worth our time, Sunny would have kicked you out. You managed to open the barrier, so you definitely belong here...for now, at least. I'd like to hear more about that sometime. Tabby and I have a bet about the cause of the barrier, so I want details. Later, when I have time. She's hung up on that *vengeful ex* theory, but I refuse to believe it. Acanth's livelihood didn't fall apart because of a second-rate CSI plot."

"What do *you* think happened?" I pressed.

We had spoken so little that I wanted to keep her talking as much as possible.

Her face lit up, another flash of light across the flawless black of her eyes. She stood and began moving her hands.

Her feather-covered arms, which looked like a sweater, ruffled cutely with her motions as she exclaimed, "It was a vampire!"

I blinked. My first instinct was to say *that's nice* and walk away slowly. I didn't want any part in that.

With effort, however, I forced my feet and my face to be unmoved.

"A vampire?" I repeated.

"Yes!" She either ignored or didn't notice my surprise. "I think that there's a vampire buried in the mountain, from way, way before we ever got there. It's been trapped there for who knows how long! Whoever trapped it there put a curse on it so it would never escape. On the day the mine closed, I believe that someone tripped some ancient magical alarm that activated a trap!"

I continued to blink, looking to the side and noting the Spawn figure crouching beside three different versions of Dracula. A fourth incarnation of the old Count sat on her desk as we spoke.

"That," I said diplomatically, "is a very different theory from Tabby's."

"I can't wait to be proven right. Anyway, I don't have time to chat. I was just taking a short break to clean my feathers."

"Have a good day," I said.

"Mmhmm."

There didn't seem to be much else I could do, so I left.

Walking back down to the kitchen, I found Tabby in the hall beside the stairs. She was polishing and re-polishing the glass on the photos on the wall.

"I'm off," I said. "Tell Sunny I'm in the mines."

"No," Tabby said. "Wait for her. It's dangerous for you to go in there alone."

Goblins hadn't shown up near the main cavern since the day that Tabby and I taught them a lesson, so I felt secure enough going most of the way on my own.

"I'll wait at the entrance."

"Why?"

"Because if I wait here," I reasoned, "she'll probably sneak past me to get to the bar and get her drink on. If I go over there, she'll need to come to me, to make sure I'm not doing something stupid like entering the tunnels alone."

Tabby raised an eyebrow. "Are you going to do something stupid?"

I signed a contract to own a mine. Of course I'm doing something stupid.

"No, I promise."

"Well." Tabby sighed. "It'll keep her away from the bar for a while, so fine. I'm grateful for that, at least."

"Happy to help. Be back later."

It hurt to leave the house, as always. Tabby's cleaning had taken on a darker light every day I lived here. At first, it'd just been a little strange. Seeing a woman perpetually in loungewear, battling the concept of dust, had been a weirdly attractive oddity.

Now, it was sad. She wasn't cleaning the house; she was holding it together. She had to move because the other two in the house wouldn't contribute to its upkeep. Eo made figures to be sold. Tabby handled orders, shipped packages, cleaned the house, and prepared meals.

Sunny...drank and played pool.

The money-draining habit was a strain on the house and on the dynamic of the people who lived in it.

Thankfully, a clear alternative presented itself. Like Tabby had once said, Sunny was a natural in the mine. So, I waited for her in the quarry, leaning against a cart full of ore that I'd excavated by myself over the past few days.

Please don't let Tabby find out about this unless my idea works.

It took a long time for Sunny to appear, so I spent much of the morning moving clumps of the ore to crates, trying to find an amount that we could feasibly carry into town.

Eventually, she showed up with a coffee and a yawn. I'd come to believe that her wardrobe consisted entirely of graphic tee shirts and denim. Today's outfit was simple: all black except for block capitals exclaiming *YOU DIED* in red font.

Once again, the text was stretched across her breasts.

"Good morning," I said.

"Hooow is it good, exactly?" she replied. "I was told that you were going to do something stupid. I was worried that I had to babysit you."

"That was a lie."

"Caaalled it. Why are there a bunch of boxes with iron ore?"

Here it goes.

"I was hoping you could help me carry some into town, to the smith. We might be able to sell some of it."

Sunny's tail began to swing back and forth, forming question marks as she tapped her foot. Clearly, she had no interest in the business. That was the problem. She had the talent, strength, and ability. She just had no interest whatsoever in...anything, as far as I understood.

After a while, she said, "We can carry someee so she can see the quality, then I'll come back with Gretchen's cart and grab the rest. She's got a special magic one that makes them weigh nothing! Oooh, and I get to take half the money off the top, for my efforts."

"A quarter."

"Why would I accept that?" She frowned.

"The rest goes to Antrum House. We'll use it to budget for groceries and Eo's supplies."

"Fiiine." Sunny chugged her coffee and jumped into the quarry. "But we're not taking any more trips than we have to." She took one crate, dumped its contents into another, and hefted it onto her shoulder. "Ready?"

"Of course."

Soon, we were marching into Acanth Village, loaded down each with a crate of ore.

I'd made a point to spend a few hours every day in the village. Part of that was for necessity. Karma had the documents I needed to understand the business side of things. This was for logistics and history. Most of the original employees had left the village altogether, which meant that I couldn't get firsthand accounts from anyone except my housemates. With my own searching—and the chameleon's help—I'd managed to get an idea of how things were meant to work.

Ore was mined from Antrum and transported to the village. There, it was either smelted and treated or sold directly to the smith at a reduced cost. For now, we'd have to settle for the latter.

Sunny led me to the Acme Anvil Smithery. The proprietor was outside, sharpening a sword against a grindstone. Sunny and I walked toward her and waited for her to notice us. Once she did, I said, "Hello."

"Hey," she replied calmly as she stood to her full height.

The blacksmith was an orc woman named Gretchen. I'd made a point to say hi and wave whenever I came to town. It also helped that Fran told me her name.

Gretchen was nothing like Tolkien led me to expect of orcs. Her skin was a two-toned mossy green. A long black braid hung down her back, pulling her hair away from her face and the many tools in which it could get caught. She wore a thick brown apron over a thin white tank top and dusty brown cargo pants. The best way to describe her look was a blue-collar craftswoman. The clothes had been worn, battered, and lightly torn in some places.

She had green eyes that almost matched her skin. Most of her teeth, I noticed when she laughed, were human. The only exception was two canines that curved upward from her bottom jaw, pressing gently against a full upper lip. Her long ears came to a rounded point.

When Gretchen saw us, she clapped. "Yes! Today's the day, huh? Please tell me that today is the day."

Very different from: Grr, me orc, Want ore. Make weapon. Grr.

"Whaaat day are you talking about?" Sunny put her crates down near Gretchen.

"Jack hasn't been subtle." She looked at me. "Is it true that the mine is open again? Do tell me that the mine is open again. It's so nice to be able to pick up supplies locally. It's been brutal trying to live off repairs and importing materials from outside. If I could get ore and metal straight from you guys, it'd be great for business. Seriously, tell me that Antrum is working again."

I looked at Sunny. Her face pulled back in surprise. There was a declaration of pure sincerity and hope, unlike anything I'd seen Sunny exhibit since I arrived. It had a clear effect. It was everything I'd hoped for but hadn't dared to expect.

"We're working on it," I said diplomatically. "We're still getting everything sorted."

"You only have old equipment," Gretchen said. "It's dangerous and inefficient to go into the mines with stuff that isn't up to date. Make sure that everything is up to code."

"Okaaay," Sunny said. "I get the excitement, but don't give us a sales pitch."

"No pitch, don't misunderstand," Gretchen said with a smirk. The lopsided smile, combined with the push of tooth on lip, created something playful and mischievous. "I'll sharpen your picks and one set of weapons for free. You must be safe."

Thank you, Gretchen.

Once again, her sincerity left an impact on Sunny.

Sunny nodded, uncertain. "There's a bunch more crates back at the mine. I'll go get them."

While she was gone with the cart, Gretchen and I discussed rates. We also talked about the miners who used to work there.

This, more than anything, was what I'd been trying to prepare over the last several days. Visiting the civic center every day had helped cement the fact that I lived here now. The people were kind, and accepting. Most helpfully, they were excited for the mine.

As with any small town, rumors spread quickly. Spending a few hours a day asking for records about the mine suggested to them something about my future plans. The smith wasn't the only one who wanted the business to return.

It also helped that I told Fran to drip-feed news of the barrier's removal to the townsfolk.

In other words, I wasn't the only one encouraging Sunny and Tabby to give Antrum another shot. The entire village was doing so.

When Sunny returned, Gretchen and I worked out a price. The orc smith and I joked through it.

When I accepted the money, she said, "Consider this a down payment. I expect more from you."

"I'm going to the bar," Sunny said suddenly. She was off before either of us could react.

As she marched away, I couldn't hide my groan.

"Everything okay?" Gretchen asked.

"I don't get it," I replied. "She was so excited at first. She was right there when I broke the barrier. I had to sprint after her into the mine. I had expected her to be so excited that it'd become a problem in itself. Now, she won't touch the mine. Where'd that enthusiasm go?"

Gretchen nodded. "How drunk was she when it happened?"

"Pretty drunk? I don't have a lot to compare to."

"Was she giddy and talkative drunk, or was she jumping around and rubbing her boobs against you drunk?"

"Bit of both."

"Oh, she was plastered. If she'd been sober, or even tipsy, she wouldn't have rushed into the mine like you say she did. I'm sure it was exciting when it first happened, but now she has to come to terms with it."

"Come to terms with what?"

"Nobody told you." Gretchen covered her mouth.

From the look of concern on her face, I guessed the tone of what was to come.

"People around here don't tell me much," I said. "It's sort of becoming a theme."

Gretchen put her hand on mine. "It's about Sunny's sister."

"Oh boy..."

"Her name was Dawn. They were together all the time," Gretchen said. "They worked in the mines together. On the day the mine closed, there was a lot of confusion. Nobody knew what to do. Most of the miners left Acanth. Dawn was one of them. She had argued that there was nothing left here, but Sunny didn't want to leave the place where they'd been born and grown up. Dawn left. Sunny didn't take it well, and..." Gretchen hesitated a moment, then said, "That day you broke the barrier was the only time she'd ever set foot in there without her sister. Yes, it's like home to Sunny, but it will also be a painful reminder of the family that isn't there anymore."

"Okay," I nodded, thankful that Dawn hadn't suffered a fatal mining accident as it had initially sounded. "Is there any chance we could call her sister and have them talk?"

Gretchen shook her head. "Jack, I'm sorry. She died working in another mine."

Oh.

THIRTEEN

There weren't a lot of people in *The Monkey's Paw*. It was a Wednesday, so I guessed that wasn't much of a surprise.

Sunny was at the bar, which only surprised me because I'd expected her to be by the pool table or the dart board.

Even more discouraging was her posture. She sat leaning over a drink, her fingers tapping the glass. There was no yelling or chugging, or flirting. The glass wasn't even empty.

Behind the bar, Fran gave me a concerned look.

I sighed.

After selling the ore, I'd gone back to the house to look through photos. With Tabby's help, I found some of Sunny at work. Sure enough, several of them showed another monkey girl. Dawn looked similar to Sunny, but she had not shared her energy. The cat, monkey, and owl held the foreground in most pictures. Dawn stuck to the background in all but one, which featured the sisters arm in arm.

Tabby had explained it all to me in greater detail. After leaving Acanth, Dawn and most of the crew went to other mines. They tried to stay together, united into a team through years of working together. Most of them managed to find a place that allowed them to continue working together. This job came from a massive mining company, one with the resources and necessities for a large group.

All forms of this work came with risks. This new job, however, took them to a scale that they had never experienced, working with bigger crews and larger equipment against deadlier creatures.

The tragedy had been a horrible mix of factors. During excavation, the crew disturbed a nest of giant spiders. The spiders attacked. The commotion brought instability, causing a partial cave-in. Dawn—every bit as talented as her sister—had been on the wall, near the ceiling, picking at the hardest-to-reach prizes. That meant she was the furthest from the exit, and the closest to the spiders.

She'd been the first to notice the issue. Her warning had come just a moment before the eight-legged assault, giving the others just enough time to prepare their weapons. Keeping the monsters at bay so her companions could escape, by all accounts, she had died a hero.

I didn't ask for more details. It already felt like I was overstepping to learn this much about Sunny's family and past. Now, at least, I understood. Being able to enter the mine that first day had brought back a million memories for Sunny, as well as the horrible fact that those days could never return.

KIRK MASON

Dawn would never see Antrum reopen. She couldn't even learn the news.

With all this in mind, I looked at my housemate with pity. Was there anything I could say? Was it right to say anything to her? I didn't know, but I couldn't let her stew alone at the bottom of a pint.

Well, time to be a friend.

I planted myself on the stool beside her.

"Do you have any amber ale?" I asked Fran.

"Of course," she answered, grateful for a distraction from the serious atmosphere. "Local or import?"

"Local, thanks."

"Certainly."

I waited, saying nothing. Sunny didn't look at me. She didn't even move. Her tail wrapped around one of the legs of her stool, like a sad drunkard leaning on a streetlamp for support. It seemed unlikely that she was entirely drunk, though. That would've involved more volume and swaying.

At least, I hoped that she wasn't wasted. There was a chance that this was some new level of drunk previously unseen.

Or maybe she's just having a rough day.

I bit my tongue and waited. The most I gave was a thanks to Fran when I got my beer. No talk of business. Nothing. Fran moved on to other customers.

There was only awkward silence for a painfully long time.

At least the beer is good, I thought.

"Sooo," my lead miner said in her drunken tone, "You gonna keep up the *Good Will Hunting* routine? You're a good dude, Jack, but your vibe is nothing like Robin Williams. If you want to talk, just talk."

"Okay," I said. "I was worried that I hurt your feelings before, because of something I didn't know. I wanted to check in on you."

"I'm fiiine, mostly." She pounded the rest of her beer down in one go, then slammed the bottom of the glass against the counter so hard that I feared it would shatter. "Fraaan, refill."

That didn't seem like a good sign. I decided to change tactics. "Thanks for helping me carry the ore earlier."

"Nooo problem. It was nice to do some work for Antrum. It's been a really long time."

"I'll bet."

"Maaan." She shook her head. "I can't believe that I charged in there when you broke the barrier. It was just so...exciting. Does that make sense? It was so cool! I've worked there all my adult life. It's part of me, you know? It felt like home almost as much as the house."

She took a long sip before continuing, "That makes it weird. You heard about Dawn, right? She left, fine. I understand why she didn't want to be here anymore. We had other friends in the crew, and she wasn't as attached to Acanth as I was. The barrier was just...her reason to leave. What happened to her was something that could happen to anyone but...I wasn't with her."

Sunny gripped her tankard with both hands. A sneer cracked across her face in a wince, as if she were recoiling from pain. "If I'd been with her, we both would've made it out. Or we would've gone somewhere less dangerous. Or...something!"

When Fran brought a new drink, Sunny downed half of it in one go. The bartender and I shared a nervous glance as Sunny smacked it down onto the bar.

"Ugh!" she groaned. "I don't knooow! It's my fault!"

Her normal volume was returning, in a bleakly horrifying form.

Unsure what to do, I took a sip. Her head dropped, so she rested her cheek on the bar, staring listlessly at nothing. We continued in silence a little longer. There was nothing good to say.

Maybe change the topic?

"Nice shirt," I said. "I wouldn't have guessed you for a Dark Souls fan."

Her eyes moved to me before the rest of her face. It felt like a miniature version of Eo's habit. There was no answer for a moment. Perhaps she recognized the attempt at filling the silence for what it was. If so, she agreed to it. "I'm not much of a fan. Eo is. It was a gift from her for my birthday."

"Ever played it?"

"Yeeeah. It was fine, I guess. I played with Eo after Dawn left Acanth. She basically told me how to do everything. Kept talking about stats and min-maxing and equipment. I prefer the 'jump on baddies and get shiny things' style of games, but it's fun to play with Eo. You'd be amazed how energetic she gets when she's into a game."

As she spoke, a smile slowly crept up her face, returning color to her cheeks and lifting the corners of her lips. "Man, I could probably rattle off a dozen names and places and items from that game. What does any of it mean? No idea. Still, it was a fun time. Eo was beside me the whole time, cheering me on to keep fighting bosses over and over. She screamed sooo loud that Tabby had to check on us. Then, we made Tabby try." She shook her head. "You should have seen it! Imagine Tabby trying to figure out *Dark Souls* controls in the middle of a boss fight. It was hilarious!"

She started doing impressions, complete with tail re-enactments, of Tabby at a controller. The impression was awful, but the more it went on, the brighter Sunny became. After a while, though it didn't last long, the memory brought out a deep belly laugh. It shook through her. Afterward, she sighed. As she leaned back for the laugh, I noticed that nobody stood at the pool table.

Let's see if we can keep the mood light.

"Want to play a round?" I pointed to the table.

"Of what?" she looked over. Suddenly, her head swung back to me. She was still smiling, but it read, *Oh, you poor naïve soul* instead of, *That will be a good time.* She looked me over again, appraising. "Are you serious?"

"Why wouldn't I be?"

In the corner of my vision, Fran rubbed her eyes and said something under her breath.

Sunny tapped her fingers on the bar for a while. "Loser pays the winner's tab for the night."

Instantly, Fran's tail struck out as if she'd been electrified. Her golden eyes bore into mine, pleading silently but clearly that I not accept the terms.

"How about," I asked, "the winner gets twenty bucks?"

"Fifty."

Another look at Fran. The fluffy tail settled a little. Panic lightened to concern.

"Thirty-five," I said.

"Fooorty."

"Deal."

Fran crossed her arms.

"Let's gooo, Jackal." Sunny pushed away from the bar and confidently, though clumsily, walked to the pool table.

"Jackal?" I asked.

"Jaaack Calvinson. Jack Cal. Jackal."

Behind us, Fran snorted.

"It's a bit sinister for my taste," I said. "If you think of anything friendlier, let me know."

"Sure thing, Jackal."

"I walked right into that one."

"You sure did, hee-hee!"

I liked that she gave me a nickname, but I didn't much like the one she chose. It didn't get better after the game started, either.

She told me to start, chanting, "Ja-ckal! Ja-ckal!" as I cued up.

The distraction, unfortunately, got to me. It was an awful break.

"Suuucks to be you," she said as she got ready. She swung the pool stick with the same familiarity as her pick. "Heeey, have you checked out the basement yet, Jack?"

"We have a basement?"

"Hee-hee!" She hit the cue ball. It sniped a striped ball and sent it directly into a corner pocket. "There's a pool table down there. I've been playing this as long as I've been playing Mario."

"Oh..."

Wallet, forgive me, for I knew not what I did.

Sure enough, she cleaned me out. My rusted ability managed to get two balls in, but she didn't allow me the opportunity to finish. I could only imagine how good she would be if she were sober.

"Weeeell," she said at the end of the game. "How about a second round? Double?"

Her smile was massive, confident, and contagious. With lids half shut, hips cocked to the side, arms folded, and tail holding the cue, Sunny was a woman in her element. Every part of her radiated comfort and certainty in her ability.

"Twenty-five," I said. "I also need to pay for drinks after our game."

"Oooh? Where's your confidence gone, Jackal?"

She teased me, but she also agreed to it. As she set up the next game, an idea appeared. Sunny was good at pool, but she was brilliant at mining. She knew it, too. Maybe the way to get her interested in Antrum was to use *her* confidence.

"You were right, Sunny," I said as she set up the next round. "This clearly is where you belong. You're a master at pool."

"Riiight?"

"You sure showed me."

"It do be like that." She chuckled as she set up the pool balls. I bit my tongue and let her run through her chuckles. As she stood to take the first shot, she said, "Once you see the best, you know it."

"Exactly. I respect your decision. We'll work Antrum without you."

"What?" An ugly thwack filled the air. Sunny hit the cue ball off course. It missed the triangle entirely.

"Tabby can fight the goblins. Eo knows the routes. I'll pick until we can hire some others to join the team. Gretchen should be able to help with that, I think. We won't bother you anymore. You can live your life."

Please, let this work. Must maintain a straight face. Do not look worried.

"Buuut," she stammered. "You got Eo and Tabby on board?"

"I have their support," I lied.

My first strike required power, not finesse. I struck the cue ball into the triangle. Nothing fell into a pocket, but it was a good, clean break.

I continued, "Eo gave me the login info for the shared drive. I can look at the charts. Tabby has shown me how to fight. Don't worry about us, Sunny. We've got this."

"Nooo!" Sunny struck the cue faster than I could see. It bounced off a side, hit a solid-colored ball into one pocket, then rolled into a perfect position to hit another. "Antrum is my home!"

She marched up to me. Rather, she marched up against me, almost pushing me away as she shoved herself into my side. My much shorter housemate pushed me against the wall and pinned me there with her breasts and her eyes. Her body and her gaze emanated warmth, energy, and determination. This was a woman who knew exactly what she could do and what she was good at.

In this unexpected, unintended intimacy, she continued, "I'm the best in this village at working a pick. I have a sense for ore. I know where it is. I can reach it. I'm the best. I'm the greatest. Do you know why they call me Sunny? My name comes from Sun Wukong. You know who that is? Only the coolest, most badass character in all of mythology. Look it up, Jackal."

The game began.

She knocked in ball after ball. This was a woman in control. Because of her short height and, as such, short arms, she had to partially climb onto the table for some shots. Each strike came with a loud, decisive crack.

It looked like I might not even get a chance to fight back. Fran, and everyone else in the bar, watched, stunned as she demolished me.

"I thought," I said carefully, "that you would rather stick to *The Paw* and play pool?"

"I can do both!" she said. "Watch me! You won't believe how much ore I get."

Her confidence gave me a sense of elation. Never before had I felt so happy to be losing so badly. Still, there was something important that needed to be said.

"If you say so," I told her as she prepared to hit the eight ball. "Only if you say it again when you're sober."

At that, she hesitated. The pool stick lifted away from the table. She looked at me with an expression that I couldn't read. "Just wait and see! I'll show you tomorrow."

She hit the cue ball. It hit the eight ball. She destroyed me in the quickest, most merciless game I'd ever seen. And I couldn't have been happier about it, considering the circumstances.

"Looking forward to it."

FOURTEEN

The sun rose, casting fingers of light over me as I lay in my bed. I stretched, feeling a little hungover, but still fresh and ready to start the day.

I went through my routine. Situps. Some stretches. Watching the sunrise and enjoying the sight of Tabby doing yoga on the yard. Then I headed downstairs, humming to myself.

Over breakfast, Tabby asked, "How was Sunny last night?"

I resisted humming the *You got a new weapon!* jingle from *Zelda*.

Tabby and I had become more comfortable around each other. Though our conversations never went deep, we always chatted over our morning coffee. I was confident that she would be willing to get back in business if I could get the others in the house to agree to it.

"Better at the end of the night than at the beginning," I said. "She took a bunch of my money."

"Did you play pool against her?"

"Yeah."

"Then it's your own fault."

When she thought I wasn't looking, she bent down to the bowl and lapped at the milk. That adorable sight—complete with her cheekbones flushing in delight—was better even than the sunrise stretches.

Tabby had switched to wearing leggings in the morning. They were always cool colors that contrasted her ginger hair. Because of them, it became more important and more difficult to ignore her when I opened my blinds. Antrum had been her home since long before I'd arrived, after all, so it felt wrong to ask her to wear something else.

I don't think I'd want her to, either.

Every morning, she entranced me with slow, deliberate undulations. On more than one occasion, I'd wondered if she was trying to goad me. Her routine emphasized her body. That body couldn't have had a better figure if she'd sculpted it from marble. It was so toned, but it didn't lack any feminine suppleness. The curve of her legs rose into a perfect ass that lifted, dropped, and twisted for me every morning.

"Jack," Tabby said. "You look distracted. Everything okay?"

"Hmm?" I asked, clearing my throat to shove away the thoughts of her round ass. "I'm fine. I was just thinking about Sunny. Last night, she said that she wanted to return to the mine."

Tabby rolled her eyes. "That was just drunk talk."

"Probably. I can still hope." I shrugged.

We looked at each other for a while over the rims of our coffee mugs. Behind the mask of cynicism, I saw a little hope in her. A glimmer of something that hadn't been there when I first showed up on her doorstep.

"Tell you what," she said at last, "if Sunny is up for it, I'll join you."

I almost spat out my coffee. "Really?" I asked, trying not to sound too excited, even though I was elated.

"Yes, don't look so surprised." She stifled a laugh behind her hand, then turned serious once more. "I want it to work, you know. The problem is that it's unrealistic."

As are catgirls and magic, so you ought to understand why I'm pretty hopeful.

"Maybe," I said. "Let's see. I'll go check on Eo."

As usual, I dragged some coffee and granola bars up the stairs to my avian roommate. When I got to the loft, I found Eo passed out at her workstation, resting on the feathers of her arm like a pillow.

Now, how am I going to get you interested in Antrum? I wondered, watching as she took in a breath and nuzzled deeper into the fluff of her arms.

Was it too optimistic to start thinking about Eo? I still wasn't sure about Sunny, let alone Eo, who seemed to be hyper-focused on her figures and nothing else.

I shrugged and let her rest, deciding I'd figure it all out in time.

Passing the door with the sign of the monkey, I hesitated. This needed to work, and Sunny was the first piece I needed to fall into place. If she didn't join the team, we wouldn't have one.

Suddenly, a shrill buzzing blared from the other side of the door.

"I'm awake! Shut uuup!" Sunny yelled in time with several smacks, and a crash that I could only assume was the alarm clock hitting the floor.

"Sunny?" I asked, tapping my knuckles against the door. "You okay?"

"Jack?" she asked, her voice high-pitched with shock. "How many times did I hit snooze? Oh shit! Hold on!" There was a heavy thud in her room, along with the sound of rustling cloth and fabric. "Dammit," she groaned. "Uuugh."

"Are you okay in there?" I asked.

"Just hold up. Wait, okay?" The sound of a bull raging through a narrow store followed her voice.

I leaned closer to listen, more than a little concerned.

Suddenly, the door yanked inward, and I nearly fell forward. I pulled back in surprise, righting myself with the doorframe. On the other side was a sleepy but coherent Sunny. She'd draped blankets around herself into a sort of robe. It was clearly a rush job. A smooth, plump leg stood uncovered by the blanket, exposing her skin from toe to hip.

She was naked under the blanket, I realized with a hard swallow. Her nudity either didn't register or didn't matter to her.

"We're going into the mine today!" she yelled. She pumped a fist into the air to punctuate the point.

Two things happened then. I noticed that her hair was a mess of black, tangled bedhead, and the blankets unfurled so that it was held up only by one arm draped across her breasts. Both shoulders, her upper chest, and the entirety of her arms revealed themselves to me like a blooming flower.

It was a hell of an image. Pure determination gleamed in her sleep-crusted eyes. She was confident in her barely-covered body. The leg exposed from a gold-colored blanket was smooth and flawless.

She looked like a Renaissance painting with a tail.

Wait, what did she say?

"Awesome!" I said, just a little too late. "You're sure?"

"I said it, didn't I?" She beamed. "We're doing it! Just gimme, like, half an hour to shower and caffeinate." She leaned out the door and angled her head toward the stairs. "Hey, Tabby!"

"Sunny?" came a call from below. "You're awake?"

"Yeeep. And I'm going to Antrum today. You're coming, too." She smirked. "Antrum is open for business, baby!"

Suddenly, there was a rush of movement downstairs. I looked over the banister to see Tabby leap into view. She jumped onto the stair railing and flew up with quick, light steps. Near the top, she grabbed the banister and pulled herself over to land beside me. It couldn't have been more obvious how much she wanted Sunny's declaration to be true. The only thing that impressed me more than her desperation was her dexterity.

"Are you still drunk from last night? Are you feeling okay?" Tabby grabbed Sunny's shoulders with a tight, hopeful grip, like she was about to shake the answers out of her.

The sudden grasp startled our monkey-tailed housemate, making her hand slip, so the blanket fell more. Her hold on the cloth remained, but the inches held up by her wrist slipped away. The Renaissance look completed itself. She was a part-simian angel, flesh overflowing above and below a wrist that covered only the most private area.

I coughed and tried to look away modestly.

"Oh, come ooon," Sunny said with a flirty note. "We live together. It's surprising we haven't seen each other in the shower yet. You're not the type who wouldn't get the hint if I were 'stuck in the dryer,' are you?"

I began to turn back. "Nope."

Tabby reached up and painfully pushed my head by the cheek, so I remained looking at the stairs to Eo's workshop.

"Okay," Tabby continued. "This is a lot. I'm happy about the mine. That's great. Better than great. Sunny, put some clothes on."

"Why? He lives here, too? I'm just being comfortable."

"He's a guy!"

"Exactly! That's why he's so fun to tease. Do you have any idea how long it's been since I've seen a viable dude? It's nice to feel sexy. I know that you're just as pent-up as me. Or what, do you expect me to believe that the private show you give him every morning is normal?" She wiggled her eyebrows and grinned.

From the corner of my eye, I saw Tabby's tail begin swiping aggressively and her ears flatten. "I've done yoga every morning for years. You know that."

"Suuure. You always used that much hip work, in leggings and a sports bra. You toootally didn't angle your mat so you'd throw your ass up and bend your tits toward his window."

"Don't be vulgar." She folded her arms over her chest and stuck her chin stubbornly into the air.

"It's not an accusation, Tabby. It's an observation."

Okay, it wasn't just me, I realized. *She's sending some signals. This conversation is doing wonders for my self-esteem.*

Tabby snapped to look at me, eyes large and teeth bared. "What are you so happy about?"

"Oh me?" I shrugged, eyes intent on the stairs. "I'm just appreciating the architecture. Hmm, yes, stairs. So practical. Important for going up, and also for going down."

"Heh-heh," Sunny snickered. "I know where you want to go down."

I coughed to hide a laugh.

Sunny, you are now one of my favorite people on this planet.

"Don't encourage him!" Tabby said. "Go change."

"No fun. What if I want to look at stairs? You ever think of that?"

After a slight rustle of fabric, Sunny fell onto the banister beside me, entirely nude. Her breasts poured over the banister, deliberately placed to tease me. Her position looked uncomfortable, leaning down so that the banister pressed the generously giving flesh back up against her. So smooth, so flawless.

I was powerless to look. And my crotch was powerless to contain my painfully-sudden hardness.

From the playful shake of her monkey ears and twist of her tail, that was her intent. She relished my attention, feeling the way my eyes moved appreciatively over her. Her tail tapped her back, taking my attention. My eyes watched it stroke gently down her spine. At the bottom, her tail whipped around, so she smacked the right cheek of her massive ass.

"*Damn,*" I said.

"Stairs. I know, right?" she said as I stood transfixed. "We need them. We're not like the elves in *Morrowind.* No levitating for us."

"Right," I swallowed, relishing her beauty as much as she enjoyed showing it off. "You know that game because of Eo?"

"Yep."

Unbelievable, I thought. *They're a bunch of nerds. Have I died and gone to heaven?*

Just as my eyes followed the line of her waist to the skin that met between thigh and belly, a blanket fell on her.

"Okay," Tabby said, wrapping her friend like a rushed Christmas present, "we're all adults here. Do what you want, fine. But please, at least do work before you play. Can we agree to that?"

Tabby huffed, one hand on her hips while the other pinched the bridge of her nose.

"That seems fair," I said.

"Fiiiine," Sunny agreed.

I can't complain. This has been fun. Best not to push my luck.

"We can celebrate later," I said, heart racing.

"Damn right!" Sunny said.

As I began to walk away, however, the door to Eo's loft flew open, and she wasn't happy.

"Why are you guys so loud?" she demanded. "I know for a fact that you understand how hard it is for me to sleep. Given that, why, tell me, are you making such a fuss when I'm trying to?"

Taloned bird feet began to descend from the stairs which had held so much of our attention. The bird feet melted into pale, slender legs and supple cheeks. All three of us on the second level looked in stunned silence as Eo carried a laundry hamper down the stairs, in that revealing work/sleep top she wore the last time I saw her, showing all the curves on opposite side of her breasts.

The feathers really do look like a sweater. It's so cute!

Her messy brown hair fell around her head like a curtain. Heavy eyelids drooped over sleepy black eyes as she let out a little yawn. The feathers of her wings covered her arms. There was no other way to view it than like the sleeves of a sweater, extending from her shoulders to her ribs like a cardigan. They were glossy, smooth, and well-kept. The full forest brown of the feathers contrasted the pale skin of the girl who rarely left the attic. After seeing only her bent on a stool in shape-swallowing shorts all this time, I now noticed how shapely she was.

Unlike Sunny, she clearly had full awareness and zero interest in how revealing her clothes were. She walked up to us, the laundry basket propped on her hip. I was the closest.

She shoved her laundry basket into my hands and announced, "One of you take care of my laundry. I'm gonna sleep in my bed for the first time in who-cares-how-long. Nobody is to enter my room for at least thirty hours. Ideally, more. Leave the clothes, some coffee, and the next two days of meals by the door. If you hear me crying or sobbing, it means I started a new playthrough of Final Fantasy VII and am already anticipating the inevitable. Do not be alarmed. Please be quiet. Good night."

She turned and left, yawning and stooping her feathered shoulders as she left. I couldn't help but watch the tensing and untensing of her glutes with each step.

Moving to this house was the right decision. I already knew that, but this confirms it.

"Heh," Sunny said. "That's our Eo."

"Yeah," I said. "So, I'll throw this in the laundry and meet you guys at the mine?"

"Yeah," Tabby said. "Both of you are serious about doing real work down there today, huh?"

"Of course," Sunny said.

"Yes," I said.

Tabby nodded. "Okay," Her features softened with calm determination. "As promised, I'll join. Today is just an experiment though, alright?"

"Say it," I coaxed. "Everyone except you has said it, Tabby."

Sunny and I both looked at her expectantly.

Tabby gave a caveat. "Today is just a test, but yes. Antrum is open for business."

CHAPTER
FIFTEEN

Sparkles.

Iron, gold and copper glinted in the light of the lamps suspended from the ceiling. Above us and around us, the cave was full of ores just waiting to be mined. It felt impossible that this was real. It was too good to be true.

"Hee-hee-ha! It's good to be back!" Sunny's laughing declaration rumbled through the tunnels, claiming the stone and warning any creatures from facing us.

We'd gone through a westward tunnel that curved down into another cavern. Tabby had remembered it from their previous work, and we'd followed it until we reached the end. There were no signs of any creatures in the area, not so much as a mouse, let alone a goblin. We did, however, spot some obvious signs of precious metals.

Sunny—dextrous and quick despite her thick mining gear and a heavy pickaxe—sprang up the crags of the wall and set to work.

Tabby hung back, ears and eyes darting around to check for threats. "Too bad there isn't anything in our reach," she said.

"Are you sure?" I asked.

One iron vein caught my attention. The shape across the wall, curving down toward the bottom, held my interest. It faded away, but my eyes kept moving. A strange gut feeling kept my gaze scanning the area. My feet moved before I noticed taking a step.

"Uh, Jack?" Tabby asked. "What are you doing?"

"Just hang on a second." My pick moved to my free hand while my other hand touched the wall of the cavern.

Too deep. Too faint.

Here.

Ore was nothing more than minerals. They appeared through precipitation and pressure, give or take a million other processes I didn't understand. I didn't even understand why I felt so confident that there was something at this spot, but I hefted my pick anyway. It struck the stone.

"I have a good feeling about this spot," I said.

"A feeling," Tabby said. "Well, you sound like a miner. I'll give you that."

"That's the spirit, Jack," Sunny howled from above, speaking extra loud to scare off any over-eager goblins. "Don't overthink it. Passion, effort, and strength are what you need! *Back to the Future*, not *Primer!*"

"Don't remind me about *Primer*," Tabby said. "I don't care what Eo says. It's a shit movie."

"I have mixed feelings on it," I said. "Are you going to help?"

"Why not? You got us here in the first place. Maybe you're good for a few more miracles." She hefted a pick and began breaking into the rock near me.

It was everything she said it was. Gradually, we found a rhythm. She struck, then I did. Then her, then me again.

My muscles sang with the activity. My hands hefted the pick back and above, using the force of the swing to strike into the stone. After a few minutes, a bit of stone chipped away to reveal a glint of iron in the electric lights.

"No way." Tabby slowed, stunned, and dropped her pick.

Maybe it was for the best. The sight energized me. My pick struck again and again, faster, widening the opening to reveal more of the precious metal. Tabby regained herself and joined, quickly moving her strikes in time with me. Soon, we worked through the stone and began picking at the iron itself.

"You keep going," Tabby said. "I'll clear the rubble and get totes to collect the ore."

I doubt I could've stopped if I'd tried. As had happened in our last goblin encounter, energy surged through me despite the strain on my muscles. With one heavy heartbeat, my body electrified with adrenaline. It was more than a second wind. It was a certainty. I could hit harder, faster. I had become better, stronger. The pick struck again and again, each strike bringing a small rain of sparkles.

"Hell yeah, Jack!" Sunny yelled.

"This..." Tabby could hardly speak. A few light laughs and happy gasps kept cutting her off as she scooped up the ore. "This can't be real. Antrum...Are we back?"

I kept going. My pace challenged the other two. Sunny and I began a contest for who could collect the most usable ore. Time stopped meaning anything. We worked for hours. Tabby had to wipe away the sweat and call us for water breaks because we refused to sit down. Even our feline guardian-slash-chaperone was giddy. She earned more than a little treasure from the walls.

Eventually, we huddled together against the stone, panting and heaving for breath. We powered through the exhaustion to move the ore into totes. When the job was finished, I lifted a bunch and watched the shiny bits run through my fingers. "Ba-da-da-daaa!" I yelled, mimicking the *Zelda item acquired!* sound.

My smile was so big it almost hurt. Sunny howled and lightly punched my side. "We sell our stuff separately, okay? I want to see who makes more money from Gretchen. Loser covers the tab at the Paw tonight. Sound good?"

I was too busy laughing to reply. My eyes moved to Tabby.

She was stunned, hand in front of her mouth, eyes glistening with tears of joy. "You did it, Jack. You brought another miracle."

"Miracles don't make you build a sweat like that!" Sunny yelled.

I wiped my brow. I was soaked with the stuff, and dirt smudged my cheeks, but for once, after a hard day of work, I felt satisfied and proud, not defeated.

"Alright," she laughed. "You've done a lot. Thank you." She hesitated, nibbling her bottom lip. "I was wrong about you."

"You didn't know me. Shoot, I didn't know if this would work. I just wanted to try." I shrugged, running my fingers through my hair and dislodging bits of dust and debris.

"You did well," she put her hand on my arm. "I didn't want to admit it, but I hoped that you could do this."

"All of us did well," I gestured around to my strange and wonderful new companions. "Not just me."

"Damn right!" Sunny beamed.

"Yeah," Tabby nodded. Then, she leaned closer to me.

Sunny began to guess the profits from her haul and how much I'd pay on tonight's tab—which I never agreed to pay.

My heart began to race at Tabby's close proximity.

She spoke low enough for only me to hear. "I just wanted to say...."

Tabby's cheeks went as red as her hair.

"Say what?"

"Sunny was just kidding earlier, about the yoga."

"Hmm? Oh." I gave an awkward laugh. "It's alright, don't worry about it.

Tabby shrugged. "It's a nice spot to do yoga."

"Well..."

Her eyebrows lifted. "What?"

"To tell you the truth, I've been doing some stretches in my room in the mornings. I was hoping you could show me some moves."

"You do yoga?" she asked with an arched brow.

"Stretches," I said, laughing again.

"There's nothing to be ashamed of. Yoga is awesome."

I nodded.

"I see," she said. There was a new hesitation in her eyes. Her pupils widened a little. "Let's do it. If you run into trouble, I'll show you some moves and positions."

"How generous of you. But I warn you..." I hesitated a second, then said, "I'm a slow learner," hoping she would get my intention.

"We'll see about that." She let her eyes drop to the hand which hadn't left my arm. "Yoga is just using your muscles in ways you wouldn't expect."

"The body is an amazing thing." I reached up and lightly touched her cat ear.

"Hey," Sunny flicked a pebble at my forehead. "I'm all for fun and games, but we can't get tooooo distracted, alright?"

Tabby coughed. "Right."

I rubbed my forehead.

Time and place.

We set back to work, as hard as before we'd gotten distracted.

Sunny and I went back to the walls of the cavern, picking and goading each other with threats of who would make more money with their haul. Though Tabby tried to stop us, we were like kids asking for five more minutes with a video game.

I felt invincible. The rush of adrenaline came again and again, fueling me like I was a machine. Only after a while did I begin to wonder about the safety of our work. Not from the rocks or the goblins, rather, I worried about the rumors that had been floating around since I'd arrived.

I tried not to think about it. We were doing well. So well! It seemed wrong to mess with that flow. I bit my tongue until Tabby called for us to stop. We needed to make sure we'd have the time to haul it to Gretchen.

Exhausted and coated with sweat, I allowed myself to ask the question which had been bugging me, "Hey, what's down here other than goblins?"

"Probably a demon somewhere," Sunny said with a shrug.

"Don't," Tabby warned. "That's just a superstition." She turned to me. "Where did that come from?"

"Well." I decided to be honest. "I'm still new to a lot of this. I don't know what to avoid. I mean, I don't know what there is to avoid. For all I know, there's a dragon, or a mimic, or a portal to Hell."

"Mimics are rare," Sunny said. "I don't actually know about dragons."

Tabby shrugged. "I've never seen one. Few people have. They're not very common anymore, I don't think. You might need to go out of your way to a conservation area."

"Conservation?"

"Yeeeah," Sunny added. "They are rare."

"I see," I said, my head spinning with thoughts of dragons and what they might really look like. "Is there anything else I need to worry about in the mine? Seriously, what is there other than goblins?"

They both shrugged.

"Pretty much what you'd expect. Goblins. I think we cleared out all the spiders," Tabby said.

Sunny gave a thumbs up. "We were thorough. We never explored aaall of the mine, though. So, there's not a zero percent chance of a cursed artifact. But yeah, pretty unlikely. The only thing we need to worry about is what put the barrier on the mine in the first place."

Oh, is that all?

From the way Tabby lifted her eyebrows and turned her mouth into a straight line, she had the same thought as me.

How can you leave it there?

It's a good thing she stopped us, too, because we were exhausted by the time we left the quarry with our haul. It was obvious, too, that I was the only one of the trio new to the work. Sweat poured off of me in rivulets, but Sunny and Tabby merely looked tired instead of ready to collapse.

When we got to Acanth, however, some energy returned. People noticed us. They did double and triple takes between our mining gear, our load, and our faces. Excited chatter built.

Eventually, we made it to Gretchen's. She saw us coming from a distance and waved excitedly. "Oh, yes!" she cried. "Yes! Please tell me that the mine is open. Come on!"

Sunny and I looked at Tabby. She rolled her eyes.

"For now," she said through a tired smile, "Antrum Mine is open."

"Yes!" In her excitement, Gretchen grabbed our hands. "Please keep it up. I mean it. Not just for me, but for the town." She drew away from us, raking her fingers through her hair and taking in a breath to try to calm herself. "Oh man. This is so big! I need to assess what you brought." She paused, then cleared her throat. "Um, wow. Please forgive me. I got carried away."

"No problem," I said. "We're all riding a high."

"Yeeeah." Sunny said. "By the way, count our stuff separately. We have a bet. Loser pays for drinks at *The Paw*."

"Sure thing." Gretchen was so happy that she could barely contain it. "This is just such a huge relief. You have no idea how much simpler it's going to become if I can buy direct from you guys. I'll even send my helper to come and get it with my cart, so all you have to do is mine it." She flashed her unusual grin. "I'll tell you what, first round is on me."

"Deeeal!" Sunny stuck out her hand. Gretchen took it, not realizing what was about to unfold.

In for a pint, in for a pound.

"Alright," Tabby said. "Sorry to kill the mood, but we're tired. Can we get that appraisal?"

"Sure thing. Please wait here while I do the calculations."

We waited to the side as Gretchen counted and weighed our ore. I was so exhausted that I almost fell asleep leaning against the wall, but I shook myself awake, rubbing the sleep from my eyes.

"By the way, Sunny," I said. "I never agreed to the bet."

"Oooh? You're backing out?"

"It's for your benefit. You worked at a disadvantage."

"Yeah," Tabby said. "You do know that I was working on the same vein as him, right? My share will be counted as part of his."

"Whaaat? No. I thought you'd separate it."

"No need. It's a dumb bet and I had no interest in it anyway." Tabby shrugged.

"Thank you, Tabby." I said.

Sunny pouted at us like a child who'd had their Christmas present taken away. "Uuugh. Fine. Gretchen, you can count it all together."

"Sure. Please just wait a bit."

My foot nudged Tabby. "Thanks."

Her tail rubbed against me. "I ought to thank you. Want to join me for yoga tomorrow?"

"Yes, I do."

"Then you're gonna have to get up earlier. I won't wait up for you."

"Just promise that you'll still wear those tights."

She rolled her eyes. "You'll have to put in some work tomorrow, you know? You sure you want that distraction?"

"You say distraction. I say motivation."

"Oooh, sure," Sunny interrupted. "I'm weird and kinky for being honest, but you get to make goo-goo eyes at each other. I see how it is."

"I was not!" Tabby hissed and crossed her arms, turning away.

I couldn't resist looking at her body. A healthy sweat coated the small of her back, that gorgeous ass of hers bouncing in syncopated movements as she moved, the cheeks fighting for supremacy.

Gretchen piped in, "It's a shame you canceled your bet, Jack. Please, forgive me for intruding, but your haul is higher quality. I still need to weigh the rest, but my first impression is that you've earned more."

Thank you, Gretchen.

As Sunny paid close attention to the price tally, I pulled out my phone and checked the drive for our tunnel routes. Tabby and I went over everything there. Today was lucky. I was under no delusion that we could keep this up every day by ourselves. Tabby and Sunny had remembered the last place they'd been digging before the mine closed. That's all there was to it. Still, from those memories and the areas Eo had already charted, we had several days' worth of work ahead of us.

When Gretchen found a total and gave us our profits, we felt ecstatic.

"To *The Paw*!" Sunny howled.

We followed after her, Gretchen in tow to cover the first round. As we entered, still covered in dirt from the mine, hands black with work, and hair filthy from sweat, we were conquering heroes. Everybody turned to us, saw the signs, and guessed.

Fran leveled her golden eyes on me, gave a beautiful smile that lit the room, and asked the big question: "So, is Antrum open?"

I turned to Tabby, she nodded. Sunny gave me a light push on the back. "Antrum Mine," I declared, "is now well and truly open for business."

CHAPTER
SIXTEEN

I set the alarm back an extra fifteen minutes so I could meet Tabby outside the next day.

"Morning," I said, arriving in the garden to see she was already spread out in a pose, her whole body straight and arms pushing her body up as if it was an invitation.

No, don't be silly. She's just doing a yoga pose. She's not exactly bent over doggy style.

I positioned my mat next to hers, and she instructed me to mimic her in the pose, putting her hands flat and arching her back in a backward C.

After a few moments of my panting, she asked, "Not so easy, is it?"

"Push-ups are easier," I said, laughing. "Holding this isn't."

"Back straight!" she scolded, and I quickly readjusted. "You'll be a master by the time I'm done with you."

Tabby got up from her mat and placed her hand against my lower back, adjusting me where she wanted. I felt the heat of her palm through my clothes and struggled to focus on what we were doing.

"I'll have to show you a few things in return," I said, staring at the trees. My voice sounded a little thick to my own ears.

"Like wha—yes, maybe," she said, then quickly removed her hand from the small of my back.

Did she say, 'yes, maybe' because she was afraid of what I would respond? I wondered. *Or, was she saying yes to what she thought I was suggesting?*

Or was she saying maybe?

I churned this over and over and over in my mind until she spoke again.

"Now, go to this one," she said, returning to her mat with a somewhat shaky voice.

Lowering into an upright stretch, she kept her hands on the mat and pushed her whole body back in what was the yoga equivalent of doggy style.

Damn. I had a hard time ripping my eyes away from that perfect ass.

"Jack," she said sternly.

I quickly mimicked and felt all my joints stretching—first, it hurt, but gradually that pain turned to relief.

I decided that Tabby had a point about yoga, and this was beneficial regardless of the partner I performed it beside.

"By the way," I said, in an effort to bring us back to a less stressful conversation, "You'll need to come up with a better nickname for me than Jackal."

"Yes, it's not very nice, is it?"

We both laughed.

She continued, "Usually, there isn't this much talking."

"Is it usually this much fun?" I asked.

"No," she said, then quickly added. "Yoga is not supposed to be fun. It's to clear your mind and relax your body."

Then why is it so much busier and tenser than it was before I started? I don't need yoga. I need a different kind of release. Fuck.

"Nicknames are given to people you're close to," she said coldly. "You can't just ask me to give you one. It doesn't work like that. Now, turn this way."

She turned on her side, resting her forearm on the mat, as well as the side of her foot, to do a sideways plank.

Tabby's eyes met mine, and we stayed frozen there, staring at each other for a moment. I glanced down at her neck, where it led to the exposure of her bare, smooth flesh, as well as gravity doing its wonderful work on her breasts as it pulled them toward the mat.

She quickly said, "Well, it's nice to have company, I suppose. But your form is trash, so you'll need to come back again tomorrow to work on it."

My eyes met her again as I said, "Gladly."

"Now, shut up. I'm trying to clear my mind." Her cheeks turned a faint shade of red that almost matched her tights.

"Gladly," I repeated, smiling to myself.

I swore I saw her mouth flicker in the hint of an upward curve, but she quickly straightened it.

And so, several days passed like that in a happy blur.

Every day, we did a yoga routine with the sunrise. Yes, it was healthy and good for the body, but that aspect didn't factor much into my enjoyment. The sunrise never got old, nor did the feeling of the crisp air filling my lungs, but my favorite view was even better.

Tabby.

In those moments when the sky was pink and night had barely left, she was something I'd rarely seen from her: playful. She started with simple stretches, testing my ability, but she would randomly throw in advanced positions to mess with me. Sometimes, I did a passable job. Other times, I made an absolute fool of myself and collapsed in a heap.

Usually, this made her laugh so hard that she lost balance and fell on her mat beside me.

Those first couple of days were full of flirts, jokes, and distractions. I held the more strength-based positions for a long time, showing off my endurance. She responded by having me try a leg position that was impossible for someone with testicles.

Yet, I came to appreciate these mornings more as they grew quieter. We spoke less, moved more. We became closer, physically and mentally.

She would give a little moan when she twisted, parting her lips and pushing out her chest. I would flex my muscles and offer a low, throaty grunt.

After these sessions, the shared space continued. We would have our morning coffee together, as well as a light breakfast. I brought food and coffee to the door of Eo's bedroom instead of her loft. Our statue expert's break lasted longer than expected. Sunny and Tabby all but begged her to take more time off. We could afford it now with the mine work. She didn't believe us, it seemed. Still, the exhaustion was obvious. She agreed to rest, so we heard occasional sobs and cheers and JRPG orchestras throughout the day and night.

Each morning, after we double-checked that Eo was fine, we waited for Sunny. Once she was ready, the three of us marched into Antrum. Our shifts were much the same as always, returning to the places they remembered or were marked on the charts. We swung our picks, collected the ore, and made jokes. At the end of every session, Gretchen sent her apprentice lad to come and collect the ore.

The only variety here came in the form of the pests. Goblins showed up once in a while, waving their primitive weapons at us in challenge. Because of this, Tabby gave me some basic practice in weapon handling. It was similar to yoga in that she walked me through simple movements, how they related to each other, and how important it was to be in total awareness when doing them.

A small part of me enjoyed the encounters. When goblins came, or as on two occasions, a hobgoblin, I charged them. That adrenaline burst came periodically. Each time, I could have sworn that I was a better fighter. With the first hobgoblin, I swung so hard that I broke the ax from its handle and had to improvise the rest of the fight.

This had prompted me to get a new ax from Gretchen, one that better suited my size and strength. Thankfully, she forged it for me at a discount. Of course, there had been a catch. She taught me the process of smelting and smithing so that if I ever needed extra money or if she didn't have the time to work on our projects, I could do it myself.

This learning experience helped me understand the only thing that I felt needed to be kept secret from my companions. When working at the smithy, I felt the adrenaline burst. Here, in a context without the same type of peril and exertion as the mine—or even the same intentional physical push as the gym—I was able to analyze the feeling. At first, it happened often. That first day, it happened three times. I'd been so wired for energy that I hadn't noticed how exhausted my muscles were. By the time I got home, I collapsed like Guts after slaying a hundred men.

Hurt and tired though I was, it was too intriguing to avoid. I went to the mine and the smithy back-to-back for days. Tabby and Sunny were concerned, but they chalked it up to my excitement and desire to prove myself.

Quickly, I realized that the bursts became less and less frequent. It took more time and effort to reach that level of rush again. For a while, the theory occurred to me that I'd become a literal adrenaline junky, losing the ability to appreciate a hit. It horrified me, but it couldn't be the case. Each time it happened, I was lucid. Each one was more intense. The primary feeling it brought was a certainty that I had become better at the skill I was practicing.

Whether that was in Antrum, or the smith, or even back at the gym in my old life, it always happened like that.

I'm leveling up.

There was no other way to look at it. Even with the goblins and animal girls, this felt like the most absurd thing ever. Thus, I said nothing. We had enough to worry about. I couldn't afford to be distracted in the mines.

For better or for worse, something happened soon after to push that from my mind. We finished every part of the mine listed on Eo's charts, having combed through them for every bit of ore we could get our hands on. Of course, the three of us didn't want to admit it, not when we didn't know where we should dig next. We ignored it right up until the morning we were set to enter the mine. There, at the breakfast table, we finally had our meeting.

"So," I began. "What are we going to do?"

"Weeell," Sunny looked across our existing charts. She pointed to a cavern with unexplored tunnels, which went upward into the hills. "I think this one should be alright. We found some good ore in here."

"I don't think so," Tabby said. "There might be a little bit of high-value minerals, but right now, we need quantity. That's always been deeper."

Slowly, Sunny shook her head. "I don't feel comfortable going down into unexplored territory just so we can rely on memory to get us out."

"Memory?" I asked. "Can't either of you update the charts?"

They looked at each other sheepishly.

"Not my skill set," Tabby said.

"That was always Eo," Sunny added.

I nodded. "Okay, so we're getting Eo on board."

Sunny sucked in a breath through her teeth.

Tabby put her hands on her hips and sighed. "I mean, we knew that she would need to join sooner or later."

"Riiight," Sunny nodded. If she was bothered that I had lied about Eo already being involved, she didn't show it.

All their expressions reminded me of college students who'd put off the essay until the night it was due.

"This has bugged me for a while," I said at last. "Why is it that you two don't talk to her? There's no question that you care about her or anything like that, but I haven't actually seen either of you have a conversation with her. You always clam up and get quiet whenever we talk about her."

"It's complicated," Sunny said. "The model-making is her hobby, buuut..."

"She's making all the money," Tabby said. "She'd always locked herself away in the past for her hobbies, but after Antrum closed, it became a lot more intense. After she started taking orders and selling the work, it went from eccentric to disturbing. I don't actually remember the last time she left the house."

Sunny held her head in her hands, brows furrowed and cheeks red with obvious guilt.

Tabby's tail turned limp as her ears curled down. "Did we turn her into our crazy woman in the attic?"

Sunny shook her head. "If that's a reference, I don't get it. Still, that makes it sound like we're the ones that messed up, so I agree with it."

"Okay then." I nodded. Once again, I had landed in the middle of roommate troubles. This time, however, it seemed a lot more severe than the last. "It sounds like there needs to be a conversation with Eo outside of the mining business."

Tabby and Sunny shared a pained look together, then sighed and nodded in unison.

"Should I stay out of it?" I asked. "A lot of this is between you three. I'll understand if you want to do this on your own."

"No," Tabby said. "You're part of the business and the house. You should be there to talk with her."

"Alsooo, we may need you to moderate if things go bad."

"Sunny," Tabby hissed. "We don't know if that'll happen."

At that, Sunny shrugged. "Would you blame her if she flipped on us?"

In response, Tabby lifted and dropped her finger on the table. "Is it bad," she said at last, "that I'd be relieved if she freaked out at us?"

Well then. This turned dark quickly.

"Let's go," I said. "It'll only get harder the longer we put it off."

The three of us walked up to Eo's room. As we approached the door with the owl logo, I glanced back at the two of them, taking in their nervous expressions and the way Sunny shifted her weight between her feet as if doing an anxious dance. I faced the door and knocked, "Eo, all of us want to talk. We need your help."

To my surprise, we got an immediate response. "Of course you do. I don't wish to come across as egotistic, but this is not a shocking revelation to anyone. Come in. I'm at a save point anyway, so this is about as good a time as we're going to have for whatever it is you want to talk about."

"Huh," Tabby said. "Good start."

I turned the knob and entered the owl room for the first time.

"Holy shit," I said as I looked around inside.

The walls were lined with glass cases. Inside these were figures and statues ranging in height from three inches to three feet. Dozens, no, hundreds of them filled the cases. My jaw hit the floor as I stepped further in and saw the other side of her room. "Holy shit," I muttered.

Beside me, Sunny said, "Yeeeah."

A life-sized statue stood in the corner. It was colorfully hand-painted down to the smallest, most intricate detail. It had blue hair, red eyes, and a white skin-tight suit that I couldn't mistake.

All personal and professional concerns abandoned my thoughts. "Why is Ayanami Rei standing in the corner?"

Tabby sighed.

Suddenly, all of Eo's attention turned to me. As usual, her head preceded the rest of her. She sat literally perched on a board at the foot of her bed, holding a controller and hunched in front of a massive TV.

"Isn't she beautiful?" Eo asked as she muted her game. Her words came out quickly and excited, the speed and volume building into a crescendo of excitement. "She's beautiful! You possess excellent taste for knowing Rei. I'm still trying to get Sunny and Tabby to give the series a try. Sunny watched the show but doesn't want to try the movies, which I don't understand at all, given that they're likely to address all her issues with the original twenty-six-episode run. More importantly, what do you think of her? Be honest. I try to do a life-sized model once a year. I'm still not the best at it. I have help with the clothes and hair from people in the village, because there's only so much you can do with your time, am I right? I think the one I did two years ago was my best. I did a Haruhi Suzumiya in her Playboy Bunny outfit. That was painful to sell. Still, I think it was a necessary step in my evolution as an artist. Not only did we earn a five-figure sale with it, but I think it's also important to 'kill your darlings,' as the saying goes. I've been trying to..."

Minutes passed without her slowing, taking a breath, or registering the lack of interest on our faces. As Eo spoke, I pulled up the charts that the three of us had tried to update, walked up to her, and put them in her hand.

She continued to speak even as she looked at them, "Perhaps it's not advisable to have such a slim barrier between hobby and profession, but given our financial situation... What the hell have you done to my charts?" she concluded with a yell that made me jump.

Eo bolted to her feet, standing on the board above us. Her talons gripped it so hard that they cracked into the wood as her feathers bristled. A dark flame of hurt and fury blazed in her eyes.

This reaction, I decided, *is not what I'd originally wanted, but I think I can work with it.*

"We've been working Antrum," I said.

"Right." Tabby stepped up to help me. "We didn't have much to go on, so we've been using the tunnels you'd already mapped to help us get back into the swing of it."

Eo's anger went unabated. "I had a system. You know that! Everything I do when charting or labeling things involves a very specific system of terms and labeling so that it's easy to read for anybody involved. Which of you wrote 'no mo rockz' on one of the caverns?"

Tabby and I looked to Sunny, who nodded without a shred of guilt.

Eo gaped at her. "*No mo rockz*? You need to be joking with a note like that. It's a mine, in a mountain. The entire location is comprised of rocks. Arguably, the entire thing is a single rock! This is ridiculous!"

Her posture changed. All attention left the charts and focused squarely on the other two. There was a change in the air that made the hair on the back of my neck stand up. This was no longer about the charts. Tabby and Sunny braced back slightly as Eo exploded.

"I can't believe you two!" she shouted, waving the charts at them. "I work more than a hundred hours a week, not getting fresh air for days at a time, to make sure that we don't drain what little inheritance we have left, and you're messing with one of the few things I can be unambiguously proud of in my life without explaining a dissertation's worth of pop culture significance and the psychology of storytelling and shared hobbies! No, I will not stand for having the work which means the most to me tampered with by a cat who cleans to hide her insecurity and the fear that she's lost control over her life, a monkey who wastes my income on the least healthy coping mechanism for unprocessed trauma, or a guy who showed up out of nowhere and...and...frankly, I don't know much about you other than the fact that you check on me daily and seem genuinely concerned with my well-being. Thank you for that! Sorry if that sounds sarcastic because of how angry I am, but said anger is not directed at you!" She took in a gulp of air.

"Wow..." I said, rubbing the back of my neck.

That had gotten much more personal than expected. Tabby, the older sister of the group, looked like she'd been physically struck. Sunny sniffed. Her whole body began to tremble as tears welled up in her eyes.

Things were more fraught in the house than I had realized. Eo's blow-up, it seemed, was a long time in the making.

How long has it been since these three sat down together and had a full conversation?

Not for the first time, I put myself into a situation that may not have been my business. "Eo, one of the reasons we're going into the mine is so that you won't need to do all that work. You're crucial to making this house run. We know that. That's why we need you. You understand the layout and construction of things in a way that we simply don't."

Our cartographer remained standing above us. Her feathers, however, began to settle. Her breaths remained quick and angry. "Antrum is open again. I recall you saying that. Do you have a system in place so that we can reliably earn a profit?"

Tabby explained our setup with Gretchen, as well as the fact that I was learning smithing so we could sell some items directly.

Sunny jumped in nervously. "And I'm helping. I'm working Antrum, and I'm not getting shitfaced during the week."

Slowly, Eo lowered herself. Only her legs bent. Her torso remained perfectly still as she crossed her arms, bent her knees, put one bird foot to the ground, and then placed the other. A doubtful pout bore a hole into Sunny, then into Tabby, and finally into me.

"All three of you are serious?"

"Yes," Tabby said.

"One hundred percent," Sunny added.

Eo's black eyes moved over us. Her posture began to change. The pout softened, as did her gaze. "You're serious about reopening the mine? I need to know that this is actually happening."

"Come ooon!" Sunny charged Eo and dragged her into a bear hug. "We need you! I'm sorry for leaving you up there! I'm sorry for distracting you so much when Dawn passed away and then leaving you alone. I'm sorry I never invited you to *The Paw* or asked if you were okay or checked if you wanted anything! I'm sooooorrrrrrryyyyy!" Sunny wailed.

Eo tried to look unbothered, but her face cracked with emotion. The hard line of her mouth twitched. As she jolted with the heavy embrace from Sunny, she looked more and more surprised.

"Dammit," Tabby said as she rushed in. "I'm sorry I stopped talking to you, Eo! I thought you wanted your space and I felt confused because I didn't know what you wanted, and I didn't ask and...please join us! We need you. We've always needed you. I've known you all my life, and it's killed me every day because it's my fault that you're hurting alone."

"Nooo!" Sunny shook her head into Eo's shoulder. "It's my fault! I'm the one who kept wasting our money."

Tabby and Sunny took turns apologizing and confessing. They overwhelmed Eo with tears, holding her tight in their arms, begging for forgiveness, and praising their friend, who seemed more like a sister. So much unsaid, unprocessed emotion rushed out in a weeping eruption that I thought it might never stop.

For Eo, it started with tears. They fell without reaction. "You guys..." Her thin arms lifted slowly and rested on her housemates. Soon, she pulled them in, returning the hug in a startled but meaningful hold. "I shouldn't have said it like that."

The two refuted her apology and repeated their own.

The emotion and honesty overwhelmed Eo. A sob broke her breathing. "I did it for you...I thought that it wouldn't matter if I took on more orders to be with you two. I love

Antrum. I don't dislike the work, either. I ran away into it. That was the problem."

"It's different!" Sunny yelled. "We'd be nothing without you! You keep this house together!"

"No!" Eo said. "That's Tabby. She's the one who keeps everything clean and handles the orders."

"Hardly!" Tabby said. "I'd be useless without Sunny. She's the one who knows how to talk to people in Acanth. I'd be a hermit if not for her."

Thus, the apologies turned to compliments. They praised each other, denying anything aimed at them and redirecting the good. They wept, hugged, and eventually, they smiled.

Even I teared up. The messy moment was the last thing I'd expected, but seeing it play out, I felt how necessary it was. When I was sure that things were going well, I left the room so they could have their privacy.

CHAPTER
SEVENTEEN

While the three women hashed out the remainder of their feelings, I waited in the kitchen. I wasn't sure what to think about being witness to it all.

On the one hand, it was none of my business what was going on between them. On the other hand, they had asked me to be there.

However, our cohabitation may have started, we were a community now, and I couldn't be happier to be part of that.

After several minutes, a door opened upstairs. I sat up slightly in my chair, listening to the sounds of footsteps on the stairs.

Soon, the trio appeared in the kitchen, their eyes red and puffy from crying. Still, they each had a weak but no less meaningful smile on their faces. Sunny had her arm around Eo's shoulders, and she gave her a squeeze.

"I want to go into the village," Eo said. "It's been...too long. I haven't seen people in forever."

"You need to spread your wings," Sunny said.

Eo gave a fake laugh. "I'll let it slide this one time because it's literally true."

I nodded. "Sounds good. Anything you want to do today; Eo, we're here with you."

"I just want to see my friends. If *The Paw* is open, I want to play darts."

They took some time to wipe their faces and change.

I'd never seen Eo in anything other than her loose-fitting model-making outfit, but her new casual look suited her.

She kept the purple shorts, since they contrasted nicely with her feathers. For her top, she wore a black tee shirt with the Umbrella Corporation logo on the front. The sides had been modified so that they could open from the sleeve down, with buttons to hold them together. It looked like it must have been tedious to get her wings through the shirt and to button up the sides afterward. The color of the top mismatched her feathers and shorts, but we didn't care. She didn't care. All that mattered was that Eo was getting out of the house.

When she got to the front door, Eo paused. "Is it weird that it feels strange that I'm stepping out of the house? A big part of me feels guilty that I'm not working on more orders or trying to keep up with my own schedule."

"It's not weird," I said. "Unhealthy? Maybe. But we'll work on that. You're allowed to enjoy yourself and have a life."

"In fact," Tabby said, taking her hand. "We encourage it. Come on, let's go."

With that, the four of us stepped into a beautiful day in Acanth. The sun shone brightly overhead. The only clouds were so white and fluffy that I'd swear God had placed them there for the aesthetic. Basking in the light, Eo beamed. Her feathers practically glistened as a light breeze ruffled through them.

Her arms spread, the feathers of her wings turned down, almost seeming to elongate into curtains that flowed down and out from her arms. Her eyes closed, and she began to speak quietly. From the few sounds I heard, I guessed that it wasn't English.

"Stand back juust a bit," Sunny said, pulling me a few steps away.

Holy shit, is Eo going to fly?

Suddenly, the air around Eo changed. The breeze refracted around her, sucking in the grass from all sides. Her eyelids shot up. Kaleidoscopic colors flashed across her eyes, spinning together until they formed white, then returning to their brilliant black.

Instantly, she leaped high into the air. Her wings carried her toward the sky. Even from a distance below, we could clearly see the massive smile on her face. She luxuriated in the feeling as her hair blew back in the wind.

"Yeees!" Sunny cheered. "Do a barrel roll!"

"Technically," Eo yelled, body spinning in smooth arcs and swooping down over us, "it's an aileron roll."

She rose again and flew around the house. After a few circles, she perched on the top and spread her wings. From there, she must have had an incredible view. The village, the hills, and the forest which separated us from the non-magical world all lay out before her, nothing out of reach. The girl who'd been cooped up in the attic now stood atop the world.

Arms outstretched, she leaned forward. Soon, she fell from the roof. The wind caught her wings and scooped her up without any effort from her.

She darted out beyond us. "Let's go!"

I may as well have been a kid who'd just discovered that Superman was real. Sunny whooped and ran after her. Tabby lightly jostled me, "Come on!"

The three of us ran to the village, unable to keep up with the brilliant brown bird girl.

"Hello Acanth!" Eo screamed.

Windows opened. People stepped out onto porches.

As we rushed into the village center, the front doors of *The Monkey's Paw* burst open. Fran ran out and howled in joy, tail wagging exuberantly. "Welcome back!"

"Fran!" Eo flew around the village square a few times, then curved down and whooshed in toward Fran.

Our owl damn near knocked Fran to the ground in a high-speed hug that could have been an attack. Fran, however, seemed used to it. She caught Eo and spun with the momentum, lifting onto her toes and spinning like a dancer as she embraced her old friend.

It took several revolutions before Fran could put out her feet to stop the spinning. "It's been so long!" Fran said as we approached. "It's good to see you, Eo."

"It's good to get out," Eo said.

"I was worried about you. Anyway, please come in. Would you like the morning usual? It's on me."

"Yes please." Eo fell to her taloned feet and began flapping at the elbow. "You still have a dart board?"

"Of course."

"Good." Eo walked into the pub.

"She's popular," I said.

"I mean," Sunny replied. "How could anyone not like her?"

"Good point," I nodded.

The three of us followed inside. Eo stopped to greet the others in the bar. A few of them raised an early drink or a cup of coffee to her return. A goat woman gave her a hug and thanked her for helping around her shop. Gretchen ran into the pub to say a quick greeting before darting back to her business. Through it all, Eo nodded and even gave a few rare smiles.

"I'll get your breakfast," Fran said. "Make yourself comfortable."

"Can do," Eo made a beeline for the dartboard. It hung on the wall in the corner of the building, a good few feet from the pool table, so players wouldn't interrupt each other's game. She grabbed all the darts and skipped backward to a yellow strip of tape that marked the throwing line.

"Watch," Tabby said, anticipation clear on her face.

The first dart went so quickly that I didn't see it. It hit just off-center. Eo scrunched her face in annoyance. With intense concentration, she flicked another, just off on the other side. The next four darts flew rapid-fire at the target. The last two were bullseyes.

"Niiice!" Sunny cheered.

Eo returned to the dartboard, oblivious to the rest of the world, and repeated her quickfire attempts. The darts flew. Her throwing style was like a sneak attack. Before long, she got consecutive bullseyes. Since that task had been accomplished, she started practicing on the other sides of the dartboard.

"She'll be at it for a while," Tabby said. "We may as well sit at the bar."

The two of us did. Sunny stayed on her feet, cheering Eo all the way. I shook my head in wonder. "How?"

Tabby chuckled. "When Eo becomes interested in something, she becomes focused on it until she's mastered it. It's impressive, terrifying, and helpful. Her skills have saved us more than a few times, both inside the mine and outside. She's as good with throwing knives as she is with darts."

Eo began doing trick shots, throwing at various angles and once with her eyes closed.

Meanwhile, Sunny's cheering could have matched the most rabid sports fan when their team scored.

It was so heartwarming to witness it all.

"The darts," Tabby said, "started with one of the *Paper Mario* games. Apparently, there's a bird enemy that can use its feathers as projectile weapons. That's all it took. Ever since, she's focused all of her combat on throwing. She thinks it looks cool."

I nodded. "I have to ask about flying. Can she fly naturally, or does she use a spell? From the wind and the eyes, I'm guessing there's more to it than just flapping."

"There's a lot more to it. Eo can glide naturally, but actual flight is more difficult. She has the most magical ability of anyone in Acanth, thankfully. The magic you saw is a combination of two spells that she worked on for a long time. First, she made herself weigh next to nothing with a spell designed for moving large obstructions. Next, she caused a massive gust of wind that's usually used to stun enemies or knock projectiles out of the air."

"Wow," I nodded. "What about the eyes and the wind change and all that?"

Tabby rolled her eyes in mock disapproval. "That's just her being dramatic."

"I am not dramatic," Eo said, deadpan. "Style and showmanship are secondary only to efficiency and efficacy. If it is possible to do things flashily, it is a necessity to do it flashily. The only excuse for doing things without drama is to provide something for others, so that they might be able to use it to show their own flash. Everything a person does tells you something about the person who is doing it."

"Hmm," I nodded. "That's either incredibly inspirational or incredibly stressful. I'm not sure which."

"You," Eo pointed at me, "have just described what it's like to be in my head at any given moment. Anyway, coffee!"

Fran came out with a wooden bowl full of hot oatmeal. It was topped with blueberries, chopped strawberries, and a dusting of cinnamon. Even the spoon that stuck out of it was wooden. A mug of steaming coffee followed, with a tiny metal pitcher of milk beside. Eo clapped excitedly. "It's been too long!"

Sunny shook her head and sat on Eo's other side. "I still don't get it. You come to the best pub we have and you get oatmeal."

Fran chuckled. "Thank you for saying that as if we weren't the only pub in Acanth."

"You are the best," Eo said decisively. "And your coffee and oatmeal are also the best. Before I get too distracted, though, Jack, I believe it would be a good idea to explain to you my usual role in the mining process, as well as what other magical abilities I possess and how we usually go about the process of expanding our excavation territory. I take it that one of the reasons you wished to inquire for my help is that you've either come close to or have entirely exhausted the available resources in the parts of the mine which have already been charted? Is that the case?"

"Yes," I nodded. "You can enjoy your food first if you want to talk business later."

"It's no problem. I'm honestly feeling a little overwhelmed with how many people there are, so talking business and giving me something to focus on might actually help me stay present. That said, I reserve the right to stand and go to the bathroom at any point if I feel that I need a few moments to myself to reorient my thoughts."

"More than fair." I pulled out my phone and brought up the charts of the mine.

As Eo ate, I guided her through our efforts, explaining our business agreement with Gretchen again. She asked some questions about our resources and plans, as well as about the monster activity in Antrum.

When I caught her up on all we had done, I added, "I have a question for you now. What magic can you use and how does it feel? I can't understate how cool it was to see you fly, and I want to know more."

"Why, thank you, sir. I don't have a lot of magic, you should know. All the spells I practice are focused either on practicality or on heightening my pre-existing senses. Reactionary magic, if you will. I see in the dark, my aim is impeccable, and my reflexes are quick. Things like that. Aside from that, I can create a ball of light to illuminate any tunnels or caves we explore. If there's any debris, I can make it lighter for removal purposes."

"Any healing magic?" I asked.

"No, sadly. It's not like it is in video games. I would need to either join a convent or dedicate upward of fifteen years of my life to the Restorative Arts before I could heal physical wounds. The effort doesn't interest me. I'd rather just get magical potions and salves."

"Wait," I looked between Sunny and Tabby. "Why didn't either of you tell me we had magic potions?"

Sunny shrugged. "I thought Tabby told you."

Tabby said, "It kind of slipped my mind. We just have it in the cupboard in case we need it."

"I see." Eo sighed. "Jack, one of us will explain the details to you later. The effects are much more specific than 'healing.' You'll need to be able to recognize them all and know what situations to which each one best applies. For now, however, I need to focus on my breakfast for a bit."

She turned to it and savored each bite. The other girls, Fran included, were overjoyed to see their friend out and enjoying herself.

Later, as Eo finished her last few spoonfuls of oatmeal, she asked, "Any other questions for now?"

"A lot of them. The main one, I guess, is what goes into your decision-making? I literally don't know anything. Do you use magic, or is there some science to predicting where the ore will be?"

"Hmm," Eo looked pensively at her coffee for a while. "The proper explanation to that question would take us much longer than I think you're prepared for, and Sunny has told me that I should warn people before I go on to a deep dive that could potentially last longer than ten minutes. The shortest answer I'm willing to give is that you need to understand the whole in order to understand the parts."

"Hmm," I nodded. "I have no idea what you just said or what you mean."

Tabby shook her head. "You've explained this to me before, and I'm still lost."

Eo pointed to my phone and gestured to the map of Antrum Mine. "My mother explained it best. She handled the charts before me and taught me everything that she knew. So, look at this part of the mine. This little circle is a cavern. Inside that cavern is ore. The ore is the valuable part, but to get there, you need to go to the cavern, and to go there, you need to enter the mine. The ore is part of something which is part of a bigger thing, and all of that is connected as a united system. The minerals and ore and such are like the details of my models. If you look at any one place, you find details. Those details all contribute to the whole."

She took a sip of coffee and continued, "My job is to notice and understand what most people do not, as well as to be able to relay the information that people do want to know. Most people would enter a mine and only look for the ore. That doesn't work, though. You'll miss things, or you'll be inefficient. You need to understand the stability of the caves, the nature of the tunnels, the ecosystem of the monsters within, the weather patterns and geographic history of the area that have contributed to the density and layout of mineral deposits."

She paused to take another mouthful of her coffee.

Eo's amazing, I thought, *but no wonder they worry about her so much. The girl is obsessive.*

She continued, "In other words, if you go looking for one thing, you won't find it. Every part leads you back to the whole, and if you don't understand all the components, you won't be able to find how they relate to one another. Once you understand that, you can reliably predict and locate things. It's possible to guess what monsters we'll find and how many. I can chart out which tunnels are likely to lead to our biggest paydays."

My eyes shut and opened several times. *Okay then.*

"I'm not sure I understand," I said, "but happy to have you on the team."

"That's the spirit!" Tabby said.

"Thank you," Eo said. She raised her coffee cup toward me. "I'm excited to get back into the mine."

With that, our team was complete.

EIGHTEEN

The troll roared again, bringing down its great club for another strike.

I barely dodged out of the way of the attack, feeling rubble bounce off my boots and the floor of the cave rattle slightly.

"Eo called it!" I yelled. "A damn cave troll."

"She knows monsters," Tabby said, holding off a small group of goblins with her sword.

"Hee-hee-ha!" Sunny leaped from high on the cave wall and brought a battle hammer down onto the base of the troll's skull with practiced ease.

It yowled in pain and lurched forward. I took the cue. My ax rose up to the troll's neck as it fell toward me. The blade bit several inches into the monster's thick skin. The awful, ear-splitting bellow it released shook the cavern.

"That's what you get!" Sunny yelled as she jumped from the beast's shoulders and struck at its knee.

Immediately, two kunai knives flew into the creature's other knee.

"Don't get too cocky," Eo said with a flat voice.

She stood at the mouth of the cavern, throwing her blades as she held an orb of magical light above the unexplored area. The light was the vibrant blue of a full moon. She unleashed another throwing knife in one swift, graceful motion. The spark of it flew through the air like an unleashed lightning bolt. A moment after it soared into the darkness, there was a sound of something gasping. A goblin collapsed off the wall and onto the stone floor.

Meanwhile, our troll kept up its wail, torn between the agony in its busted head and that at its legs. The knees buckled beneath its weight. Its animal eyes narrowed on me with a bloodlust that seemed to chill the air around us. The club rose one last time as the huge body collapsed toward me in a murderous fall. I rolled to the side, but not fast enough. It seemed certain that the brute would crush me.

Suddenly, Sunny's hammer struck the beast in the side, knocking it off course. It slammed into the ground behind me. My chance appeared! I jumped back toward it, raising my ax in an arc. It rose and fell onto the back of the noisy monster's neck, cutting through to finish what my first strike had started. Its head rolled off its shoulders.

The adrenaline surge hit, and it hit hard.

How much XP for decapitating a cave troll?

I turned to Sunny. "Thanks. You saved me back there."

She nodded, looked me dead in the eye, and spoke with a disjointed cadence, "You were almost a Jill sandwich!"

I frowned. "Hmm?"

"Hoooow do you not get that reference?" she said, hand on hips. "It's a classic!"

"Banter later," Eo said. "Two goblins hiding in cracks in the walls at ten o'clock. Three goblins from four. A cave lion from seven."

Tabby was at seven.

I rushed to her. Rather, my body rocketed toward the threat.

She struck down the last of the three goblins she'd been handling just as a mass of gray fur and fangs appeared in the tunnel beyond her. I hesitated as it arrived. It was the size of a pick-up truck, with saber teeth and long, thick fur.

It charged Tabby, running horrifyingly fast for something its size. As the cave lion roared into the light, I panicked. Its claws and fangs surged hungrily at Tabby. The moment it attacked, her legs split open and her back twisted down to slide in the narrow gap beneath it. At the same time, she stabbed her sword upward into its belly.

It yowled, taking Tabby's sword with it in its lunge. The beast was so enraged at Tabby that it didn't notice that it'd landed directly in front of me. The great paws barely hit the ground before it spun to face Tabby with a snarl. I took my chance, attacking and driving the ax between its shoulders.

As Tabby had done, I abandoned my weapon and ducked. The cave lion whirled and flashed its claws inches above my head. Its belly, and the sword buried within, revealed themselves to me. I launched forward, grabbed the hilt, pulled it free, and leapt to the side. It roared again. As it turned its lethal intent on me, Tabby jumped onto its back and began pulling the ax from its shoulder. The bloodied cave lion freaked out, unsure where to focus its attention.

That moment of hesitation was all I needed.

I dashed. The blade struck by instinct into the beast's throat. I pushed onward, slicing out to create a spray of blood that spattered against the walls and the floor, rapidly creating an ominous red puddle. The lion gave a final choking growl, then collapsed.

Suddenly, pain exploded through my left calf. A groan of agony and shock tore from my lungs. The leg wouldn't hold my weight, no matter how hard I tried to stay on my feet. I collapsed helplessly against the corpse of my foe.

"Jack!" two voices yelled.

Something whirred behind me. I heard the heavy, wet crunch of a hammer hitting flesh and breaking bone.

I turned to see Sunny, panting and covered in monster blood, holding her hammer over a puddle that had been a goblin only a moment ago. Its knobbed fingers clutched a dagger that was red with my blood. The little bastard stabbed into my calf while I'd been distracted with the bigger opponent.

"Any others?" I asked, looking around.

"We got them," Sunny heaved.

"All clear," Eo confirmed, rushing to me. "I have healing salve."

"Please and thank you," I said through gritted teeth. "Either that or I'll be on painkillers and crutches for a while."

"Hurry!" Tabby said.

As soon as Eo pulled a small jar from a pouch, Tabby grabbed it and pulled the lid off. I barely had the chance to react before she had ripped my pants open slightly more and was rubbing it into the wound.

"Damn goblins," she said. "This is why you never underestimate them."

"That," Sunny said as she leaned against her hammer and panted for breath, "was badass." She gave me a thumbs up.

It'd been three weeks since Eo started joining our expeditions. Her job, I quickly realized, was equipment and resource management. She understood monster tracking and prediction intuitively. It also helped that she had an encyclopedic knowledge of every tunnel, cavern, and stone we'd ever come across in Antrum Mine.

After digging through some safe bets, we'd decided to gamble and go somewhere with a potential payload. Eo warned us that we'd likely encounter a troll at the same time as several goblins.

"I agree with Sunny," Eo said. "That was some impressive fighting you did back there. If I'd known there would be a troll and a cave lion, I would have suggested we hire others to come with us."

"I think," I replied, "that Tabby gets most of the credit for the lion."

"We'll split it," Tabby said as she rubbed the salve into my aching wound. "I can't believe you jumped under it like that. That was incredibly reckless."

I shook my head. "There wasn't much time to think. Considering that I didn't expect there would be any cave lions, I think I did well. I didn't even know there could be cave lions in here."

Tabby rubbed more roughly, making me wince. "What did you expect?"

"Trolls. Goblins. Maybe a rock elemental spirit or a slime beast. Maybe a big spider. A lion seems, I don't know, mundane."

"But," Eo tilted her head in confusion. "How are spiders not mundane? I found one in the shower this morning. Lions are much more exotic."

"Well," I said, grasping at straws, "giant ones!"

Eo looked at the corpse of the cave lion, then gestured to it with two open hands like a disillusioned game show host showing off a prize. "This is giant."

"Focus, please," Tabby said. "You're acting too calm for someone who's just been stabbed. That was impressive. Maybe even incredible and extremely..." She looked at me. That look halted me more than anything in the fight. Her pupils were wide, the sapphire irises seeming to absorb the magic light and glow.

Was she gonna say 'brave?' Or something even better?

Our adrenaline was high. Every muscle in my body sang with victory. She had dirt on her face and goblin blood all over her thick coveralls, but I didn't care, I wanted to—

She pressed harder on the wound. I gritted my teeth as the salve kicked in, burning like fire as it sealed the wound and stopped the bleeding.

"I did it," I forced the words through the pain, "because I trusted in you."

Tabby blushed.

"Hee-hee," Sunny laughed. "Don't be mad at Tabby. She's just mad that a different cat almost got on top of you before her."

"Sunny!" Tabby bolted to her feet. As she did, her cat ears stuck up so violently that they knocked the hard hat off of her head. "Don't say things like that!"

The light pulsed white once, Eo's signal for us to focus on her. "It's not a cutscene, everyone. We should get started with setting up the lanterns and cables for this area. The sooner we get steady light, the sooner we make it clear that they are no longer allowed in this cavern."

With that, work began on making this cavern part of our known territory. We'd prepared several lanterns and cables beforehand. In the quiet aftermath of the battle, we brought in the lights and set them up.

Even though I took part, it was a spectacle to watch them work in tandem. The orange light came in, its hue bringing a warmth and human touch, which marked the space as ours. Eo directed the other two on where to move the lights. If they passed any large cracks which might serve as goblin vantage points, Sunny prepared a torch and threw it in. Nothing emerged from our attempts to smoke them out. We were safe.

As the lights came in, we saw the telltale glints of metal. Precious, valuable metal. Technically, it was still a mineral in the state we were looking at, but all I saw was profit. A mix of gold and copper, if I'd had to bet.

"Yeees," Sunny crooned as she climbed over our discovery.

The lights also showed off the battle.

We'd endured a lot. Eo moved through masses of goblins, pulling her kunai knives from temples and throats. They were unique, I'd noticed. Instead of the simple black design which I'd seen in so many games, these were green, with a hand-painted Tri Force on each one.

"Hey," I called once we'd finished with the lights, "what are the odds of running into more trolls or lions?"

"My guess," Eo answered, "is that there are at least two more trolls left. It depends on how many tunnels there are and how deep this goes. As for lions, frankly, I'm surprised we encountered this one."

"No kidding," Sunny laughed. "Those things usually live waaay closer to the surface."

"Anything we should be worried about?" I asked.

Sunny shrugged. "I mean, there's always dangers and unknowns in the business. It's a little weird, but I wouldn't be freaked out about it."

"Still," Tabby said, walking up to me. "Caution is a good response. I appreciate that."

Eo didn't say anything. Instead, she kept looking at the lion's corpse, uncertainty clear on her face.

"Eo," I said, "it looks like something is bothering you."

"It is bothering me," she replied bluntly. "Under natural circumstances, this thing wouldn't be this deep. Something must have happened to make it go further than normal."

"That's easy," Sunny said. "It probably happened when the barrier went up. The alarm that made everyone leave probably scared it down into the depths of the caves. That wasn't exactly 'natural circumstances.'"

"I suppose." Eo nodded, though she still looked unsure. "That would be a suitable explanation. Regardless, we should report the lion to the civic center. If there are any more of those in the mine, it becomes a concern for the village. It's unlikely, but not impossible that one might leave the mine."

"Understood," I said. "Do we do that now or after we're finished for the day?"

"I say," Eo concluded, "we lay some tracks for the carts, clear the bodies, and call it a day. All in favor?"

She looked among the rest of us. We all agreed.

Sunny suggested we break for food and water first. The battle had taken most of our energy, despite how early in the day it was. We'd struck out, prepared for a battle first thing in the morning. Good thing, too. It'd turned out to be more than we bargained for.

The break came and went quickly. Together, we laid the tracks, brought in a cart, and began to transport our bloody mess. It was important to do that, they said. Otherwise, monsters might come for the bodies when we weren't around, and they might decide that they felt comfortable in the cavern.

For the troll and the cave lion, Eo used her magic to make the corpses lighter so we could carry them without having to break them down into smaller pieces first.

After several hours, we were ready to go. Eo and Sunny left first, Eo eager to report the lion, and Sunny eager to get a well-deserved drink. I paused and looked around the cavern.

The precious metal held a lot of my attention. What really grabbed me, however, was the fact that there was only a single other tunnel. Every other cavern we'd come across had several openings. This was the first I'd seen that had only one. We had come from an opening that sloped into a massive bowl. The other opening was directly opposite. I could barely see into it, but it curved immediately, preventing me from seeing any further.

It felt oddly deliberate. The bowl, the cracks for the goblins. The cavern itself felt too smooth, almost like a dome. Perhaps the goblins or the troll messed around to make itself more comfortable. This shape, I decided, was not natural.

"Hey," Tabby walked up to me, "you did some amazing fighting today."

"Just being cautious," I said, throwing her word of choice back at her.

"Glad to hear it." As we walked to the exit, she moved closer to my side. "We move well together."

"I should hope so. After all the yoga, I'd say our bodies respond to each other."

She looked at me, then to the entrance. "You might be right."

"I still can't believe that dodge you did," I said. "A full split and stab up into the lion? That was incred—"

Suddenly, she leaned in and kissed my cheek. The peck was quick and unexpected, by far the most effective attack I'd seen all day.

I stood stunned and silent.

"You were amazing today," she said. "We moved perfectly in sync."

Her hand rose to my face. As she pulled away, her fingers moved gently over my skin, feeling me.

With that, she cruelly, beautifully, perfectly, pulled from my grip and walked away.

Her tail swished back and forth in content playfulness.

I followed, all thoughts of the strangeness of the cavern vanishing.

CHAPTER
NINETEEN

I woke up a minute before my alarm.

The day was already off to a good start. Being able to catch the alarm right before it went off was a small pleasure of mine. Part of me, however, wondered if I'd been sleeping light.

Was that from nerves, or anticipation?

I was worried about Antrum. We were still working on the dome-shaped cavern. We'd mined so much from it that the walls had expanded. We'd even set up several wooden pillars and lattices to increase the stability of the walls. There'd been enough money from our finds that we could afford to hire some carpenters to help.

As much as we'd gained, I felt nervous in that cavern. The feeling didn't happen often, only when I thought about what lay beyond it. The tunnel entrance, for example, freaked me out. I had no shame or fear in admitting it. It was too clean, its edges too defined.

We'd investigated it once. It twisted back and forth for a short way, then cut suddenly left and downward. From there, it became a sloping hallway, its ceiling, walls, and floor flattened. There were only a few of the bumps and ridges we'd come to expect underground. The area had been flattened by someone—or something. It was large, too, about eight feet square, and incredibly long. Eo had cast her orb of light and sent it as far down as it would go. We saw no sign of an end to the tunnel.

How long, I often wondered since, had that lion been running before it arrived at us? Had it really heard our commotion? Had it come by coincidence? What had sent it down there to begin with?

The three of us had agreed to block it off. We used simple wooden boards and yellow caution tape. It would stop nothing, but we would know if something had come through while we were away. So far, nothing had.

No, Jack. Don't worry about it.

Worries only brought tension. Tension made yoga difficult, which in turn, made Tabby laugh at my tenseness.

Maybe, I hoped, *that's why it's easy to wake up early on the weekend.*

Tabby and I kept up our daily routine on our days off. Normally, we started an hour later on our weekends. The previous day, though, she had requested to start at the same time today. I wasn't sure why.

The house was especially quiet as I rose and moved downstairs. Sunny indulged in her liquid vice on Saturday nights. Considering how well she did through the rest of the week, none of us stopped her. She'd likely be out of commission until noon. Eo was on the opposite end of the spectrum, habit wise. On Saturday nights, she holed up in her room and busied herself with models well into the night.

I stepped outside, the cool air helping me wake up. The bigger help in that regard, however, was already on her mat. Tabby was in something I'd learned was called the *dolphin pose.* Her feet and forearms rested on the mat, spine slanted down with her head so near the mat that her hair almost touched it. Her legs were perfectly straight, tilted ever so slightly forward so that her ass was not only the highest and most noticeable part of her, but also positioned ever so slightly up and forward in a way that could only be called inviting.

There was no way that was the intended way to do the pose.

My eyes moved across the view, down her firm stomach to those amazing breasts which gravity now pushed up her body.

I'd seen those from just about every angle.

I damn near whistled at the view.

"My eyes are down here," she said. My eyes move down from her chest to her upside-down face. "If you're done ogling me, we can start. Or would you rather look at me than the sunrise?"

There's no competition there, and you know it.

"Right," I said, unfolding my mat and preparing to start the routine. I was, of course, wearing yoga pants. The loose-fitting apparel was itself a motivation to stay on task. If I ever got too distracted, she would well notice. Considering all she had done and how well I had focused, I felt like I was on the path to Enlightenment.

"For today," she said as she pulled out of the pose and moved to her hands and knees. "I wanted to check in on the basics. Did I show you cat-cow?"

"Not you specifically. I saw a bunch of video yoga routines with it, though."

She scrunched her face disapprovingly.

Is she disappointed?

"Well," she huffed, annoyed for some reason, "let's try it together."

She walked me through one of the most basic moves. It was a simple breathing exercise that worked for the start of simple routines. We'd skipped it most days because of how often we messed with each other. Both of us started on hands and knees with straight backs. Once it was a straight line from shoulders to hips, we took in a long, deep breath. As we did, we raised our heads and pushed our bellies as close to the mat as possible, creating a curve in our spine.

When Tabby did this, I couldn't look away. Her body curved with an impossible fluid motion. Not only did her face rise, but her chest puffed out and forward like the figurehead of a ship. The intense angle of her spine curled down from her shoulders and looped back up to her hips.

The entire point of this was to move while taking a slow, deliberate inhale. She flew in the face of that at the end of her rise. Instead of finishing her inhale, she let out a sexy little moan. Her upper teeth poked into view and bit her lower lip.

Fuck, Tabby! I like the teasing, but this is just torture!

This had a different feeling to it. Our little moments never started this intensely this early. My breath was already uneven and ragged, largely because of my distraction.

After a few rounds of this torture, she said, "Okay, now let's work on balance. Do you know about one-hand one-leg planks?"

"Go on."

"Just watch me." She went into a full plank.

Her palms lay beneath her shoulders, and her legs were outstretched, so only her toes touched the mat. From toes to shoulders was a smooth line. With her next exhale, her right hand and left foot rose and stretched away from her body.

"You try," she said, clearly focusing on staying balanced.

"Okay," I said.

It didn't look too difficult. I went into the plank position, reoriented my breath, made sure that I was steady, and exhaled. My left foot rose without issue. The moment my right hand left the mat, however, my body shook. My hand fell back to the mat, then lifted again. My entire body trembled, trying to crumple into its center of gravity. I tried to push through it. When I realized how ragged my breath was, I knew I was screwed.

"Shit." I collapsed to the mat.

"Pfft, ha—" Tabby chuckled, but that destroyed her balance. "—ah!"

She toppled to her right, rolling toward me. She rolled onto the thin patch of grass between our mats so that her shoulder and arm landed on mine. When had we started practicing so close to each other?

I stared.

She rested a cheek on the grass, her laugh still holding the smile on her face. The green played well against her hair. Her smile became smaller but more comfortable. We lay there, side-by-side in the light of the dawn, unable to look at anything except each other.

You're beautiful.

"Well," I said at last. "That's a difficult move."

"Yeah," she said, eyes fixed on mine. "You need to use every part of your body."

"Every part?" I asked.

She rolled her eyes playfully. "Just about. Try again."

As I got back into position, she didn't move. "Um..." I said, "you're on my mat."

"Is that a problem?"

"Not at all."

I returned to a plank pose, trying not to think about the fact that I'd land partially on her if I fell again.

"There you go," she said. "I'm starting to think that you only improve when something's at stake. That's a very unattractive feature, you know. It's important to value something for its own sake. Still, let's see if we can use it to our advantage."

As she said all this, Tabby moved beneath me. She pushed herself onto my yoga mat and moved her shoulders between my hands. I had never noticed how thin she was.

"What—" I started to ask, but she interrupted me.

"Don't speak. Just focus." She placed her hand on my right forearm. *No claws.* Her delicate, deliberate touch sent fire across my skin. "We have stakes now. Take a deep breath in and out to focus. On your next inhale, raise your arm."

I shook my head and bit my lip. She lay beneath me, her chin gently pushing up as if anticipating a kiss. Her eyes seemed to glow in the light. I heard her soft breaths. "Tabby," I said, "I don't want to crush you."

"Don't worry," she said, her expression serious. "I trust in you, just like you trusted in me, okay? Please, do this for me. I want to know if you've actually put effort into these yoga sessions or if you've only been here for the view. I wouldn't do this with just anyone."

What exactly wouldn't you do with just anyone?

With effort worthy of the Greek heroes, I raised my eyes forward. It was always easier to hold a position when looking ahead. I inhaled. With the breath, my left foot and my right hand rose at a glacial pace upward.

"Good, good. Keep going. That's it. No rush. Inhabit your body. Let the breath guide your movement. It's just you. Right here. Accept the discomfort. Breathe through it. Good. Hold. Hold it for me. Breathe out, slowly. Breathe in.

Hold. On your next exhale, you can lower your arm and foot. Three. Two. One. Release..."

Her hand rose to my upraised wrist, guiding it to its proper place on the mat. There she was, beneath me, hot and inviting, with no plans for the rest of the day. Even if I'd said nothing, the growing lump in my yoga pants gave away my thoughts.

"Tabby," I said, voice husky with desire.

"You talked about push-ups when we started," she said. "You were trying to impress me or something. Well, go ahead." Her eyes shut, and her arms fell to the side. *Trust. Desire. Invitation.* "Impress me."

As you wish.

My arms bent. All strain was forgotten as I lowered toward her. I couldn't stop myself from leaning my face forward to meet hers first. My eyes shut as our lips touched. It was nothing like the adrenaline burst. This was warm, delicate, and mutual. I started slow. She leaned into it. She gently pulled my lips with her own, touching her tongue to my upper lip to taste me.

I lowered my body to touch her, but not to rest on her. It seemed wrong to put all my weight on her. That wouldn't have been part of our game. Still, we felt each other. Finally, I felt the body that had entranced me since I first arrived.

When my bulge pushed against her inner thigh, I felt her lips curl into a smile. Her palm touched my cheek as she leaned further into the kiss. My mouth gently gripped around her soft lower lip and pulled.

Now, it's my turn to tease.

My arms pushed me up, lips still pulling. She followed me as far as her neck would allow, until I pulled away. When her eyes opened, her irises were wide, covering almost half of her eye.

She wants me. I want her.

"I thought," I said, "this was about push-ups."

"Not just that," she breathed. Her voice was heavy with her breath. They were deeper. Her chest swelled. Her cheeks flushed. "It's compatibility. Two bodies. Moving together." She touched her neck; I nodded.

I lowered myself. Quickly, her fingers wrapped into my hair and pulled my face to her neck. My lips pressed against her flesh, my tongue appearing gently for a moment to lick her delicate skin. I did this over and over, exploring the warm, tender skin of her throat.

When my hips lowered, once again, my bulge pressed against her. She reacted. Her hips rose to meet me, pushing and lightly grinding, shoving all rational thought from my mind. Her breath came in huffs to match the undulation of her hips. She kissed the top of my head and breathed heavily into my hair.

Gently, experimentally, I stopped holding myself with my arms. My knees rested between her legs, and my body lay on top of hers. Her breasts pressed up against me, their sweet give spreading them across my chest. I wanted to tear off my shirt so I could feel her against my skin. An animal groan of lust rolled out of me. Her warmth passed even through the fabric. I needed to touch her.

My lips rose up her neck, traced her jaw, and once again found her lips. They were soft, pulling me closer, asking me to do more. There, we held a long, deep kiss. My hips pressed down against hers. Her hands moved to my back, rubbing up and down.

All the while, I grew. She knew it, felt it. I needed all of her.

My mind went blank with sheer desire. My breath shook. Our lips came apart, but we stayed there, feeling each other's breath. Our eyes were inches from each other.

"Tabby," I said. "I'm not gonna be able to hold back any longer."

"My room," she said. "Now."

Instantly, I launched into action.

I hopped to her side, grabbed her hand, and lifted her off the ground.

"*Ah*," she let out a maddeningly sexy little sound as I lifted her off the mat. I'd meant to lift Tabby to her feet, but as I did, her legs rose and wrapped around my hips. All her limbs pulled tight and pressed her against me.

"I need you," she breathed into my ear, driving me mad with the hot moisture of her breath.

"Tabby," was all I could say.

Quickly, awkwardly, I clambered back toward the house with this amazing woman who was grinding against my cock even as we moved. When we got onto the porch, I couldn't focus. We slammed into the wall beside the door. She let out a little yelp.

"I can't focus," I laughed to myself. "You're doing too much to me at once."

She laughed, biting her tongue again. "Follow me, then." Tabby pulled her legs and one arm away. She opened the door and ran inside, one hand holding on to the hem of my shirt.

I dashed in after her, not even bothering to close the door.

We dashed up the steps, almost tripping several times, laughing and giggling like idiots. Soon, we made it to her bedroom door. As we did, I darted up against her. My hands wrapped around her hips as I pushed myself against the ass which had presented itself to me for so many mornings. I pressed her against the door.

"Eager." She laughed. "Get the door."

I did. I moved my hand from her body to the door handle and flung it open. We almost fell inside. As I stumbled in, my nimble yoga partner slipped from under me and shut the door behind us.

I turned over to see her, in a single gorgeous motion, pull her sports bra over her head and throw it to the ground. There she was, bare, beautiful, full. Her breasts whipped up with the rough pull of the bra, then bounced back and jiggled as they were set free. In response, I pulled my own shirt over my head and dropped it.

She raised an eyebrow seductively, lips curling into a devilish grin. "Were you expecting this?" Her eyes went over every inch of me, desire and lust plain in every second of the gaze.

"Were you not?" I replied.

In response, she began to pull down her tights. The thin fabric had done almost nothing to hide her shape. I'd seen her curves, her widening desire. I practically tore off my shorts, pulling free the hard, throbbing desire that she'd encouraged all this time.

Suddenly, there we were, perfectly and entirely revealed to each other. Her curtains were open, so the morning light which we'd shared so often now showcased our bodies to each other. Under that toned stomach, she was shaved. Her eyes gaped at the hard, curved measure of my lust.

"You're beautiful," I said.

She looked at me, and all teasing fell aside. "Fuck me."

We rushed to each other, then fell onto the bed. My mouth moved over her as if I were possessed. I buried my face between her breasts. She held me there. One of my hands grasped her breast.

"Yes," she gasped in a shockingly light, high sound.

I gripped a little harder, filling my hand with her warm, soft skin. My mouth enclosed on her other nipple, sucking as my tongue flicked at one of her most sensitive areas.

Meanwhile, my other hand went south. My fingers moved over the firm stomach that had already begun to move under me. Immediately, I felt her.

Wow, you're so wet already. You've wanted this as much as me, haven't you?

I laughed, letting my hot breath flow onto her. Again, she reacted. As she moaned, I rubbed up and down the inviting warmth.

"Okay," she said.

She grabbed my face and lifted me to look at her. For a second, I feared that there would be more teasing or something else to delay us. Instead, she said, "I want you, all of you, inside me."

She turned onto her stomach. Only now did I notice the luxurious nature of the bed. White silk sheets. She lay against it, her sun-kissed skin looking all the warmer against the sheets, her breasts pushed up against her. Suddenly, she rose, hips first. Tabby raised herself onto her forearms and knees into a very familiar position. Her hips shook back and forth, tail curling up, ears pointed high. "Now," she pleaded, "get back there and—"

She didn't have a chance to finish. Immediately, I was behind her, with a similar view to what I'd seen every day, now with all revealed—a perfect peach, with her soft slit between the crevice, begging to be entered.

She moved. Her hips shook back and forth. Her ass jiggled for me, tilting up and down, begging for me. At the end of the bed, she'd turned her head to look at me. Her tail curled to my face and traced its fluff across my jaw.

My hands grabbed her hips. My tip found its way to her wet lower lips. I pushed.

"Ah!" She gripped the sheets. The pupils overtook her eyes. Her tight hot pussy wrapped around my tip. My hips rocked back and forth. Over and over, I worked myself deeper, pulling back slightly only to push deeper with each thrust. "Ooh! Yes...more!"

Her moan was high, begging, so unlike the stern voice which had once doubted me. My hands gripped tighter at her slender, firm sides. I pulled back to the tip, relishing every glorious inch as she squeezed me.

Pulling her and pushing myself, I sheathed to the hilt.

"Aaah!" she squealed, moaned, and shook. "Uh-uh-ah..."

"Already?" I teased, smacking her ass.

"Ah! Shut up!" she said. Already, her arms were twitching, her body convulsing with pleasure. "Just—"

I pulled back and slammed her against me again. Again and again, I slammed myself into her ass. With each smack, I rubbed through her tip to base. The pleasure overwhelmed me. My body moved in a blind rhythm. She gripped me as my eyes stayed transfixed on the glorious body that begged for me.

Her tail wrapped around the back of my neck, going taut to help support her. I tried moving harder. Her voice caught, "Yes! Like that! Ah! I feel your balls slapping my clit. Fuck! You feel so good!"

My fingers gripped harder. I pushed and pulled harder, bringing her so far away from me that I threatened to slip out, then slamming her hard and fast down my entire length.

"Are you," she huffed, "still fucking growing?"

She reacted to me. Every twitch. Every thrust. Every motion. "You kept me waiting," I growled. "Now, you show me something."

Immediately, her ass shook. Her tail wrapped around my waist to anchor her to me. With this fulcrum, she leaned her face and chest down into the sheets and began to work only her hips. Pleasure overrode all thought as I went still, experiencing her motion and watching that beautiful ass slide up and down, soaking and stroking with each expert thrust.

Gradually, we found a rhythm. Our bodies moved together. We pulled back to the last possible moment where I threatened to slip out, then slid back in all the way with a loud wet smack. Every inch of my body blazed with the hot intensity.

Suddenly, she pushed herself back onto her arms and began to shake her hips from side to side. She moved slower, focusing on the shake of her hips, pulling and stroking me in every way.

Fuck.

"Yes, yes, yes! Oh!" she reveled in it, relishing the way my shape filled her and rubbed through her insides. Time lost all meaning in the thrusting, shaking, smacking ecstasy. "Push me down. Harder!"

So, we moved. She splayed out, resting her whole body on the bed. I leaned down over her and pounded into her. I held myself up with my hands and knees so that the sex was our only contact. She huffed and squealed with every hard thrust. I looked down and saw her ass ripple with each impact. I could barely hang on.

"Tabby. I'm almost—"

"Please! Do it!"

Instantly, I grabbed her hips, held myself into the base, and slammed into the bed beside her. I stayed inside as we turned sideways. One of my hands slid under her body and grasped her breast. The other hand wrapped under her thigh and lifted it, so I had more space to move.

I pounded. She screamed my name. Faster. Harder I thrust into her. Tabby's entire body shook against me. Her free breast swung around with the constant motions, hitting back against my hand.

My body moved faster than I thought possible. Everything shifted below. The pressure built in my shaft and the head. She squeezed.

"Please!" Her face turned to me. "Kiss me!"

I did. She demanded me, gripping with both lips. We moaned and moved together.

Finally, we climaxed.

I shoved in deep, pressing into her and holding her to me as everything erupted out of me. Her entire body trembled in my arms, her eyes fluttering up. I twitched. Again, firing out every last drop. She reacted each time, melting into me and the sensation.

"Yes..." she said, grabbing the hand on her breast and holding it there in place. "Stay..." she said. "With me...in me...Stay..."

My head fell on her pillow. I'd been awake less than an hour, but I felt like I could pass out. It was as if I'd given her all the energy I had. Still, I held myself against her and kissed the back of her neck.

"Nowhere I'd rather be."

She chuckled and fell against the pillow also. "Good thing we have no other plans today."

Oh?

Experimentally, I rubbed her nipple. "You sure?

CHAPTER
TWENTY

At some point, I fell back to sleep. The sheets were far too warm and comfortable, and the person next to me, warmer and more comfortable still.

I woke to find Tabby tracing her fingers over my chest. We were cozy and snug beneath the blankets together, her nestled tight against my side.

"Someone was tired," she said.

"Well." I chuckled. "*Someone* demanded a lot from me."

"Hmm." She lifted the blanket and rolled on top of me. Below the blankets, her tail rubbed up and down my thighs. "And you provided." She kissed my chest, eyes looking up with playful desire. Her hips wiggled, waking me up, so my cock began to lift. "There we go."

"You could just say what you want," I said.

My hand went to her head and rubbed those adorable cat ears. She leaned into my fingers and lifted her chest, bringing her beautiful breasts back into view. I leaned forward and licked her nipple.

"Ah," she muttered. "I speak with my body. Same as you."

I pulled back, and she settled onto my chest. Tabby made an expression I hadn't seen before: contentment. She looked at me like there was nothing and no one else in the world, and it stirred me in ways I never knew anything could.

"Hey Tabby," I said. "Should we talk about what we did?"

"*Did*?" Her hand moved down and felt the base of my erection. "I think we're gonna do it again. But what's on your mind?"

"Well, we're co-workers and roommates. I know that we've bantered back and forth a bunch and, yeah, I've wanted this, but I want to make sure we feel the same about it, so it doesn't get messy down the line."

Tabby nodded. She shifted from my chest to my side. There, she kissed my shoulder. "I'm happy. Do you have any regrets?"

"No. Do you?"

She put her arm over my chest and rested her head on my shoulder. "I kind of wish you'd made a move sooner, but I'm glad you didn't. I like how well we move together. I feel like I can trust you. This is just one part of that."

I nodded. "Alright. So, now the hard question; what are we?"

She shrugged. "For now? Yoga partners. We don't need to put any more labels on it than that quite yet. Are you okay with that?"

"Yeah." I let out a sigh. "Honestly, I'm relieved. I don't want to go too fast."

"Good. Let's just see how it goes."

"And if it goes somewhere?" I replied.

Tabby gave a grin. "Then, it goes somewhere."

Suddenly, as I lay defenseless, her soft fingers caressed my balls, held the base of my shaft, and began to stroke. She leaned to my ear and said, "It's my turn to be on top."

We spent that entire day in bed. It was perfect. It felt like the culmination of all of our hard work. We'd gotten Antrum Mine into production. Everyone in the house was involved. Also, the sex. The naïve part of me expected the next few days to be pure bliss.

That's not what happened.

All the individual elements of my life were at their best, certainly. Tabby and I had sex almost every morning. It'd practically become part of the yoga routine. I hit the smith some days after work in Antrum, learning the craft but mostly trying to examine the strange adrenaline bursts. I even got back into gaming. Eo brought out all the local multiplayer classics, usually decimating us. Sunny cleaned house in fighting games, however, and I could hold my own in Mario Kart.

Still, no matter how good the moments or how peaceful the nights were, the talk didn't last once we started work. A shift into silence had become a disturbingly regular part of the day. At first, it happened when we saw our makeshift barrier in front of the one tunnel entrance in the dome-shaped cavern. We never saw any signs that something—or someone—messed with it. There weren't even any more monsters there. Our only fights came from stragglers on the way down to that cavern.

Our nerves, instead of easing, grew tenser.

None of us said it, but it was obvious. Tabby, Sunny, and I always became silent when we arrived at the quarry.

That day was no different.

Eo, thankfully, didn't feel nervous until we were inside the mine.

"From the earth we came," she said as we stepped to the entrance, "and into the earth we return."

"Tabby *came*," Sunny said, yawning. "You two are so fucking loooud."

Tabby blushed. I did too, but I had to bring a hand to my mouth to cover an involuntary smile.

"Hey." Tabby nudged my side with her elbow. "Don't laugh."

"I can't help it."

"Is that what that sound was?" Eo said. "Good to know. You woke me up the other day. I almost walked over to check if you were okay when I heard the screaming."

"I'm okay," Tabby grumbled with a nod. "Thanks for the concern, though."

Sunny rolled her eyes. "I'd guess you were waaay more than okay."

"Anyway." Tabby walked faster, her cheeks still colored pink. "Once more unto the breach."

"Dear friends, once more!" Eo led us as we descended into Antrum once again.

"What breach?" Sunny asked.

"It's Shakespeare," Eo and Tabby said in unison. "Jinx!" They turned to each other. Tabby was first to say it, but Eo was first to finish the word. After a moment, Tabby said, "Call it even?"

"That seems fair."

The chatter kept up as we went deeper and deeper into the mines. Eventually, we made it to the dome, which was as ominous as ever. We grew quiet as we entered, and we all immediately checked the tunnel entrance. The tape and boards were untouched. Nothing had come in or out.

"Alright," I said, hoping my sigh of relief wasn't too obvious. "Back to work."

The dome kept giving more. More gold. More iron. More copper. We'd extracted so much that we'd almost started our own tunnel into the side of the wall because of how deep the ore veins went. Every step of the way, we were careful to reinforce the stone to reduce the chance of a cave-in.

The mood stayed heavy until Eo began humming the *Skyrim* theme softly under her breath. The rest of us didn't react. She sometimes sang to keep a pace. Her voice was soft and airy. Today, I almost laughed. She knew every lyric of the made-up language, softly regaling the stone with the legend of the Dragonborn.

We got comfortable. Our pace quickened to its usual steady flow. The picks moved, and the ore came out. For hours, things went well.

Suddenly, my pick broke through the stone. It didn't break a piece off, it broke *through*. The rock fell inward, leaving an open crack of black nothingness.

What the fuck?

My heart plummeted to my stomach when I saw it. Worse, I felt something. A low whoosh of warm air emerged from the opening. Curiosity and horror got the better of me. *This, I thought, is where the guy who dies first would lean forward to investigate. I'm not going to be that guy.*

As I turned back to tell the others of my accidental discovery, a sound emerged from the opening.

"Guys!" I yelled. "I found something weird. Be quiet for a second."

Quickly, the impacts of the other picks stopped. There wasn't even the clamber of Sunny scaling down the wall. The others were frozen with nerves, the same as me.

"Talk to us," Tabby said. "What is it?"

"I broke through. There's an opening in the rock. I can hear something. It's too faint for me to tell what it is."

"Allow me." Eo quickly pulled me to the side and looked at the crack. "Everyone, be silent. I'm going to activate the enhancements on my hearing."

"Got it." Sunny landed on the ground and prepared her battle hammer. She kept her back to us and watched our much-feared tunnel entrance. Tabby unsheathed her blade, raised her ears, and looked across the cracks in the wall. I pulled out my ax and stayed by Eo.

She looked at me. I nodded. She returned the gesture. From there, she shut her eyes and leaned slightly toward the crack.

"Something crackling. It sounds like a fire. There's something more. A low...rumbling? No, it's too smooth. It's..."

Eo leaned a little closer. When she did, we began to hear it. Crackling, just as she had said. Suddenly, a small tongue of flame jumped out from the crack. If we hadn't been so on edge, it might have seemed playful, but because of the atmosphere, Eo leaped back and shrieked. All of us turned our focus onto her.

It's a distraction!

I turned to our barricaded tunnel to see a humanoid shape appear. It raised a staff toward us. It was made of onyx, with a fist-sized diamond near its top.

"There!" I yelled—not quick enough.

A bolt of lightning flashed through the space and struck Tabby. At the same time, several loud grunts and angry, throaty snarls came from above. Tabby collapsed. The sword fell from her grip. She convulsed on the ground. I wanted to run to her, to cradle her and make sure she was okay, but I couldn't. Not yet.

I looked up to see a nightmare falling onto us. Goblins, like nothing we'd seen before, threw themselves at us. Seven of them leaped from the cracks above us. Spittle flung from their lips. Cracked and broken bits of teeth pointed from jaws with the skin torn from them. Skin had been cut and decayed away. Bone poked through the patches of half-rotted flesh. Their eyes glowed an eerie dark purple.

Are those fucking zombies?

Instantly, Eo screamed. Her hands clapped together and pushed toward them. A powerful gale, like that which had helped her fly, erupted from her. Most of the animated corpses were knocked back, bashing into the wall and falling to the ground with hideous crunches. Two kept on course, angling toward Tabby.

"No you dooon't!" Sunny's hammer smashed into one in the air, sending it crashing away.

"Fucking zombies!" I tackled the other from the air. It snarled and slashed where it landed on the ground. Sunny ended it with another strike that burst its head like an over-ripe melon. I looked up at her, angry and fearful. "Why the fuck didn't anyone say something about zombies?"

"Duuude!" Sunny yelled back. "Do you have any idea how rare necromancy is?"

"Illegal for centuries," Eo said. Three kunai flashed out toward our resurrected foes. They stumbled back but continued to shamble onward. "Did anyone see who cast the bolt?"

I whirled back to our barricade. The figure was gone. "I saw someone," I said. "Didn't get a good look. Human-shaped with a staff that had a diamond-looking thing at the top. Eo, please tell me you have a potion for Tabby!"

"I—I'm fine." Tabby trembled from head to toe, and her eyes were dazed, but she tried to grip her sword and get to her feet.

Eo opened a pouch at her hip. As she did, the cave shook. A single violent jolt knocked us off our feet as if someone had shaken the cave like a children's playset. A small glass vial slipped from Eo's grip.

"Get that!" she yelled.

I dove for it, barely catching the glass before it hit the ground. The shaking continued, sending dust and rubble falling onto us. I scrambled to Tabby, keeping an eye on the shambling remains of the three goblin zombies who still moved.

Who was the guy with the staff?

I couldn't wonder for long.

In front of the mouth of the cave where we'd entered the dome, a geyser of stone spurt up. In the middle of its upward blast, it stopped. The rocks were all connected. It rose into the shape of a colossal hand, which smashed into the ground and pushed. A great body of stone pulled itself from the floor.

Nope. Nope. Oh shit!

Sunny screamed the word I didn't want to believe: "Elemental!"

"Oh dear," Eo said as what little color she had drained from her. She stared at the barricade, her eyes wide with horror.

"What now?" I demanded.

As if in answer to my question, a feral roar sounded from the tunnel. A cave lion with ragged fur and scarred paws crashed through our barricade into the room. Its eyes glowed purple, like the undead goblins.

"Shiiit!" Sunny did something I'd never seen: she panicked. Her eyes widened as her pupils shrunk to pinpricks.

I saw all this as I poured the vial's contents into Tabby's mouth. She was limp in my grip, barely able to lift her head and trembling so hard that the glass of the vial chattered against her teeth. The moment she swallowed, she gasped. Instantly, she was back to herself.

Relief flooded through me, but it was short-lived.

"Dammit!" she yelled and grabbed her sword.

We stood. The four of us moved so we had our backs to each other. Our threats were many. The elemental was a giant, blocky caricature of a human, at least ten feet tall, with an absurdly thick body and unfairly long arms. The cave lion approached slowly, waiting for us to present the opportunity to attack. If those weren't bad enough, three of the zombie goblins hobbled toward us.

"I don't want to die," Sunny said, her voice a mere whimper compared to her usual boisterous tone.

"Don't talk like that," Tabby said.

"Why is there a necromancer in Antrum?" Eo asked.

I said nothing. I looked among all our threats. Giant. Lion. Zombies. Mystery man with a staff. Of all things, it felt like a murderous prank. The guy with the lightning could have stayed and continued the attack, but he'd left. All of this could have happened sooner. We'd been here for days. Nothing happened until I broke through the stone. Everything came after that. The sound and the small flame had come to distract us. The rest only happened from there, one after another as we were distracted.

In the immortal words of Admiral Ackbar, it's a trap!

But if that was the case, why all the pomp and circumstance? Why wait days as we excavated? Why distract us with all the drama? Who the hell was that mystery guy?

Who knows? Fuck it.

"How tough are elementals?" I asked.

"Are you serious?" Sunny asked.

"They've been known to take out platoons of trained soldiers," Eo answered.

Okay, Salvatore was right, noted.

"I have an idea," I said.

"Please share," Eo replied, a note of urgency in her voice.

The elemental didn't move. It stayed crouched like a hockey goalie at our escape. The reanimated lion crept toward us. It moved slower, more sluggishly than the one which had attacked us the other day.

"We kill the lion first," I said. "Bait the elemental into stepping away from the tunnel, and make a break for it."

"That's it?" Sunny asked.

"Honestly, yeah."

"Okay," Tabby nodded. "Jack and I will rush it and split to either side. Sunny takes the front. Eo, focus on keeping the goblins off us. Everyone clear?"

Eo and I agreed. After a second, so did Sunny. Tabby turned her eyes to me. There, I saw complete and unquestioning trust. She nodded, her gaze blazing with determination.

Immediately, we bolted for the cat. It roared an awful cry unlike anything I'd ever heard before, but we continued toward it. At the last second, we broke off, me to the left while Tabby flanked to the right. The cave lion backed up, trying to keep both of us in view, but we didn't allow it. At the same time, Sunny charged it head-on with the inevitability of a freight train.

Suddenly, it sprinted. The cave lion ran for the gap between Sunny and me, eyes focused on Eo. The owlgirl didn't notice. The elemental had begun breaking rocks from the wall and throwing them at her as she tried to deal with the goblins.

The cave lion didn't act like an animal. It ignored the threats. It made a deliberate choice to wait for this moment and make a rush like someone trying to find a route in a bullet hell.

Time seemed to freeze. I saw the great possessed beast look between us with murderous intent. If it broke through, Eo would die.

"*No!*" the word exploded from my lungs. I moved. My legs launched me at the lion. I threw the ax, sinking the blade clumsily into the hind leg. The lion yelped as if it still felt pain. It slowed, turned, and swung a single paw at me as if to say, 'silly boy, what are you doing?'

I wasn't worth its consideration. There wasn't supposed to be anything I could do.

Fuck that.

I ducked under the paw and rushed onward. My arms stretched wide as my body slammed into the beast's ribs. I tackled the cave lion, knocking it off its legs and onto its belly. "Help!" I screamed, squeezing its ribs as it shook and slashed and snarled, trying to remove the pesky mortal attached to its chest. It bent and snapped and shook. I felt myself slam against the stone floor. Its claws ripped at my back. Each impact of its paws felt like being pelted with razor-sharp stone.

Still, I didn't let go.

A heavy thud sounded. Sunny's hammer had struck the cave lion just below the eye. The lion was dazed.

"Move!"

I pushed away at Tabby's command. The moment I pushed away, her short sword pierced through its ribs and into its heart, right where I had been.

Apparently, this kind of reanimation still required the use of a heart, because the lion gasped. Its eyes faded to something more normal than glowing purple, then glazed over.

"Okay, now help me!"

We turned to see Eo frantically dodging large rocks from above and undead goblin hands from below. Her frantic jumps, crouches, and bends looked like a horrifying dance.

"Sunny!" I yelled as I grabbed my ax. "Can you deflect the rocks?"

Her eyes lit up. "No problem!"

"Tabby, you and I are on goblin duty."

"Our specialty."

The three of us charged. Sunny ran in front. She leaped as a boulder careened for Eo's head. The battle hammer shattered it to dust with a mighty strike. As a zombie goblin went for Sunny's feet, Tabby cut through its neck. Only two of the goblins remained. My ax chopped through both of them with practiced ease. With that, I felt the familiar adrenaline burst. It rippled through me and made me feel more than human.

With our other enemies dealt with, we faced the elemental. Its cragged, craterous face pointed at us in mimicry of a stare. For a horrible moment, I thought I saw it smirk. The barrage of stones ceased. It appraised the threat of our quartet.

"Any more crazy ideas?" Tabby asked.

"Did you football tackle a lion?" Eo asked in disbelief.

"You think we can beat this thing?" Sunny asked.

"Yes," I nodded. The monster was massive. Bigger than the tunnel it blocked. I ignored the pain searing through me and the blood trickling down my back as I sized it up. "Eo," I said. "For your lightening spell, can you control when that ends if you cast it on something else?"

"Yes," she answered. "Why does—"

"Cast it on me, hit me with the wind, turn me into a missile, and cut the weight spell at the last second, so we get full impact."

"What?" Eo and Tabby gaped.

The elemental grew bored. It would not move from its station, but it didn't need to move to harm us. It swung a great stone fist back and struck the wall. Again, the dome quaked. Cracks shattered all around us as dust, and small bits of rubble began to fall.

Through all the rumbling, Sunny stayed calm. Her smile grew. "Dibs!" she said. "Do it to me, not Jack. I can take the impact. You know it."

The elemental struck the wall again. Greater cracks formed as chunks of rock began to tumble from all around us. Our wood supports crashed. The floor itself began to shatter into uneven terrain as the ceiling threatened to rain down toward us.

"Figure something out!" Tabby yelled. With that, she ran toward the enemy.

Is that thing grinning?

I looked back to Eo and Sunny. "You're our best hope!" I charged toward the rocky giant.

It brought its massive fist down toward Tabby. She dodged it and slashed. The fist's impact broke the ground beneath her, so she staggered. It swiped its hand back and grabbed her. The stone fingers wrapped around her waist, pinning her left arm also in its grip. She slashed at the arm, sending up sparks from the metal grinding stone. Small pebbles cascaded away from her strike, but the golem was undeterred.

To my horror, it started to squeeze. Tabby screamed in pain and terror.

Fear and determination rocketed me straight at the beast. Its free hand raised again. The ground was already unstable, and Eo's wind was a general blast, not a focused strike. The shakier things were, the worse our chances grew.

A horrible, stupid idea appeared in my head.

Time to test if I've been leveling up.

To the shock of my companions, I threw my ax at its face. The throw was awful. It bounced harmlessly off its shoulder, but it had distracted the thing. Its swing had slowed before impact. The ground, weakened, still shook beneath the strike. I jumped at the limb, wrapped my arms around its huge wrist, and pulled.

It stared at me for a moment, confused. I thought of the adrenaline bursts. *Please*, I begged, *let those have made me stronger.* Every muscle strained, the cuts from the lion bleeding harder. The world began to fade around me from my strain, but it was working. I pulled the arm away. It tugged back, but I yanked. Its shoulder jerked toward me. It wouldn't release Tabby, nor would it move either of its feet. It stood there, wide open and confused at the idiot who tried to grapple a giant.

"Monkey Missiiile!" A great whoosh of wind drowned out the deafening crumble of the cavern. Suddenly, a black-furred cannonball launched through the air. A flash of metal hinted at the hammer that struck at a small crack in the golem's chest. Sunny hit the stone body hard, like a furry rocket. Instantly, the rock began to shatter like glass. The stone body staggered back, taking Tabby and me with it.

It struck the cavern wall behind it. The shock of the hit made it drop Tabby. Deep cracks ran all along its torso, but the elemental kept its shape. The unfeeling eyes stared hatefully at the dazed and wounded monkey woman at its feet.

Tabby struck. Her sword drove between two cracks. The giant spasmed. With its attention lost, Eo rushed to my side and put her hands on the stone I still held. There was a low flash from her hands. "It's light!" she said.

Perfect.

I redid my grip and hauled. Eo stood beside me and helped. The elemental jerked with our pull. Tabby caught on, dropping to its foot and straining to lift. Even with magic, it was like moving a car. Its other arm flailed back, smacking the cavern wall to no effect. Its foot came up, the shoulder came down. We threw it to the ground, finally opening our escape.

"Stupid stone bitch!" Sunny spat as she got to her feet.

The elemental collapsed into pebbles. We froze. That wasn't us.

Then, we heard the voice. "Points for ingenuity, but sloppy in execution. Tsk, tsk."

None of us looked to check who said it.

"Run!" I shouted.

All four of us bolted as fast as we could up the tunnel. The shaking intensified. Rocks tumbled. Dust blinded us. We tripped and helped each other back up. Sunny, still dazed, kept an arm over Tabby's shoulder and her tail around my palm as we fled. I kept an arm around Eo. Stones fell all around us. It slammed into our shoulders, jagged edges cutting into our gear.

After an exhausting, agonizing run, we made it to the next cavern. The shaking lessened to a rumble. We didn't stop. Onward and upward we ran. I dared a peek over my shoulder. The tunnel had collapsed. We wouldn't be able to go back through.

CHAPTER
TWENTY-ONE

We practically collapsed once we made it out to the quarry. The trembling had only followed us part of the way, but we'd rushed for all we were worth until we met daylight. All of us fell into violent coughs as we stepped into an overcast day.

Eo, on her hands and knees in the grass, threw up.

"Never," she sputtered, "make me turn my friend into a weapon again."

Sunny, gasping and panting, ripped herself out of her torn, bloodied gear as if it'd been choking her. "Hoooly fuck!" She kicked her helmet as she marched back and forth, overflowing with energy. "That was the coolest and freakiest thing I've ever done!"

"I wouldn't say *cool*," Tabby said, trying to rub the dust out of her tail. "Do we want to talk about what just happened?"

"We should clean up first." Eo retched a second round of her breakfast as if to stress her point. "And tend to you two." She pointed to Sunny and me. "I'm guessing that you haven't felt the pain yet because of the adrenaline, but you two have a lot of wounds that need some immediate treatment. I don't feel comfortable doing anything else until we address that." She purged again, then swallowed and composed herself, looking sternly at the monkey woman. "Sunny, I mean it. I'm so sorry."

Eo apologized several times, head shaking back and forth. Sunny rushed to console her. As she did, I saw what Eo meant. Our warrior looked like...well, she looked like she'd been turned into a missile and shot at a pile of rocks. The thick mining gear took a lot of the damage, but she was still battered. The jeans and tee shirt—this one had a picture of a broken wine glass and the words *What is a Man?*— were covered in tears and small bits of blood.

I looked down at myself. "Holy shit!" My gear was ripped apart. The lion's claws had torn through all layers, exposing flesh and shredding it in places.

How close had I been to dying? Lions and fires and elementals, wow.

Eo shakily moved through her pouches, checking on all of us as she did. The three of us had sustained the worst injuries, but Eo was by far the most disturbed. She checked on each of us over and over. Tabby, the older sister of the group, had to remind her to calm down. We agreed to clean up and meet in the kitchen.

Eventually, the four of us made it back to the house. Sunny and I took several small drinks from potions. The healing potions were a lot more specific than I'd anticipated. One was for disinfecting the wounds, and it tasted awful, but I drank it down to appease Eo.

Thankfully, I didn't need to wait for them to get my turn in the shower. The large house had more than one, and we'd long ago worked out that I should have my own. *Thank goodness for that. I wouldn't be able to handle having to wait for the girls to shower. It takes a long time to wash fur and feathers. Actually, note to self: Suggest that Tabby and I could share a bathroom.*

That could wait, though. As I scrubbed away the dirt, I thought about the battle. Fire, lightning, goblin, stone, lion. Why not hit us with everything at once? The guy could have killed us easily. But he didn't, as if he was playing with us. There was something there, too. A vague familiarity bothered me as I considered it. As I shut off the shower, I realized what it was.

Whoever it was sent them out one at a time like it was a game.

"Dammit." I got out of the shower, applied the salve that Eo had given me, put on a clean pair of cargos with a *Zelda* tee, and went to the kitchen. The sight that awaited me was one of the strangest of the day. Eo stood there amidst a sea of charts. She had a phone in her right hand. Her left hand drew through the air, literally. A glowing gold line like the trail of a sparkler followed her finger, except it stayed instead of fading away.

It took a second, but I recognized the shape. "Is this Antrum Mine?"

"No talk," she said. "Thinking."

I did as she said, shut up and watched. Tabby soon followed behind. After a few more minutes, so did Sunny. We stood back and watched the spectacle. It was simplified, with straight lines going down like those in an ant farm, but I'd recognize the mine anywhere. There were several circular nodes throughout the diagram. I guessed that these were caverns.

The last detail she added was at the bottom. She drew an extra large circle. From it, the only straight line in the entire diagram slanted downward. There was no question, this was the mystery corridor that we'd refused to explore.

"Okay," Eo said. "I realize we should report on the battle but something was bugging me so I wanted to check, and you know how obsessive I can be when something is on my mind. I made the executive decision to prepare it as simply as I could, so here it is. Hear me out."

"How did you say that in one breath," I asked.

"Alright," Sunny said. "Show us."

"Okay. I'll give you the short version. First, I apologize for the crudity of this model. I didn't have time to make it to scale. It's also frustrating to try to bend a three-dimensional space to two, because there are so many—"

"Short version," Tabby said.

"Right. Look here." Eo pointed to the lowest node on the diagram. "This is the cavern that we entered the day of the shutdown. Now, look here," she drew a straight dotted line from that point across the diagram. It ran through the upper part of the slanted corridor. "If we had gone any deeper, we would have reached the same depth. Tabby, do you remember how I half-comedically bet that we'd activated a vampire curse? Well, I think I was wrong about the curse aspect, but I think we did get too close to someone or something. It's just a hunch, but I believe that we would have activated some kind of alarm like the one that created the barrier if we'd gone deeper. Perhaps, again there's no certainty, our mysterious necromancer became impatient with us being at his doorstep and decided to take matters into his own hands. Please tell me if I'm being paranoid or if this was an improper time to address all this because I'm very stressed and mainly worked this out because thinking of your wounds bothered me too much."

I stared at her, amazed that she could say so much without taking a breath.

"I'm glad you made this," Tabby said. She stepped forward and began moving her fingers along the lines.

"It's beautiful," Sunny said.

"You're amazing, Eo."

"I need tea." She moved to the cupboard and started rifling around.

"Coffee for me," I requested.

"For all of us," Tabby sighed. "Okay...now we need to figure out what the hell is going on?"

From there, we launched into a round table. I shared what I remembered of the man with the staff several times. We returned to Eo's diagram over and over, occasionally consulting some of her other charts for specific details. For much of the conversation, I simply listened. Many of the rules of this fantasy world came up that I never would have thought to ask.

First, necromancy was illegal and had been for centuries. The penalty was damnation in one of multiple hells. The theory cropped up that there was some criminal living way under the hill, someone who had either never expected us to dig so low or had been there since before Antrum and Acanth.

What seemed more certain was that there were at least two magic users down there. It also explained the strange order of events when we'd been down there. Even the most powerful mage in the world could only cast one spell at a time. The one who'd cast the lightning was likely not the one to resurrect the goblins, and the one who'd brought the cat was likely not the one to summon the elemental.

Here, an uncomfortable subject came up. Sunny nervously asked, "What if the demon is real?"

"No," Tabby shook her head. It was clear that the day was weighing heavily on both of them. "The demon is just the manifestation of everyone's PTSD nightmares from that day. We shouldn't think about it."

"Riiight. It was my idea, so it must be stupid." Sunny rolled her eyes.

"That's not what I meant." Tabby frowned.

"No, it's fine. Why should we consider the most dangerous possibility?"

"*Sunny*." Tabby's voice was thin and harsh.

We can't do this right now.

"Eo," I said, "give me probability. Given the spells cast today, what are the odds of it being a demon versus multiple spellcasters?"

She jumped onto the question. I had no idea if she knew I was trying to dodge an argument, but it worked. Eo said, "I'm going to withhold proper numbers. When taking everything we've discussed into account, when considering only the minimum forces required to handle the battle we endured...Okay, so one had a staff which could be a spell-casting focus, typically used as a boon for those who aren't the best with magic...which would also explain why the goblins were resurrected, but the lion was merely possessed. I'd guess it's either a necromancer and a skilled apprentice or a necromancer and a demon that it summoned."

"Seeee," Sunny said, "it's a possibility."

I stood and moved to our diagram. "Okay, now the big question. How does everyone want to respond to this problem?"

The girls looked at each other, then back to me. "What do you mean?" Tabby asked.

I pointed to the corridor. "There's a necro-freak sending monsters after us, and whom we can safely bet is the reason the mine closed. I know it's dangerous, but I say we bring the fight to it."

Tabby nodded, "I agree. I don't like the idea of writing up battle plans, but Antrum is our home. I can't lose it a second time."

Eo stood. She looked pale, but she nodded. "I agree. It's not just about us. With necromancy involved, it becomes a larger matter. Acanth isn't safe with that nearby."

Sunny tapped her fingers on the kitchen table for several seconds. All of us waited for her response. Nobody rushed her. Tabby looked slightly annoyed, but she bit her tongue. After a while, Sunny stood. "No monsters in Acanth, I agree."

"Okay," I said. "Now, let's—"

"Nooot so fast," Sunny folded her arms and looked at me. The hesitance had gone. "You tackled a giant lion and still had the strength and energy to partially grapple an elemental. That's not something a normal mortal can do. I wanna talk about that."

"Huh..." Eo said, her voice dropping. "You make a good point."

Tabby said nothing. Suspicion flickered across her eyes. It hurt. I'd never mentioned the level-ups because there was no way to explain them. I didn't understand them either. I didn't know how to talk about them, or even if they were real.

"I genuinely have no idea how I did what I did today," I said honestly. "I want to explain it to you, but right now, I don't have the words or the understanding to explain it. Before we get into all that, I think we should go to the village. We should talk to Gretchen about some armor and weapons. Also, we should let people know. At the least, we should go to the civic center and check if there's any record of an escaped necromancer or whatever that might be our stranger."

The three of them looked at each other. "Huddle," Tabby said.

Fair.

The trio turned away from me and spoke in hushed whispers for a while. It seemed straightforward for most of the conversation. They pointed back and forth to each other several times. It never seemed heated. Eventually, they gave a mutual fist bump and turned back to me.

"Okay," Tabby said. "We agree. I'll go to Gretchen's to order the armor and weapons. Eo will stay back to figure out our best plan of attack. Sunny will go into town with you."

"Sounds good," I said.

Eo snapped her fingers. The diagram popped out of existence like a blown-out candle.

We had a plan. Only one thing bothered me: whoever was down there would be expecting us.

CHAPTER
TWENTY-TWO

Tabby, Sunny, and I walked to the village together. Tabby broke off quickly to visit Gretchen. As soon as she was out of earshot, and as I walked toward the civic center, Sunny grabbed my wrist and changed our direction to *The Monkey's Paw*.

"Hey," I said, "where are you going? I thought we needed to go to the civic center."

"We wiiiill, but we're doing this first. Fran will spread the word faster than Karma. Trust me."

Her eyes were dead set. Considering what she had been through, I could only imagine what was going through her mind. Seeing so many people leave Acanth, hearing of her sister's death, the danger we'd faced. Not even a month had passed since we reopened Antrum. The fantastic life which we'd set up had not fully set in. The only thing that had been with Sunny through every good, bad, and uncertain memory had been this pub. Part of me wanted to haul her toward the civic center or to turn away and go myself, but I couldn't blame her for wanting to warn Fran before everyone else.

Besides, a part of me worried that there was a more cynical reason to do so. If the bartender at the town's only pub wants information to spread, it will. If a civil servant wants it to spread, it might pass through days of paperwork before it gets out.

No, that's my old life. That's not Acanth.

Whatever the case, we entered *The Paw*. Rather, Sunny erupted through the doors like a hurricane. "Fraaan, we need to talk."

The golden-haired bartender did a double take at us. "Well, that was a short shift. You're already done with work for the day?"

"Not even close to done," Sunny replied. "We need to talk."

Sunny and I relayed the short version of what had happened. Fran's attitude changed quickly from polite interest to shock. When we finished a basic description of our list of foes, Fran said, "How in the hell did you defeat an elemental?"

"Later," Sunny said. "It was badass. I'll explain another time. Jack's idea. Anywaaay." Her eyes flicked to me. I recognized that look. It was the same one she gave when I caught a whiff of whisky in her flask at the mine. It was guilty and conspiratorial. Worst, it held the expectation that I would understand and say nothing to Tabby.

"Do you know of any rumors of escaped necromancers in Acanth? Ooor...maybe...demons?"

Ah. So, that's what this is about.

Fran looked between the two of us. Her eyes leveled at me, and silently asked if I was worried about the demon as well.

I shrugged and said, "I'm just here to make sure people learn what's going on. If you have any useful info, please let us know."

"Sorry," Fran said. "I don't. I'll try to spread the word, though. Have you talked to Karma yet?"

"We're doing that now." I stood and began to leave.

"Waaait," Sunny said. "Come on, Fran. There has to be something. Look, Karma has all the records, but you know the stories. Everyone talks to you. I need to hear this from you. Is there anything to the demon talk?"

Fran sighed and reached across the bar to Sunny's shoulder. "People have claimed to have seen everything out of that mine. They said *dragon* just as much as *demon*." Fran glanced at me. The weight of her eyes caught me off guard. "Both of you, listen to me now. If the intruder in the mine can cast necromancy, it can probably cast psychic spells. You can *not* have any doubts or fears about what's in there. All four of you need to be on the same page, okay?"

After several seconds, Sunny sighed. "Fiiine. Hey Fran, can I get be—"

"Coffee," I said as I stood. "We have a long day yet, right Sunny?"

She drummed her fingers on the table again, but finally relented. "Forget the drink."

"Be careful, both of you. Please give my regards to Tabby and Eo, as well. You have the village's support."

"Thank you," I said as I left.

As we walked out of the bar, Sunny followed me, arms crossed.

We'd learned nothing. Sunny's nerves were a little appeased, but it didn't help our strategizing. My gut told me that the civic center would be no better. We were reporting on it, that was all. We'd check the records, of course. Maybe there was a report of an escaped criminal. Maybe some old stories about the hill before the mine had opened. What good would that do?

Dammit! Just when I thought I understood Antrum, this happens!

The next several minutes were a blur. We told Karma what had happened. She made notes. All the while, something bothered me. My eyes wandered from the large, sunlit office to a wooden pillar. In it, I saw the name of the department that had been stamped on the envelope which had brought me here in the first place.

Grandpa.

I hadn't thought about him much since things had started to move smoothly at the mine. I'd looked at his orders for equipment, his business affairs. I even saw a copy of the certificate he had used to permit me to visit that one time when I'd been a child.

After Sunny and I finished our report, I said, "Is there anything from or about my grandpa that I haven't seen? Anything at all?"

Perhaps my tone gave away the worries and concerns swirling through my head.

Karma nodded. "There is one thing, Mr. Calvinson."

Sunny and I threw all of our attention at her. She hit a few keys on her computer. "Your grandfather experienced some legal trouble once several years ago. I'd elected to say nothing given that it did not fit your business venture."

Legal trouble?

I looked at Sunny. She shook her head, as confused as I was.

"What did he do?" I asked.

In response, Karma turned her monitor toward me. It showed several digital receipts side by side. "He purchased the ingredients for an illegal potion. He used the tourists which our town once received as a guise to receive them."

"What kind of potion?" I asked.

"It's rather difficult to describe. Well, you know that muscles atrophy when not used. One loses their skill with anything over time, and they can only become so strong. The potion eliminates that for humans. If you went to the gym, for example, and you exercised enough, you would eventually be able to lift heavier weights. Imagine if that new level was now your base. No matter what you did, you would never be weaker than this new base of strength. Every improvement you made would become your new base level."

"The fuuuck?" Sunny tilted her head. "If someone takes this potion they level up like a video game? That's—Why doesn't everyone take this?"

Karma shook her head. "It doesn't work on anyone capable of using magic, or anyone who grows up with magic in the environment. It's illegal because it could be sold to mortals. Your grandfather avoided arrest because it was deemed that he'd already been in Acanth too long for it to have an effect. It's as impractical as it is difficult to acquire. It was later discovered that it would need to be introduced to one's system prior to puberty, that way it would become part of the musculature as the body grew. Mr. Calvinson?"

Grandpa...

I damn near fell out of my chair. My muscles, which apparently would never weaken, felt like Jello. My mouth went dry, and my head emptied. I rushed back to my memory, Sunny somewhere shaking my shoulder.

On the day I visited my grandpa, we only had one exchange. He gave me a drink, telling me it was a special kind of juice.

You turned me into a damn RPG character. You bastard...you wonderful bastard, you set me up from the start to take over, didn't you?

Did he want me to take over the mine? Was it his awkward attempt at a gift? Was it guilt from not seeing his mortal family?

I had no idea.

"Jaaack!" Sunny said. "Talk to me."

I coughed, suddenly remembering that Karma had said that the potion was illegal. "Sorry, this is a lot to take in, and I found out that there are zombies on my property." I looked at Karma. "I hope you understand that this is a weird day for me."

"Of course," she said. "Anything else?"

"No, thanks. Sunny, let's go."

"What?"

I all but ran out of the civic center. As soon as we were outside, Sunny grabbed my wrist and turned me to her. Before she could say anything, I burst out laughing.

I'm a fucking RPG character! All those days at the gym meant something. The days at the smith. The battles. Yes!

I grabbed Sunny's shoulders and said, "My grandpa gave me that potion when I was a kid."

Her eyes widened. "Nooo..."

"Yes!"

Immediately, she pushed me toward the town center. "We need to tell the others. Now!"

CHAPTER
TWENTY-THREE

Eo and Tabby stared, jaws on the floor. "No way," Eo said, covering her mouth and giggling to herself. "That's so cool!"

"Wait," Tabby said. "That would help explain the battle with the elemental, yes, but this is...huge! Have you felt anything like this?"

I explained the adrenaline surges. During battle. During workouts. I told them when I'd felt them, feeling giddy all the while.

I...I can't believe it...

"How many times have you felt it?" Eo asked. "Do you know what level you're at?"

"No," I answered. "I mean, I never thought to keep track. I don't have a health bar or XP points or anything. It just happens sometimes. I think it's like with muscle growth. The fibers tear and grow back stronger. Maybe it's something like that. I don't know."

"But you also got it doing smith work," Tabby said. "This is..."

"Do you level up at sex?" Sunny asked with a straight face.

Tabby and I froze.

Eo shrugged. "It's not an unfair question, if you think about it."

Tabby's tail curled in a very unsubtle way as she blushed. "Well? Do you?"

"Uh, I don't think so. I've never felt it during. Not during yoga either."

"Hmm." Eo nodded. "Tabby, you said that you saw him when he came here as a child. Did you get any of this potion?"

"No," Tabby said. "If I understand right, it wouldn't have worked on me, anyway."

"Right, anyway." I pointed to the stack of charts that had overtaken the floor of Eo's loft.

We came back to discuss everything for our strike into the mine. I didn't think I'd ever make plans to invade a dungeon in the presence of a cheering Yoko from *Gurenn Lagann*, but it was far from a bad experience. The Solid Snake in mid-salute gave a little morale boost as well. "What did you find, Eo?"

"Yes!" She clapped. "Considering that details are necessary, I'll give a proper explanation this time."

She spoke for close to forty minutes. During that time, she exhaustively cited every chart, date, and person she referenced. Thankfully, it came down to a simple conclusion. We'd move to a cavern above the hollow spot where the flames had shot up, and from there, we'd dig down. I'd found a gap, so we might be able to clear into that opening.

"Sooo," Sunny asked at that point. "We hack away at the ground and hope we find it. Won't that give them a lot of warning and leave us completely exhausted by the time we get there?"

"We have dynamite," Eo said with a horrifying grin. "As well as a few Scrolls of Major Destruction that I've been saving in case we ever had the need for it."

Both of their tails stood on end. "Where did you get that?" Tabby asked.

"How could you not tell us?" Sunny asked.

Eo gave a single 'ha' of triumph. "It is not difficult for me to get what I want. All it takes is an internet connection and some patience. Some of the old Antrum crew and my figurine clients have helped me set up quite the network. I could probably gather the materials necessary to build a nu—"

"Back to the topic at hand," Tabby said. "Gretchen said that she could have high-grade armor prepared for all four of us in two days."

"Do we want to wait?" Sunny asked. "Shouldn't we attack sooner?"

Tabby looked at me. "We have an ace that they could never expect. I say we take our time and try to make Jack level up as many times as possible."

Slowly, all three of them turned their eyes to me. Tabby's eyes brimmed with respect and certainty. Sunny's boiled over with mischievous intrigue. Eo clapped her hands together excitedly as if she had a new toy.

At that moment, only part of me felt nervous. More than that, I felt at home. Antrum needed me. I was our best bet of saving this place. They were relying on me.

This feels better than the surges.

"Okay," I nodded. "I'm in. What's next?"

What followed, it turned out, was a grueling afternoon and evening of nonstop exercise. We decided to attack early in the morning on Sunday, our usual day off. It may not have been much, but perhaps the surprise would give us a slight advantage. That gave us four days.

After our meeting, Tabby did mock duels with me with padded weapons. We practiced until I was too tired to move, but we didn't stop. Eo rubbed a salve onto my aching muscles to bring back my stamina. She said that these were rare and expensive, but given the circumstances, they were worth it.

I'm basically Goku training to the edge of death and taking a senzu bean. If only we had a hyperbolic time chamber...

Tabby became too exhausted to continue, so Sunny gave me heavy objects and forced me through a DIY boot camp. The girls had me do everything. I did push-ups until my arms collapsed. I ran up and down the stairs while weighed down by my full mining equipment. I ran along the road to Acanth and back until my legs couldn't move.

And it worked.

It was hard-fought, and it only happened a few times that day, but I felt the surge nonetheless. It roared through my chest and boosted me along with a second wind. Every time, I forgot my pains and aches and pushed harder. The result was that by the time I got to bed, I crashed as soon as I laid down my head.

Like the idiot I was, I even agreed to do yoga like usual the following sunrise.

That morning was one of the roughest I've ever had. I woke up before my alarm because of the muscle fatigue. Slowly, my cramped body worked its way out of bed.

I'm going to need a day of recovery before our battle.

Yoga seemed like a good idea. It should help with the tension if nothing else. For once, I was the first one outside.

Tabby was shocked to see me. "Are you okay?"

"My morale is good, but my muscles feel like shit."

"Did we overdo it yesterday?"

Even if we did, I need to build them as much as possible.

"It was a lot, yeah. I want the day before our invasion to rest, but I think you all have the right idea. I'm the only variable to the freak in the mines. We should make that work as much as we can. For today, I should be fine after the yoga, though. I need to loosen up. Let's do something gentle, alright?"

"Of course."

We began a simple routine. Some cat-cow poses. Deep breathes. Some grounding techniques. Gradually, my body loosened up.

"Are you feeling better?" Tabby asked as the sky pinkened.

"Yeah," I answered.

"Good." On hands and knees, she moved from her mat to mine. Her hands slid one in front of the other in a gesture far too graceful. She hit me with those big eyes once again. "Your form is awful," she said with a throaty voice that meant only one thing.

"Is that a fact?" I asked.

"Yeah. You're way off your game. You need some hands-on guidance."

Soon after, she was naked on her bed, hooking the bends of her knees around my arms, widening herself so that my erection could push deeper.

"Just like that! Ah!" Tabby gripped the sheets and moaned as I slammed into her again and again. My greedy yoga partner demanded a lot from me. In fact, she wanted all of me. I pulled my cock almost all the way out. Her pussy tightened around me as if trying to hold me in place. She stared at me, demanding I give it all back.

I did, slowly at first. I slid deep into her warm wet cave.

She shook and huffed. "Yes..." Suddenly, I slammed in the last inch. "Oh!" All the way back and forth I went, each thrust making a sloppy wet slap as she shook and soaked my erection.

"Already?" I teased.

"Keep...going..."

Her flesh rippled under me. Her breasts bounced up and down. After a moment, she stopped holding the bed. Instead, she grabbed her breasts, squeezing them together, rubbing her nipples, and panting. "Oh!"

I'd endure just about anything to keep this at the start of the morning.

The shape was too perfect. I slid so deep that I almost believed she could wrap herself around all of me. It felt like she did.

"I want you to fin—"

She didn't have a chance to continue. I fell onto her, grabbed her hips, rolled over so I was beneath her, and pounded upward.

"Fuck!" She wrapped her fingers in my hair and pulled. My hands gripped that beautifully toned ass, lifting her and slamming her against me in time with my hips. I had total control, and she loved the way I used it. My pace quickened until there was nothing in the universe except that wet, glorious feeling.

"Right there, yes, please!" Her hot body pressed against all of me, rubbing her smooth skin against mine, rippling with each thrust and begging for more of me. Her back arched as her head lifted, swinging her breasts back into view. I moved my face into their gelatinous embrace. Her arms wrapped around my head and held me there, squeezing her breasts into my face. Her hot breath ran through my hair.

Nothing existed except us. It drove me wild. Pressure built from the base and grew to the point of almost being painful.

"That's right," she said. "Give it to me!"

I went harder. I didn't know if my body could keep up the pace. I was so close. I needed her. The pleasure bordered on agony.

Tabby said, "I want you."

I came hard. Pure ecstasy burst from me. Tabby gasped, clutching my face so tightly into her breasts that I couldn't breathe. She gripped me, gasping and shuddering with each spurt as I poured into her.

"Ah..." She released me. We collapsed, me onto the bed and her onto my chest. Again, she was a twitching mess. "Yes..." Her hips continued to grind on me, her sweet pussy gripping my erection, greedy and hungry for every drop.

"Do...do you need...to do training today?" She looked at me with naked desire, grabbing my hand as soon as it moved from her hips. She smacked my hands under her ass as she continued to slide up and down.

As if in answer, there was a knock at the door. "Hurry it up," Eo said. "Training today."

"Ugh," Tabby sighed. "Stupid schedules." Suddenly, she looked at me again. "I guess we need to prepare to fight a necromancer."

CHAPTER
TWENTY-FOUR

Sunday arrived before we knew it. We put on our new gear, worn only enough to get used to how it fit.

I swung the ax a few times. It was amazing how comfortable it felt in my hand. Every movie and fantasy novel had made me expect that it would feel like an extension of my own body, but it wasn't like that. Still, it did feel comfortable to be loose with it. I trusted myself to spin it, swing it, toss it. No matter what, I knew where it was and how fine the blade had become.

Was that because of Gretchen's skill, or my leveling up?

Probably a bit of both.

Gretchen had done well for us. Every blade was new. Every bit of protection had been upgraded. Flexibility was a priority. A thin mail shirt went over our torsos but not our arms. We wore the same old style of coveralls above it all to hide some of our readiness—as if that would matter. Maybe the necromancer bastard would expect us. Maybe he believed that we had run off.

Whatever the case, we would fight. Eo walked us through the specific plan for our dig. We had two backpacks worth of dynamite. Hopefully, that was all we'd need. Eo had three Scrolls of Major Destruction, but didn't want to use them.

"What do the scrolls do?" I asked.

"Eeeasy," Sunny answered. "Wrecking ball. Right there in the name."

"While that is somewhat of an oversimplification," Eo sighed, "the essential effect is the same. You open the scroll wide, get within ten feet of the thing you want to destroy, and say the word 'destruction.' The result is like if you focused the explosive power of a rocket ship launch onto a five square foot area."

Tabby shook her head. "That would cause a cave-in."

Eo shrugged, as if acknowledging a point she hadn't wanted to consider. "Like I said, I'd rather we didn't need to use them. For all I know, they're bootlegs."

The three of us stared at her.

"How," I asked, "can you bootleg a magical item like that?"

"It's pretty simple, actually. The true thing should work if you open it and focus on the target within range. The bootleg ones only work if you touch the focus. You need to have the back of the opened scroll against your target when you say the spell."

Tabby groaned. "Wouldn't force that close hurt the user?"

Eo nodded. "Exactly. A useless bootleg."

"Aaanyway," Sunny twirled a hammer. "We gonna hunt a necromancer or what?"

"Let's do it," I said.

We knew the route. An hour after dawn, we marched. From the quarry down through tunnels to our desired cavern. Like an impatient Dante, we walked deeper.

Aside from planning, few words were spoken that morning.

No monsters appeared to stop us. A passing whim told me to check out the dome-shaped cavern from which we'd been chased. That, however, was not going to happen. It was impossible to get to, though we'd get close. We'd be in a cavern above. Eo said that if we were lucky and she'd done her calculations right, we'd be either in the hollow space that I'd found, or the top of our mysterious corridor.

As we went along, I wondered what kind of person our necromancer would be. The thought didn't hold my attention long. In the end, I guessed that it wouldn't matter. We had to get rid of them, for the sake of the mine and the people of Acanth.

Finally, we reached the cavern. It was cragged and uneven. Stalactites stuck out in random places. The floor was a mess of bumps. In other words, it was a natural cavern. It also had no further tunnels branching from it. The four of us nodded and set to work. After examining the ground, guessing which would be the best spot for our explosion, and cross-referencing that with Eo's mental charts, we chose a location.

As we set it up, Sunny said the first words from any of us in the last twenty minutes: "Fran had beeetter give us all free drinks after we kill this thing."

Tabby turned back, a look of surprise on her face. Surprise, but not necessarily disapproval.

"I could go for nachos," Eo said. "It's been a long time since I had the nachos there."

"It's not on the menu anymore," Tabby said. "That does sound good, though. Some nachos, maybe a glass or two of wine."

"It's settled," I said. "We celebrate our victory with nachos and drinks. Fran's buying."

Soon, we were ready. We ran back to the tunnel from which we'd entered for cover. Eo held a detonator that looked like...a Super Nintendo controller.

It actually was.

Of course Eo has a customized detonator.

She began hitting buttons. True to herself, she put in the Konami code. When she hit start, the Select button began to glow green. Her black eyes turned to us. We prepared our weapons.

She hit the button. Immediately, a shockwave cracked the air. The tunnel made a single, violent heave as if thrown by a child. "It will stabilize," Eo said as the stone shook around us. The explosion had been a blink. The shockwave lingered for close to half a minute.

As soon as the shaking ceased, we ran back into the cavern. There, we saw something impossible and lucky. A huge hole, about ten feet in diameter, had been punched through the floor, surrounded by a halo of sooty debris. Instead of a crater, we saw an opening. It dropped several feet into inky darkness. Eo cast a spell, so a bulb of white light bloomed in her palm. She let it float into the darkness like a dandelion on the wind.

"Okaaay," Sunny shook her head.

Our dynamite had punched through about three feet of rock. Below was a rectangular space. The walls were impossibly smooth and flat. A caved-in tunnel stood to one side, blocked by rubble. On the other side, there was a long corridor slanting down.

It's the tunnel.

"Okay." Eo nodded.

Sunny shook her head. "I hate this. I hate this. I haaate this."

"Hey," Tabby said. "Let's focus on the plan. Kill a necromancer. Stop the zombies. Get wasted at *The Paw*."

"I do like *that* plan."

"That's the spirit." I nodded and took the rope from my pack.

As I began tying it around a stalagmite, the others prepared a long cord with electrical lanterns at every ten feet. It was bulky, frustrating, and necessary.

Soon, we lowered ourselves into the top of the corridor and began moving down. Eo's magic light led the way, while its caster moved behind me. Tabby held the back while Sunny carried our light cable.

Down and down we went, careful with each step. Before long, there was no visual mark of our movement. We heard our steps, yes, but there was no sign of progress. Below was the light reaching feebly into a void. Above was the cable. It didn't take long before we could barely make out the top.

Someone needs to say something. This tension is killing me.

"Huh," Eo said as if hearing my silent plea. "This kind of reminds me of the really long hall in *Silent Hill 2*."

"Bad comparison," I said.

"Yeah," Sunny said. "Why not go with the endless staircase in *Mario*."

"Conceptually." Eo rotated her head all the way back as she walked. "I'm not sure that's any less grim."

"Eyes forward," Tabby said.

We kept on walking. Soon, the cable reached its full length. Frustrated, we continued without it. Only a few steps later, we saw a dull orange light at the bottom. Eo dimmed her magical sphere. Sure enough, the corridor ended ahead. It opened on the right, where red firelight crackled to illuminate the end of our descent.

I looked up, to where the comfort of our electric light had reached its limit. "That doesn't feel like a coincidence," I said.

Nobody replied. With a mix of determination and resignation, we marched on.

At long last, we made it to the bottom. To the right, the stone opened into yet another cavern. This one was also shaped like a dome. The ceiling was impossibly smooth, as were the walls and floor. There was a hole in the center of the roof, to which the smoke of a five-foot pyre rose.

The flames roared in the center of the room. Something sat in front of it. The figure was humanoid. The bright fire behind it sent shadows running across its features. We saw only the red irises. Short, thick horns swept sideways from the top of its head, breaking through wispy white hair. It leaned on a golden staff with a diamond at its head. The figure smirked, the firelight glinting off porcelain teeth.

That was the one I'd seen in the previous battle. I was certain. It stood and walked forward. As it moved, the fire illuminated it so we could get a better look. As it did, our tension broke into confusion.

It was a bison woman. The curled horns which poked from her temples were those of a buffalo. Gray, ashy fur covered all her skin, save for patches of scars and scabs. The hair was uneven. Tufts of it poked out at different lengths. The snow-white hair on her head was a mess of tangles. She looked at us with a strange sneer. Her lips twitched outward instead of up, as if they couldn't handle that effort anymore. A black robe, slightly too big, was draped over her.

"Now," the figure said with a nasal rasp, "this is just disappointing. Ye hast kept us waiting."

"Who the fuck are you?" Sunny asked.

Something else stuck out to me.

"Us?" Tabby said it before I could.

"Oh, mine dear fools. Ye knowst nothing. Tell me, doth Acanth still stand?"

I looked at the other three.

Tabby shook her head and stepped forward. "We're not interested in your story."

Her ears twitched back. I heard it, too, a low shimmering. We looked at a wall of light and fog like *Dark Souls* covering our exit. There was no escape.

"Cute," Sunny said, unbothered.

"Heh," the necromancer's laugh was a rasp. I knew that our enemy would be old, but I hadn't expected her to be... ancient. "My story," she repeated. "Yes, I doth suppose there is none left. I ended my life when I made my pact with Radec."

I gripped my ax and looked around the cavern. There was nobody else.

"Who's Radec?" Eo asked.

The necromancer clicked her tongue. "The true dweller of these tunnels. The Lord of our Dark. Our host. The one who brought me to his home and taught me the true art of Magick."

The reality of what she was about to say hit me before she said it. All three of my companions tensed.

Please don't say it.

"The demon of Antrum."

Shit...

The other three stiffened. Sunny looked at the back of Tabby's head. "You saaaid that it didn't—"

"I didn't think it did!"

"Ha!" The necromancer raised a staff. "Fear not my master." Her pained smile fell. A hideous scowl leveled at us instead. "It seems that centuries do naught to change attitudes. Even as I helped lay the very foundation stones of this village, none recalled the name of Bianca. Now, I need them not."

She raised her staff.

"Game time!" I yelled.

"Ye know not your place, mortal. Thank ye for your entertainment. I grant thanks to Radec that I may slay you myself for the sin of—"

She kept talking. I looked at the other three. All of them varied between horrified, confused, and angry. There was a lot to unpack and no time to do so. I clung to the fact that Bianca had said that she would kill us herself. Also, her villain monologue gave us the time to process the info.

God bless these arrogant assholes. The old hag probably hasn't had non-fiendish company in centuries. I can almost pity her.

"We good to fight?"

They all nodded.

"Okay," I said.

As we held this quick meeting, Bianca shouted at us. She yelled about the true nature of power and the true inhabitants of the stone. Probably some other stuff.

I lifted my ax. "Shut up!"

Her eyes narrowed on me. "Mortal..." she spat the word.

"You broke the barrier. Our recent displeasure is because of you!" Her staff ignited with light. I dove to the side as a bolt of lightning shot out. I wasn't fast enough. The bolt struck my side. Every muscle tensed so hard they felt like they'd snap. I collapsed as the other three flew into action.

Eo's kunai flew. Bianca ducked under one. A second sank deep into her shoulder, but she didn't react. Instead, she gripped the staff with both hands and screamed, "To me!"

In the rock ceiling, several openings burst to life. The stench of rancid meat hit before the dust. Zombie goblins fell from above, snarling into reanimated existence and forcing us to look all over the cavern. One fell directly toward me. For a stupid moment, I wondered if I'd killed this one before.

A flash of steel returned it to death. Tabby cut through it and knelt to my side in one fluid motion. She plucked a vial from her belt and poured it into my mouth. "Guess we're even," she said.

Another bolt flashed. We turned to see Sunny leap above a shower of sparks. She'd jumped to the wall and began to dash along the curved ceiling.

"Die!" Bianca hissed.

Sunny pushed off the wall, turned in the air, and bounced off the ground. She rushed back and forth, ducking and rolling to avoid bolts. There was a moment, barely as long as a blink, when the staff glowed before the bolt flew. Sunny scrambled around that. She sprinted full tilt, her fur standing on end from the static as she dodged.

Meanwhile, Eo struggled to clear a path through the goblins. Tabby and I moved quickly to help her. Sunny couldn't get close, but she forced the necromancer to keep all her focus on one place. I hacked through the undead on a path toward her.

Bianca noticed. She tried to turn to us, but Sunny would dash in, not letting Bianca take her eyes from her. It looked like the battle would not cost us much.

Bianca became annoyed, then enraged.

"Damn you all!" She hefted the staff again. This time, dust exploded up in front of her. A cave troll's fist punched through the ground like the shot in every zombie movie.

"No you don't!" I screamed.

I rushed to the beast and leaped. Its head erupted from the stone as my ax came down. The downward strike met the rising skull. My ax cut straight into its brain. The purple glow drained from its eyes while it broke through the rocks like a whale breaching water. I had to jump back to avoid the momentum of its massive body. A quick look told me that Tabby and Eo didn't need help with the goblins. I pried my ax from the twice-dead skull and turned to our enemy.

Maybe we didn't need to worry.

Bianca backed toward the fire. She was too pitiable for me to hate. Her skin had become sallow as a corpse. The blood which trickled from the wound in her shoulder was thick and black. She hardly counted as alive.

That demon bastard is sacrificing her for his own entertainment. That monster is probably laughing his ass off at this.

Sunny charged with a roar. I was silent.

Bianca screamed. A howl of terror and disbelief cracked her voice, "Save me!"

Suddenly, the pyre shifted behind her. The flames twisted and curled toward her glowing staff. They whipped toward her via a silent wind. The fire wrapped around her in a deadly, blazing blanket. It crackled and hissed as it formed an orb around her.

Sunny and I halted.

We glanced at each other, then at our companions who'd just dealt with the last of the goblins. The flames had left their place. A charred spot of soot and ash remained where the fire had been set, but the fire now blazed independent of kindling. It whirred around Bianca, a deadly giant marble of heat. Hot air spread out from the thing.

I began to sweat.

The heat intensified. The flames turned brighter. The fire blossomed from crackling flames to a whooshing inferno. Burning wind whipped around us, blowing smoke and stinging our eyes. Sunny yipped as embers began to flick in all directions. One singed her monkey ear.

"Um," I asked, "what does this mean?" The whooshing storm of suffocating wind stole my voice.

"What?" Sunny yelled back, but I had to read her lips. There was nothing. The constant devouring wind swallowed all sound.

Eo ran forward and threw out her hands. *The wind spell!* Cool wind erupted from her. It pushed against the flames, which bent at her pressure, but it bounced back into shape. The spell had done nothing.

Suddenly, the orb of flame broke open like an egg. Bianca, half-burnt and with her clothes aflame, stood there. Embers skipped across her clothes and hair. The fire pulled back and took on a new shape.

It began as a tail to her clothes. It rose into a pillar, but it split at the top. Two long curling arms stretched out, their ends parting into fingers of flame. In the center, two specks of white-hot flame signaled eyes while a wicked grin appeared from the same.

She has a Stand. That is a fucking JoJo's Stand!

Sunny, Tabby, and Eo stepped back.

Bianca looked at us. Her irises and pupils had vanished. There were only blank, veiny eyes. "Kill!" she ordered blindly.

Her fiery servant laughed. A high, ethereal wind shrieked through the air. Its flames spouted up to the cavern's top and began to spread. It bathed us in red light. I turned to my friends. They were stuck, horrified as the flames threatened to melt us on the spot.

CHAPTER
TWENTY-FIVE

I charged.

There was no time to think. The longer we waited, the worse the heat became. Already it scorched my skin. I felt like I was burning. Sweat poured. Worse, the air became hard to breathe. Each breath felt dry and uncomfortable in my nostrils. Asphyxiation was a greater threat than the creature itself. The worst thing we could do was wait until this thing burned our lungs. Besides, it was fire. Not a solid. Maybe I could run through it and cut her down.

Not likely.

The Fire Stand struck toward me like a snake, still connected to Bianca. Its needle-like fingers melted together into a single pointed flame. As I charged, the attack changed. The hand thinned and heated into a white-tipped drill.

Nope!

"Move!" Sunny rushed to me and bodychecked me to the side.

We narrowly dodged the strike. The white-hot attack broke through stone, breaking it into dust and scattering smoldering pebbles.

Sunny and I ran to Eo and Tabby, who stared in silent horror.

"You. Can. Not. Win." Bianca's mouth moved, but the words came as a hiss on the burning air.

Eo, shaking with frustration, threw another kunai. Bianca did nothing to dodge. The blade struck directly into her chest. There was no reaction. Tabby tore one of the carefully secured Scrolls of Major Destruction from Eo's belt. Sunny and I dove to the side to give a clear path.

Eo yelled something as Tabby unrolled it flat and aimed it at Bianca.

I recognized the word on her lips, a desperate plea as much as it was an attack: "Destruction."

A sound like a hundred simultaneous cannon blasts shattered the air. The attack tore the scroll apart as pure destructive force distorted the air in front of Tabby. A merciless hurricane of wind whipped toward Bianca. She hissed and stepped back, with her Stand having the same reaction.

But that's all it did.

The wind had an aftershock. Tabby collapsed back as if shoved. Her fingers were crooked. Eo fell to her knees with hands already moving for a potion.

She screamed something and began to violently fidget in terror. Sunny rushed over. All three of them screamed, but I couldn't hear a damn thing over the storm. Bianca shook her head. The flame spirit looked ready for a new attack.

We need to get out of here. Now!

Every second was an advantage to this thing. Was it right to attack it directly? Charge from four directions? Could we even focus enough to do that? The team was falling apart.

They were wrecked with terror and confusion. There was a demon. It was real, but it wasn't here. The necromancer had a spirit. We couldn't get close to an enemy that didn't dodge attacks. Communication was impossible.

"Dammit!" The wind ate my voice.

I looked at Bianca. Her jaw hung limp in a lazy, empty smile. Some of her hair had burnt off her head. Her eyes were empty. It looked like there was nothing left of her. Either all of her life was in the fiery spirit, or she'd sacrificed her life so this thing could use it.

It's killing her...The fire thing will kill her. Radec, you sick monster.

My eyes moved to the fiery creature. It looked at us with an unnerving understanding. It stretched out an arm and waved its hand for us to approach. It knew that it could take its time. It would have been happy to suffocate us.

It was too hot. Already, it felt like the sweat was evaporating off my skin. Every inch of my flesh felt like it was hovering over a hot stove. The other three looked worse. Sunny patted her fur. Eo took a vial from her pouch and poured it down her shirt, onto the feathers that must have been near combustion. Tabby shouted something, trying and failing to look calm.

As we fell apart, Bianca walked closer. The flame spirit approached with her. There needed to be something. Anything! My eyes frantically scanned all over for a weak point. Finally, I looked at the whirring cap of yellow on its head. It touched the stone ceiling.

Maybe, a horrible thought occurred, *we don't need to be the ones to kill her.*

We were deep underground. Eo still had two Major Scrolls of Destruction. Maybe we could activate those and cause a cave-in. The rocks would fall and crush her. Then, maybe... maybe we could sprint up the hall and get out in time.

Maybe...

I looked back to our exit. Still, the fog cut us off. There was no doubt in my mind that we wouldn't be able to pass through it, at least not until we dealt with this thing. Radec didn't care about his protégé any more than he cared about us.

I grabbed Sunny by the shoulder and pushed her toward the fog. I did the same with Tabby, mouthing, "Go! Go!"

Bianca helped my point. She walked to us. The flame spirit reached out. As a group, we scrambled toward our inaccessible escape. Sunny rushed the fog and struck at it with her hammer. As expected, she bounced off it.

I fell in front of Eo and pointed to the scrolls which had been carefully secured to her belt. I tried to speak, but she couldn't hear me. She shook her head, more and more flustered. She couldn't understand.

Dammit!

Suddenly, I remembered the ax in my hand. My hand had been wrapped around it in a tight, unbreakable instinct of terror. That would do. I slashed open my left palm with the ax. All three of my companions freaked out, momentarily forgetting our impending doom.

Immediately, I wiped blood onto my finger and wrote onto the floor in front of Eo: CAVE-IN.

I pointed once again to the scrolls, then to the ceiling above our enemy. I yelled out a plan, knowing I couldn't be heard. Hopefully, my hands would give the idea. I would take the scrolls and try to do...something!

Eo nodded. Sunny and Tabby screamed in muted disapproval.

Bianca, meanwhile, crossed her arms. I began to wonder if she wanted us to have a slow death. Or, maybe, she couldn't think. All her hair had melted to sludge. The pallid skin began to burn in places so she looked like a patchwork version of Two-Face in *The Dark Knight.*

I turned back to Eo to see her pulling the scrolls from her belt, one in each hand. Tabby and Sunny leaned in close, demanding something from us. An explanation? Offers to help? Pleas? I couldn't know.

Eo grabbed Sunny's arm and pointed to the fog. "Go!" she mouthed. And the same to Tabby.

I reached for the parchment. She ran past me. Then, tucking them under her chin, she tore out of her mining overalls. Her wings glistened in the red light. The air sent them fluttering in waves. They looked ready to ignite as the fiery wind blew at them. Her wings spread, one hand clenched the scrolls, and she looked dead into my eyes as she yelled again, "Go!"

Her determination horrified me almost as much as the flame spirit. Her eyes became a kaleidoscope. The rest of us jumped to her. She mumbled something. Instantly, a huge gust of wind lifted her off the ground. Eo flew to the patient enemy. It swatted at her with playfully lethal attacks. The brown blur of our friend weaved around, over, and under the attacks. She had to flap to dodge. Terror kept a tight grip around the scrolls she had in each hand. There was no chance to unfold them. She reached out her hand to open the scrolls, but the flames returned. The hand shut. She had to keep flapping to dodge.

My feet ran before I could think. Eo had created an opening.

Bianca was so focused on Eo that she didn't notice me until I was only a few steps away. Tabby and Sunny were at my side. With each stop closer, the heat intensified. I felt like I'd combust with every step. Breathing felt like swallowing a lit match.

The flame spirit noticed us at last. It swiped a flaming fist at us. We jumped back. Sunny and Tabby flanked the demon without a word of communication. Extra arms sprouted from the incorporeal body of heat. It lashed at each of us with blind, desperate swings. Bianca's face did not show fear. It showed nothing. There wasn't enough of a face to express emotion.

I threw my ax. The clumsy throw was far from her, but it made an arm swing. I waved to Eo. She saw my open hand, swooped down, and smacked the scroll into my hand like a baton. I grabbed it, fell to the ground, unrolled it onto the stone, and screamed, "Destruction!"

It felt like I'd punched into the earth's core. The spell hit so hard that the sound itself made my ears ache. The cavern lurched as cracks broke out in all directions in jagged forms like lightning. Everyone jostled and trembled. Everyone, that is, on the ground.

Sunny fell to all fours for stability. Tabby struggled to stay on her feet. Bianca shook and stumbled to her knees. The fiery demon wavered in its connection.

Eo dove. She fell like an arrow through the spirit's arms and struck Bianca. She unrolled her final scroll onto Bianca's chest, shut her eyes, and screamed the word.

Suddenly, a painfully loud boom brought the cavern into silence. The spirit blinked away as if it'd never existed. The sudden lack of light and roaring flame knocked me off my feet almost as much as the shaking. My ears continued to ring with the howl of the wind. They rang with the aftereffects of noise. The only light came from the light gray mist of our exit. Sure enough, it faded.

Meanwhile, the cavern's shaking stabilized.

Soon, I lay still in the deep dark. Pain racked my hands and chest. My lungs felt like they'd dried out. Every breath hurt. Still, we'd won. In a stagger, I forced myself to my knees and slapped at my belt. After a moment, I found my flashlight. With it flicked on, I found the others. Tabby and Sunny were clutching their heads, recovering from everything that had happened. Eo lay beside a pool of blood. Her fingers were gnarled and her feathers singed. Tears rolled down her face. From her expression, she must have been wailing. The ringing in my ears drowned her out.

With shaky steps, I marched to her. Sunny beat me to her. Sunny reached a hand to Eo, and our savior gripped it. Eo wrapped herself into Sunny like a wounded child clinging to her mother. Sunny held her. Even without hearing, I recognized the message: "I've got you."

I turned to Tabby. She reached out and grabbed my arm. She looked dizzy and ready to pass out. I wasn't much better. We leaned against each other. I waved my flashlight and pointed for the exit. Silently, we hobbled away. Nobody asked Eo to cast her spell. There was no feeling of victory. At this pace, it would take more than an hour before we left the mine.

As we approached the tunnel which had intrigued us so much, I looked over my shoulder. There, in the darkness, I saw two glowing points of crimson red. The eyes watched us leave. For a moment, I could have sworn that I heard the demon's evil laugh as we hobbled away in the worst victory of my life.

CHAPTER
TWENTY-SIX

The fatigue from the battle hit as we walked away from the mine. The heat had dispersed as the barrier had fallen. One of the few lessons I remembered from science class: hot air rises. All that heat had shot up like Antrum coughing up smoke while we got a fresh return of oxygen. My ears rang, blocking out any trace of sound.

As we cooled down, the fatigue grew. Our limbs became heavy and leaden. With every step, I wondered if the demon would come for us and launch a surprise attack. It felt safer once we were back with the electric lights, but no better. Aches set in. My clothes shifted painfully, still hot and irritating on my skin. I could only imagine how uncomfortable it felt against fur.

Tabby kept her eyes on her feet. Sometimes, she or I looked at the pair beside us. Sunny half-carried Eo through much of the climb. I felt horrible seeing singe marks on some of her feathers. Eo wept and sobbed. Sunny, on the other hand, may as well have worn a mask. She ran through words of comfort without them being heard.

We had few scars. Only minor cuts from falling rocks. Still, three of us had broken fingers. All of us were rattled. I didn't know if they also had intense headaches, like someone had dug screwdrivers into my temples and began to twist, or if it was just an effect of the lightning strike.

One thing I knew for certain was that we were all thirsty. We all should have stopped to take a sip from our canteens. At the same time, none of us were willing to stop. There was a fear that we wouldn't be able to keep moving if we killed the momentum.

The corridor drained most of our energy. That unending incline was brutal on our sore muscles. My legs wobbled by the time I climbed out from the hole and into the caves that I knew.

Slowly, my hearing came back.

The first thing I heard clearly was Sunny saying, "You'll be okay."

Tabby blinked back tears. Eo seemed no less distraught, but she'd gotten her bearings. She walked along with Sunny.

"I thought..." Tabby muttered. "I didn't think that it was real." Her head hung low in guilt.

"Hey," I said. "There was no way you could have known."

She didn't reply.

Eventually, we made it to the quarry. There was no sun to greet us. Overcast clouds loomed above, hanging low and foreboding.

Great...just great.

As we stepped into the fresh air, Sunny said something. It wasn't clear. I turned to her, pointed to my ear, and said, "What?"

She made a gesture of lifting a mug and taking a drink, then pointed toward the village. Eo shook her head and clung to Sunny. Tears shone in our fighter's eyes. Sunny led Eo toward me and moved Eo's uncertain grip to my hand. All the while, Sunny never looked at Tabby.

They started to talk, but they still sounded muffled.

Tabby said, "I didn't know—"

Sunny cut her off with a middle finger, not even looking at her. "There's a fucking demon. I told you. There was no point."

Eo sniffled, saying nothing as she hung her head.

I put my arms around her and said, "Let's get some water."

Sunny waved us off and walked away. Tabby took a few steps after her, but she stopped. She didn't need to say anything to communicate how guilty she felt. The four of us may as well have lost the fight. None of us knew what to do.

Tabby tried to clench her fists, wincing in pain from her hands.

Oh, right.

I gently nudged Eo's shoulder. She looked up. When I showed my hand, with the index finger bent forty-five degrees at the wrong angle, she nodded. The task gave us something to do. We all sat on the gray rocks and passed around potions, salve, and water. The potions, as far as I knew, numbed the pain. One of them fixed my headache, at least.

The last thing Eo gave me was a little orange capsule. I tossed it back and chugged some water. A few seconds later, my hearing returned in full. "What the?" I asked to check my own voice. I snapped my fingers by my ears several times. Sure enough, everything was fine.

"That should be enough," Eo said. "I hope you feel better." There was no sarcasm or double meaning in her words. The volume was little more than a whisper. I'd never seen a person look so frail as the woman who'd saved us all.

I hugged her. "Eo, you saved us. Thank you."

Tabby hugged from the other side. Now, after everything, she too began to weep. "I'm so sorry, I'm so sorry, I'm sorry!"

Eo barely reacted, even as Tabby lightly shook her. "I'm tired," Eo said after a while. "I don't want to be alone right now." Her legs pulled back until she began to hug her knees. Slowly, she rocked back and forth.

"Of course," Tabby said. With effort, she stood and helped Eo to her feet. "Come on. Let's wash the soot off and get some rest."

"Everyone was excited," Eo said blankly. "We were going to be heroes."

Neither of us responded.

That was the awful thing. She was right.

"Don't worry about it," I said. "I'll go into the village and... yeah. Most of Acanth knew about our plans for today. So, I guess I'll break the news."

What the hell am I going to say? Hey guys. Turns out there's a demon. So, now we're traumatized and unsure what's going to happen.

Eo dug into one of her pouches. She pulled out another capsule and gave it to me. "Don't let Sunny be alone, please."

"Right," I said.

What the hell are we going to do now?

It felt as if everything had vanished. *Antrum.* All the hope and happiness that we had earned since we first got here all disappeared. It was too much for me to accept. I may not have known a damn thing about demons or how they worked, but I couldn't simply accept that it was now off limits.

No! Why the hell hadn't they helped us with the necromancer? If the mine was such a big deal, why were we the only ones fighting for it?

As I walked into Acanth, I turned away from the bar. I trusted Sunny to stay there. Instead, once again, I found myself in the civic center.

A few of the workers looked up with surprise when I entered. A few of them tried to make it look like they were working. They kept their heads pointed down at the polished wooden desks, or suddenly became interested in their locally crafted coffee mugs. I'd already come to recognize some of these faces. I saw them every day. They cheered us on, but they wouldn't help us.

As I approached Karma, one of her eyes flitted up to me. "I am surprised to see you so early in the day, Mr. Calvinson," she said. "From your expression, I take it that something unexpected and of import has arisen?"

No point in sugar coating it.

"There's a demon in the depths of Antrum."

Instantly, every person in hearing range snapped their heads up to look at me.

The scales of Karma's face lightened toward yellow. "Oh." A tiny change in pitch was the only surprise she revealed. "Are the other members of the Antrum Estate okay?"

"Um...physically, yes. They're going through a lot. We just killed a damn necromancer who claimed to be centuries old."

People stopped pretending to ignore us. There were no dividers between these desks. I liked the setup. Everyone worked together and could easily keep in contact. Now, they gaped at me and Karma. From the twitch of her left eye, she recognized the audience. "That's an incredible feat which you four have accomplished. Your courage and deeds shall be properly compensated through a grant. If you provide any proof of the deceased, we can—"

"Look." I leaned forward. "I am going to be very blunt. Sorry in advance if that makes me come off like an asshole, but I need to be fucking quick because a lot is happening, and I don't want to throw shit onto your plate that you don't need. There is a demon in Antrum. The necromancer said that its name is Radec. Since there is a demon, is there any way that we can call in...I don't know, an exorcist or an army or whatever it takes to kill this thing? My friends are traumatized and horrified, and I can't blame them after what we just endured. The mine is important to this village, right? Help us."

Karma swallowed nervously. Her eyes flitted to the area around her. "Would you be willing to join me on my break, Mr. Calvinson? Perhaps I can answer your questions with some fresh air."

Shit...

I didn't like it, but I got the hint. With a grunt and a nod, the two of us stepped out of the office. As soon as we were outside, Karma said, "Do you want the result first or the explanation?"

"You sound like Eo," I said.

"I take it that you'd prefer the result. Nobody is coming to help you with the mine."

I stared at her. It was frustrating enough when Tabby and the others had convinced me not to request help in fighting the necromancer. But this? This was an entirely different scale of threat. How did we even compute this?

"You have to be kidding," I said. "This thing is a threat to all of Acanth, isn't it? And...it's a demon! How is that not something that people are willing to send help for?"

Karma shook her head grimly. "I would like you to imagine something, Mr. Calvinson. Imagine if there were a hurricane, and that this hurricane were a horrible storm that you knew would cause major destruction. However, that hurri-

cane was deep underground and, thus far, held no suggestion of going somewhere inhabited."

"What? It's not a damn hurricane! It's a living embodiment
of evil, isn't it?"

"Perhaps." Her eyes darted around to check for nosy eaves-
droppers. "Still, such evil has not bothered anyone until it
was encroached upon."

"Encroached..." I shook my head. "This thing isn't Smaug,
okay? The four of us haven't wandered across the country-
side to get to this thing. People have been working this
mine for decades and decades! It's a danger to us. Besides,
aren't demons escaped from hells or whatever? Can't we
call its parole officer or something?"

Karma shook her head. "Your grasp of the situation is not
quite correct. Demons belong to the hells, yes. Because of
this, as far as most legal and law enforcing authorities are
concerned, they are completely outside of mortal jurisdiction."

Every sentence made me angrier. Before I could speak,
though, she cut me off with a gesture. "That's the proper
explanation. To be more blunt, nobody wants to risk their
own lives to go fight something so dangerous for a town
that most people have already forgotten."

"No way." I pointed at her. "I know that that's not true.
There are adventurers and mercenaries willing to fight this
thing."

"And are you willing to pay them, Mr. Calvinson?"

The direct question stole all my momentum and emotion.
She continued before I could respond, "Those with the

experience for this job require tremendous prices. They would charge more than Antrum earned in a month as the height of its business. Even if higher authorities were interested, they would demand bed and board. The city can't afford that. This is a poor city of exclusively women, Mr. Calvinson. Keep that in mind when you suggest what kinds of people you wish to bring here. We respect all that you've done, and I'm personally grateful to you. But I'm afraid that this is all we can do. Perhaps there is a workaround. Is there any chance that the four of you can mine in the areas above the demon?"

Slowly, my head shook back and forth. I could only gape at her. "I'm sorry, what?"

"Perhaps," she said. A slight nervous pause hitched her voice. The ever-polite expression remained, but I saw it crack. Here was the person, not the civic employee. "Well, Mr. Calvinson, while I don't know much about your industry, I do understand the typical patterns of demons and demonology. Typically, they express a degree of territoriality unparalleled in sentient beings, which should allow you to continue to mine in the areas located above that in which you located it."

"Uh-huh," I gave her a slow nod after listening in careful, polite silence. "So, you want us to stay in the mine where we know this thing lives and *hope* that it doesn't attack us?"

"I didn't—"

"This is the same creature that cast a barrier closing us out of the mine in the first place. A monster so big and frightening that some people in this village would be traumatized to know that it merely exists. This thing has already corrupted one person and convinced them to give up their humanity. Nobody wants to stay in their homes when they find out that there's a demon!"

"Most of the time," Karma sighed, "they have to do so anyway. Mr. Calvinson, there's nothing I can offer you. I'm sorry, personally, but I can't offer you funds or resources that our village does not have."

As she spoke, her composure returned. This wasn't about her. This was about Acanth. She was doing the job that I'd once wished I'd been doing. The mine on the edge of town had been out of business for a long time. If it died, so be it. She had the rest of the village to worry about.

So, we were alone...

I felt like Sigourney Weaver in *Ghostbusters*. The evil spirit wasn't in my fridge, but I was stuck with it all the same. I didn't know what to do about it. I was stuck with the mine just like she had been stuck with the apartment. Unfortunately, I couldn't ask Bill Murray for help.

I slumped back. "Dammit," I muttered under my breath. "Sorry I snapped at you, Karma."

"I can hardly blame your emotionality, given the circumstances."

Huh, I thought, *that's the coldest form of sympathy I've ever gotten.*

But that was it. There were no reinforcements. We were on our own.

Karma re-entered the building. I was alone. When I lifted my head, I saw *The Monkey's Paw* sitting across the square.

For better or worse, there was no time for me to pity myself. There was still a horrified monkey woman getting herself drunk to deal with trauma. I had to make sure that she was okay.

No, not even that. I cared about her. She was hurting. She needed someone near her.

CHAPTER
TWENTY-SEVEN

"Gimme another ooone!" Sunny's voice rang out from the Paw.

A rabbit woman beat a quick retreat from the pub, food crumbs still on her mouth.

I grabbed the door before it shut and walked inside.

The energy in the room was both lonely and chaotic. The tables were almost all empty. The sole remaining patron, a goat woman, saw me enter. As soon as she did, she pounded back her coffee, threw money on the table, and left. Fran stood behind the bar as another server stood to the side. From the look of mild panic on the server's face, I guessed that she wasn't used to drunken noise this early in the day.

What time was it anyway? A look at the old grandfather clock above the pool table told me that it was barely noon. Everything we'd endured had only lasted the morning. Sure, we'd set out early with that in mind, but it still stung to see that our entire world had changed in a few short hours.

Fran, for her part, looked more uncomfortable than I'd ever seen her. She kept scratching nervously at one of her dog ears. As I approached the bar, she glanced at the server and nodded toward the door. The server nodded and rushed off on an impromptu lunch break.

Meanwhile, Sunny pounded down a tankard. As she drank, she stabbed her index finger onto the bar, demanding a replacement for the drink she'd barely started.

Fran's golden eyes swung to me, torn between concern and a plea for explanation.

"Whaaat?" Sunny sputtered through her beer. Several foamy drops splattered onto the bar and her shirt. Sunny whirred to look back. When she saw me, she rolled her eyes and sighed. "Well, you're fine, I guess."

What the hell does that mean?

She turned back to the bar. My arrival had deflated most of her energy. The change from bitter and angry drinker to moping drinker did not inspire any confidence. Fran and I shared another look, equally concerned.

Well then...

I sat beside the strongest fighter on my team. Fran's eyes drilled into me. The weight of her scrutiny almost hurt. The fact that her business took a hit for the day likely didn't matter much. One of her best friends was now fuming into a drink. It didn't look great.

"Coffee," I requested.

The Paw's owner knew the bar so well that she set to work without looking away from me. She may as well have grabbed me by the shoulders and demanded an explanation. Was it safe to pour a coffee when looking away from it?

I guess it's best to just rip off the bandage.

"There's a demon in Antrum," I told Fran.

She froze. The coffee splashed over the rim of the mug. "Shit!" Fran yipped and put the pot and mug on the counter, shaking her hand.

As she ran her hand under cold water in the sink behind the bar, Sunny sighed again. "Riiight. I fucking called it. But nooo. We don't trust the monkey. It's all just ruuumors. I told Tabby over and over and over! Physical attacks? Fine. Magic? Tricky but doable. Spiritual or Psychic? No. No fucking way! I can fight trolls, monsters, but—"

She stopped as suddenly as if someone had cut her off. Sunny stared ahead blankly. Her eyes began to moisten. Her breaths came faster. "We— I—" she stumbled through a few words, gestures getting bigger. She smacked the table as her breaths became shallow. Her entire body rose and fell with the gasps. A frantic, frightened pitch broke the breaths.

"Sunny," I said. I reached out toward her.

She let her forehead fall and hit the dark wood of the bar. "Ugh!" Her hands clenched the back of her head as she smooshed her face down. After a second, she began to bang her head against the bar.

"Okay," Fran placed a coffee in front of me and slid her palm under Sunny's forehead, cushioning the impact. When she plopped onto the hand, Sunny stayed there. Fran was stiff, uncertain. Sunny slowly lifted a hand to hold Fran's wrist, then turned her head so her cheek rested on the palm. Tears were running down her face. "I can't," Sunny spoke with a flat and lifeless tone that turned my blood cold. Her eyes turned to me as she forced out the next words. "I can't keep us safe."

There was no good way to respond. She didn't want a response. The look she gave me was empty. To her, there was no question in the truth of that awful sentence.

This is so out of my depth.

I decided on honesty. "We'd be dead if not for you."

Sunny shook her head. "Don't, okay? I appreciate it, but pleeease don't. You're new here. You don't get it. I shouldn't get mad at you, because you didn't have any reason to think that there'd be anything like that down there. You didn't have to say goodbye to most of the people you'd ever cared about, or find out about their death from a phone call." She swished her drink in the cup for a while. "I wasn't there. Even if I had been, it wouldn't have done anything. I'm useless.

"No," Fran said before I could. Her tail stiffened as she poured herself a drink and downed most of it. Sunny raised a disinterested eyebrow. Fran met her eyes. "I'm not letting you pity yourself."

An ugly scowl pulled back to reveal Sunny's canines. She shook her head. "Fraaan, please don't. Stick to the drinks, okay?"

"I've given you years of my time and patience, so now you better give me fifteen seconds. If you need space, a pool table, and a bottle to deal with everything you've been through, that's your business. I've watched you try to drown your thoughts with booze for a long time. I can't tell you what to do, but you need to stop pretending that you don't have people who love you nearby."

"Shut uuup," she said into her drink.

"Relax, it isn't like I'm going to cut you off or anything." Fran grabbed the tankard and refilled it. "I won't tell you how to live your life. I will tell you that I won't allow dishonesty. If you don't want to talk to me, at least talk to the guy you've been crushing on for weeks."

Suddenly, life returned to Sunny. She bolted upright as if an electric current had shot through her. "Fraaan! Don't say shit like that when he's right here!"

Fran rolled her eyes, topped off her drink, and downed it. She was back in her element, clearly. Instead of taking a simple drink, she leaned her hips against the bar, stuck out her leg to lightly stomp her boot to the floor, and threw her head back for the drink as if she were some kind of Musketeer pinup model.

"Don't pretend." Fran pointed a finger to her while the other three held her drink. "Just because you won't talk about your feelings doesn't mean you can hide them. You've been making full-on Disney princess goo-goo eyes when you talk about him. Actually, it's worse, because I didn't hear Belle talk about how hard up she was!"

"Shut uuup!" Sunny seethed. She flared her nostrils and glared at Fran, who gave a shake of her hair and took another drink. She owned the bar, the gesture said, as well as the situation.

But wait. Would Sunny be the Beast here since she's the one with animal features? No, stupid, what am I thinking?

"Jaaack." Sunny turned the full force of her mixed emotions on me as I chastised myself for the stupidity of my thoughts. "Why aren't you saying anything?"

Brain, I know that we've had our disagreements, but help me here.

"Well," I said. "I thought I'd try the *Good Will Hunting* approach again."

Unimpressed annoyance hit me like a wave. She rolled her eyes. "If you start saying 'it's not your fault' over and over, I'll punch you in the face."

"Okay." I shrugged. "Instead of that, I'll just be here."

I turned back toward Fran and had some more coffee. What was I doing?

"Whyyy?" Sunny asked.

"Because I care about you, and I want you to know that you're not alone."

From the corner of my eye, I saw Fran's eyebrow shoot up. Her tail wagged lightly as her fingers tapped on her tankard. She may as well have been typing up the night's local gossip.

Sunny, meanwhile, pulled back, surprised. Her ears twitched and she cocked her head. "Huh." She looked back to her tankard. "Huuuh." Her other hand moved to the tankard. All the muscles in her face scrunched into intense thought. "Um, Fran? Can I borrow the guestroom in the back?"

Fran tipped her glass to a door at the side. "Of course you can."

"Oookay." Sunny nodded and stood. "Jack, follow me. I... Let's talk. Just not here."

"Alright." I stood and walked after her.

Along the way, Fran stepped up and tapped my shoulder. "That woman has the biggest heart I know, even if she's bad at showing it. A lot of that heart, she's already given to you. Don't hurt her feelings, please."

"Jaaack," Sunny called. She had her tail on the handle of the door, leaning forward to us and using her tail to keep her from falling like a sloppy parody of the Smooth Criminal pose.

"I'd better go."

We entered a short hall. A door to the kitchen was on the right, a bathroom on the left, and one marked with the word 'guest' on a carved wooden plaque. The interior was a small bedroom.

"In case someone overdoes it," Sunny explained. "There used to be some nights where I couldn't make it home, or when Fran felt too tired to go back to her place."

There was a single mattress with a wool blanket. Beside it was a small nightstand with a shaded lamp sitting on it. Across from these was a fireplace. There was also a shelf made of black-painted wood. Tucked into it were several books about recipes and drink mixing.

The walls were decorated with paintings and photos of Acanth through the years. One caught my eye. It showed a younger Fran, still in full getup, draped over Sunny while the other leaned on the pool table. They were laughing so hard that they could barely stand.

"Weeell," Sunny called back my attention. She sat on the bed and tapped the spot beside her. "Let's talk."

"Right." I moved toward her. After a deep breath, I said, "I'm sorry that I didn't listen to your concerns more. You were really freaked out and it was a dick move for me to not take your concerns into full account. I'm so, so sorry about th—"

The moment I sat on the bed, she wrapped her arms around me. "Shut uuup..." She pulled herself into me and buried her face under my shoulder. The strongest person I'd ever met clung to me. The difference in height startled me, even after living together for a while. The warmth of her face, arms, and body filled me. Then she began to shake lightly in sobs. "Please...I need this."

Slowly, I put my arms around her in return. Her squeeze tightened. The strength was amazing, almost interfering with my breath, but she made sure to never cross that line. She clung to me like she was afraid I'd slip away. I slid one hand in her hair and began to gently pat her head.

We stayed like that for a while. There was nothing to say. The only thing to do was be there. "I'm sorry, Sunny."

"For what?" she said into my torso.

"Asking you to be a weapon against an elemental? To march into a mine when you were still dealing with stuff? To get over your drinking in a rush without taking your time? Feels like there's a list."

A soft sigh of a laugh eked out of her. "I forgive you. I'm sorry, too."

"For what?"

For a while, there was no answer. Eventually, she looked up. "I'm not enough."

I didn't say anything. Instead, I looked at her. Her eyes were swollen with tears. Dust and soot from the fight still marked her cheeks. I got a static shock from her hair, likely from the lightning at the start of the battle. It killed me to see her doubt herself like this. "Talk to me, Sunny. Why do you think that?"

"Because it's true!" she said into my chest. "I didn't do shit today! Eo brought the scrolls and the light. You killed the troll and knocked the necromancer off balance. Tabby kept the goblins off us and was the first to use a scroll. It's not the first time, either. With the elemental, it was one of the coolest moments of my life, but I was ammo!"

She began to weep openly. Warm tears soaked through my shirt. "I didn't do shit against the zombies. Eo has barely been back in the fight, and she's already pushed herself waaay too hard! Did you see how hard she was crying? She won't say it, but she's fucking exhausted! Working with all those charts? Her sleep schedule is still complete shit. Aside from how tired she is...she had to kill that necromancer basically with her hands! Eo is the gentlest, sweetest girl in the world. She shouldn't have to do that.

And it fucked her up sooo much to shoot me at the elemental."

Sunny pulled back slightly. As she did, her hands grabbed my side.

She continued, "Aaand Tabby. Ugh." The fingers tightened to keep me with her, even though there was nowhere else I ever wanted to be. "She taught you to use a sword. Showed you the mines. Killed the lions..."

Again, she looked at me. The grip tightened. She leaned in and wrapped her arms around me anew. "And the 'yoga.'" Her tone gave it air quotes. "I saw the way she looks at you. The way you talk to her..."

Suddenly, Sunny pulled back and scratched her hands through her hair. She snarled and pushed her fingers violently back and forth in her head. "Do you have aaany idea what you did here? You brought happiness back to Antrum! Tabby is putting on real clothes, leaving the house for things other than chores, and laughing. Eo got out of the house. She has fun. She sees people and wants to see people."

Her hand slid across the top of the blanket to my hand. "I haven't felt happy to be sober in a looong time. There used to be nightmares all the time. I saw Dawn. Ooor Tabby or Eo or whoever. Dying in a cave-in. They would scream for me to save them, and I couldn't. The drinking made those dreams not happen...as much. Since you got here, I have those dreams less and less."

She squeezed my hand. "Buuut there's more. It's not just the demon. You have to know that. You have Tabby. Neither of you see me as much. Eo doesn't need me anymore. She's carried. I'm worthless in a fight. Aaand...I'm no good with you guys anymore."

"That's not true," I moved over and hugged her. She flinched. "You dodged fucking lightning. You think the rest of us could have done that? We'd be dead if not for you. You practically knocked a troll down by yourself with one hit. There's no way we can move the ore without you. There's no one who can move or climb like you."

"Stooop," she said weakly.

"Fine, then let's talk about Antrum. We don't have it without you. You are the energy. The smile. The muscle. This whole thing doesn't function without you!"

"Stop." Her palm smacked against my sternum and knocked me back. "Oh shiiit!" She gasped as I fell back against the bed. Numb pain rang through my head as I impacted against the wall. The mattress was too thin. She moved up beside me and cradled my head. "Are you okay?"

The hit was a reminder that I hadn't eaten or drank anything since we'd been air-fried. I felt lightheaded. The hit shouldn't have bothered me much, but my vision blurred for a second. I blinked several times. "I'm alright," I muttered.

When my vision returned, she was right above me. Her eyes were puffy with tears and drooping from booze. A red glow brightened her cheeks. The crying left streaks in the dirt and rubble from the caves. Her lips quivered as she breathed. I felt her warm breath on my lips. She leaned closer, pressing her breasts to my side.

Here she is, the woman. The fighter, the jokester, the pool player, the survivor, the protector. And in pain.

She moved in glacial slow motion to me, her breasts giving across my arm and onto my side slowly. As she moved, the lips pulled back toward a sob. She cried again. "I'm an awful friend." Again, her face landed on my chest, her fingers bunching up my shirt.

"Hey," I said. "You're okay. You're okay."

I wrapped one arm around her shoulder and patted the small of her back with the other. "I'm nooot!" She sobbed. "What about Tabby? It's not a secret. The two of you are a thing. I can't...You don't need me and she doesn't need me anymore..."

She turned her face up to look at me. A weeping smile met my expression. "You get my references. You laugh at my jokes. We have the same energy. You have a niiice body, too. And I can't stop myself from wanting you, but..."

"Sunny," I leaned forward and kissed her forehead. Surprise washed over her features. "Tabby and I are scared," I said. "We're terrified. She says what she needs to keep all of us focused. I still have no clue what I'm doing. Yeah, we have sex, but we've been perfectly honest with each other about what it is. It makes us less afraid. We're confused, frightened, and looking for someone to help us." I took a breath and said, "You're honest, Sunny. I admire the hell out of you for that. When you're scared, you say it. When you're horny, it's the most obvious thing in the world. I hide behind sarcasm. Tabby puts on a brave face. You're the one who charges at a fucking lightning attack like it's nothing and distracts an entire storm. Besides." I lifted her chin and pressed my lips beneath her eye. "I'll say it again. There's nothing wrong with wanting someone."

We looked at each other in silence for a while. She nestled halfway on top of me. Her open palm lay over my heart, a finger doing light circles over it. Suddenly, she leaned forward and kissed me.

Our lips were dry and cracked. The taste of coffee, beer, tears, and dust mingled together. Still, neither of us pulled back. We breathed each other in, experimenting with how comfortable we were. Her body moved gently over mine. I brought my hand to the back of her head and gently held her there for a kiss.

Later, she pulled back. Some of her energy returned. She pushed herself up so she was above me rather than beside me. "Tell me again. Be honest. There's nothing serious between you and her?"

I shook my head. "We've made a point to not define it."

"Sweeeet," she said. "I don't want anything with a title or a label or anything. I just want you, in me, now."

As she spoke, the sadness left. The playful energy turned into a declaration of fact. She'd wanted to say this for a long time, I realized.

"Okay." I nodded. "But one request."

"Yeeeah?" she looked concerned.

"We both wash our faces and drink water. The two of us look like shit."

"Ha!" She brought her head down and playfully nuzzled my neck, her hair tickling me. "Sure."

TWENTY-EIGHT

We freshened up as much as possible in the bathroom. A splash of cold water helped us both feel better. I was shocked at how much clearer headed I felt as I dabbed the back of my neck dry. So clear headed, in fact, that I wondered if this was the right decision.

Sunny told me that she'd wait in the room while I went to the bar for water. A small lunch crowd had gathered, those who had not witnessed Sunny's outburst. I had to wait a minute at the side of the bar before Fran walked up to me. "So, what's happening?"

"She's a lot better. She wants to...rest for a while back there. Can we get some water?"

"Rest," she repeated. A knowing glance and a twitch of her dog ears told me that she saw right through me. "Call it what you want. I've told her to fuck you and get it out of her system. So, I guess she's just following my advice."

I blushed. When she returned with two large glasses, she tsked. "Your only problem, Jack," she said as she leaned over the bar and gently patted my cheek, "is that you take things too seriously. You're allowed to breathe and enjoy the moment."

"But," I said, "so much is happening at once."

"Exactly," she replied. "Those are the times when reprieve and small pleasures are most valuable. Now, I need to get back to work. Don't worry, I soundproofed those walls a long time ago." She gave me a conspiratorial wink and a flourishing whip of her shaggy tail.

"Right." I took the glasses and returned to the room. As I got there, Sunny sat looking up at the amber-colored electric light. She gave me a small smile. With that simple act, life returned to her. I passed her the glass. "Cheers."

"Cheeeers." She tipped her glass against mine and downed half of it in one go. As I sat beside her, she threw an arm around my waist and pulled me close to her. "Thanks for everything."

I put my own arm around her in response. "No problem," I said. My arm barely landed across her shoulders before she grabbed my hand, pushed it onto her breast, and pressed my fingers so that I held and lifted it.

She downed another swallow of water and put her glass on the nightstand. "Come ooon, already. Let's do this."

She grabbed the hem of her shirt and lifted. As expected, she wore no bra. Her breasts heaved up with the fabric. Gravity brought them down with impact, jiggling back into place as her nipples perked into view.

The sight knocked me out. I hesitated as I pulled off my own shirt.

"Huuurry it up." Sunny slid to the floor between my legs and roughly undid my belt. She shook me back and forth as I pulled off my shirt. With the way cleared, I helped her pull the denim and my boxers down. As they fell, the beginnings of my erection sprung free. She stared for a moment and watched me grow. With her right there, with that amazing, hot body right there, how could I not?

"Hurry it up," I threw her words back at her.

She obliged. She pulled my pants and boxers off my feet and, before I could react, wrapped her lips around my cock.

"Sunny," I huffed.

My hands gripped at her shoulders.

She moved one again to her breast, pushing my fingers into her so I squeezed. I did as she wanted. My hand pressed her breast back and rubbed.

She moaned, the sound muffled because of my cock in her mouth. The vibration ran along my shaft like a current of pleasure. She focused on the tip, stroking back and forth, wrapping her lips to cover me from all sides. Her fingers curled around my shaft, her thumb tracing a vein, and she began to give quick strokes with a tight grip.

Suddenly, her tongue ran along the underside of the tip. "Yes!" My free hand moved to the back of her head. Pure instinct put me there. "Just like that." Her head stayed still. She stayed focused, swirling the tip of my penis all around with thorough lolls of her wet tongue. Her hand moved to my balls. She slid her fingers all over them like she couldn't get enough of the texture. My erection reached full height. Every inch of my body belonged to her.

"Deeper," I said. "Take all of me."

It was instant. Her hand shifted to the base of my erection to keep me balanced. Sunny's head moved back and forth. Through wet sounds of glugs and gulps, she greedily devoured me. She pressed her lips around me. My cock slid back and forth over her tongue, feeling the glorious wet warmth of her mouth.

Slowly but surely, she took me into her. She worked her way along my cock with pleasure. The motions became longer and deeper. The pace slowed as each push went deeper and pulled back farther.

This...this is incredible.

My eyes rolled back from the sheer pleasure of it. Nothing existed except the sensation. She put all of her focus on my cock. I just sat there and received it. I felt like the most important person in all the world to feel this and see her work to make me feel this way.

I have to be amazing if she thinks I'm worth this.

When I looked back down, I caught her eye. That same playful gleam took on a new tone. As soon as she saw me, she pushed all the way down. "Sunny, yes." My erection pushed over her tongue and into her throat.

She stayed there for a moment, as if to show off that she could take so much of me. As I felt myself twitch, she slid back slowly. She opened her mouth and let me free. Then, she kissed my erection. Her hand held it from the other side as she kissed and licked along the shaft. Every touch felt amazing. It was a slow, gentle pleasure that, to my own surprise, made me harder.

"Yeees," she breathed the word onto my shaft. Her tongue slid to the base and lapped at my balls. The wet warmth tugged at me. Sunny kissed my balls, then spread her lips. She pulled me into her and began to stroke my dick again.

The two-fronted assault of pleasure absorbed me. The feeling was amazing, but seeing her do it to me was mind blowing too. I leaned down so I could keep touching her breast. I gripped. She moaned again. "Um-hmm," she gave a full-throated approval.

The sound, the sight, and sensation brought me to the edge. "I'm gonna come," I said.

"Noooope."

Instantly, she released my balls and held her index finger over my urethra. She stared up at me with lust, confidence, and yearning. "I know that you've had a chance to work on endurance. Now, don't disappoint me."

As she said this, she pulled down her pants. Those curves were unfair. She was so thick that my mouth watered at the sight of her. Her thumbs hooked through the hem and worked to pull her jeans down from the great curve of her ass.

She stood between my legs, naked and wet. I'd seen this body before, but not like this. I saw it all. She was all smooth flesh and curves. Her slit was pink and already wet. As soon as she kicked away her pants, I pulled her to me. With me sitting and her standing, my face landed squarely between her tits. They were so full that they overflowed in my hands. My face nuzzled between them, licking and kissing the nipples. I slid my hands down her sides and grabbed two big handfuls of her ass.

"Lay down," she ordered.

I flopped back onto the bed. As I did, she knelt on the mattress between my knees. "That's right, just like that." She brought a hand to her mouth and licked her fingers. Her eyes stared at me, relishing my reaction as I watched her hand move down. Her fingers slid into her wet folds and rubbed.

"Come on," I said. "Just get on me already."

"That's the spirit."

I aimed my erection up. She positioned herself over me. The labial folds gently met me as her lips had. Sweet, soft, warm, wet. The tip of my erection found the opening. There was no hesitation.

She pushed herself down. My cock pressed through the tight opening. Sheer pleasure overwhelmed me as she worked herself all the way to the base. "Hot damn, you have a nice curve," she said in a huff.

I couldn't respond. Her pussy wrapped tightly around me. Before I could move, she planted both hands on my chest and began to move.

"Yeees, stay. Stay just like that."

I gripped the bedsheets and tried to think about baseball. She grinded herself up and down my cock. The sweet rhythm of the sex entranced me. She pulled and pushed herself from tip to base, her massive ass smacking my balls and thighs with each descent.

All the while, her tits bounced. Those glorious breasts swung up and down in hypnotic swirls as she moved. I grabbed them both. "Yeees!" she said.

I pushed her breasts against her, squeezing so that her flesh spilled between my fingers. I loosened and squeezed in intervals, sometimes shifting my grip to lightly pinch her nipple.

"You got it, just like that. Smack my ass!"

My hand lashed out and spanked a beautiful, massive cheek as she smashed down onto my dick. The smack filled the room. "Oh!" she called out. Her pussy squeezed tightly around me. My cock twitched so hard that I almost worried I'd finished.

"You," I said, "are amazing."

"Say my name." She leaned forward and braced her hands on my lower chest. Her eyes stared into me as her hips worked. Instead of grinding back and forth, she lifted that perfect ass up and down. I saw the beautiful jiggle whenever she reached the top of the arc. She slammed herself down onto me. Each impact took me to Heaven. "Spank me and say my name. Please!"

"Sunny." I spanked her ass. Again, her pussy squeezed tighter. "Sunny, you're amazing. Sunny!"

The heavy smack of my hand on her ass filled the air, joining the wet slaps as she used my dick to please herself. "Yes, yes, yeees! Give me your hands."

Frantically, my hands moved up to her shoulders. She took them and wrapped her fingers through mine. Her lips went to my neck. She embraced me and pinned me down at once. All of her pushed against all of me. I gripped her hands back and reveled in the experience. Sunny had so much that she needed. She'd been pent up for a long time, and this was her way of taking everything that she needed from me, through me.

Sunny's breath grew faster. My erection twitched again. "Sunny...I'm gonna—"

"Yeees!" She pushed herself up. Her torso swung up as she kept pounding herself on me. She leaned back and braced her hands on my legs. I grabbed her hips and intensified the rhythm. I swelled inside her as she brought me toward my limit. "Yes, yes, I need you to come in me now!"

The pleasure and pressure reached the end. My hips thrust up to meet her. I pushed myself all the way inside her as my white-hot climax surged into her.

"Aaaah!" Her body went still, except for spasms, as her hand smacked over her torso. I reached for it. When she found my hand, she once again pressed it onto her breast and squeezed my hand so I groped her.

"Yeees," she moaned. "Oooh fuck!" The orgasm roiled through me and into her. We stayed there, huffing and spasming for several seconds. When the last of it left me, I fell back against the bed.

"That's good," Sunny said. "Oh, shit, I needed that."

Then, her hips began to move again. She clenched my dick anew and kept right on grinding. She stared at me. Instead of playfulness, I saw a hungry demand. "You can keep going, right? I need more."

That day, I learned that Sunny liked being in charge.

She made me sit at the edge of the bed so she could reverse cowgirl. I wrapped one hand around her breast while the other rubbed her clitoris. She heaved and moaned as she pressed and wiggled her ass against me. We kept going for hours. When I couldn't keep it up any longer, I used my fingers. We stayed there until I was drained and she was exhausted.

Both of us heaved for breath. "Holy shit," I said. "Sunny, you're amazing."

"You've said that a few times now," she said with a smile. "You're pretty good yourself."

There, in each other's arms, we fell asleep. It was just going to be a short nap. My fatigue had vanished when I opened my eyes. I sat up and noticed the angle of the sunlight. "Hey Sunny. We should probably get going. The other two are going to worry about us."

I turned around.

What the fuck?

I saw myself lying beside Sunny, both of us asleep with content smiles on our faces. Red marks from bites, grips, and smacks dotted our bodies.

What was happening? I looked down. I saw myself. I was transparent, like a ghost.

"Let's talk," a low voice spoke.

I screamed and jumped back in a less than dignified manner. Across from the bed, leaning against the wall, stood our enemy. A purple-skinned figure stared at me with burning crimson eyes.

The name slipped out of me as my heart seemed to clog my throat. "Radec."

CHAPTER
TWENTY-NINE

He guided my spectral body out of the room. We wandered through the bar. Nobody saw us. I would have expected someone to feel something from us. A chill? A tripped magic alarm. Yet, there was nothing. As we walked by Fran, she glanced toward the back room, but quickly refocused on her work.

While we moved, Radec said nothing. He'd told me to follow, and he knew that I was powerless to do anything against him. He may as well have been Freddy Krueger. He showed up in my sleep just after I had sex.

The main difference between him and Krueger was the ambiance. Radec had no flare. He walked with confident, casual steps. By reflex, I covered my crotch with my hands as we went, but luckily, I saw I was fully clothed. That brought the weirdest part of the experience. I didn't feel anything. No temperature. No touch. As we walked, we may as well have floated an inch off the ground for all the impact we had.

Radec led me out of *The Paw* and began walking toward Antrum.

What's he doing? Well, if he'd wanted to hurt me, I guess he would've done so by now. Right?

I moved faster to walk—*float?*—beside him. In the light, I got my first good look at him. He seemed less like a demon than a technicolor gargoyle. Radec was only a little taller than me, but much thicker. His purple muscles were those of a sculpture, impossibly well-defined and solid. His pecs were huge slabs and his biceps almost as big as my head. Eyes that were a flat crimson, lacking pupils like Eo, lazily took in everything around us. He had horns the same shade as his skin, curling up from above his temples. His battered gray vest and slacks had been mostly worn away by time.

"What do you want?" I finally asked.

"We're almost there."

I rolled my eyes. "Why couldn't we talk at the pub? Did you make me sleep walk through town?"

"Yes." He nodded and looked at me. There was no malice in the glance. No sadism or joy, or much of any emotion. The bluntness unnerved me more than any pervy laugh might have.

"Hey," I said. "Were you watching Sunny and I while we were..."

"I placed a spell on you while you fought my former disciple. It was set to activate when you next slept so that we might speak to each other. I did not expect you so soon. I'm disappointed that I couldn't go through my routine." He sighed. "I would have stood at the foot of your bed, amplifying the light of my eyes. It would have been a delight to see how you scrambled in the dark. I looked forward to your cries as you screamed for your companions, wondering why no one came to save you."

My spectral body felt nothing. No heat or breeze or chill, but I got goosebumps all the same. "Well," I said, "aren't you a bucket of fun and roses."

So, this is what Sunny meant about demons being dramatic.

Radec gave a soulless 'ha.' "I have been away from company for a long time. Indulge me."

I shook my head. "What about Bianca? She trusted you."

"A fine woman indeed."

"You could have saved her."

"That," he said as he looked me dead in the eye, "is not my nature."

His tone put me off. Was it a threat? A statement of fact? Both? He had no emotion or intonation in it, yet he clearly wanted me to take those words to heart. After some more walking, we arrived at the quarry.

"What do you see?" Radec asked.

"I don't want to listen to a damn monologue," I said bluntly.

"I shall try to be blunt with you, Jack. Your little nap has altered my schedule for the day as well. Let us try to solve this quickly and like adults, shall we?"

"Your schedule?" I spat. "What, did you have a brooding appointment with Batman in the afternoon?"

He gestured to the hill. "Look, mortal. This is not a network of tunnels. It is a series of hills. You do not understand because you are new to this place. Many of the tunnels below were dug long before you arrived. This place is older than Acanth. Do you truly believe that the only things living down there are goblins and myself? Did you suspect that Bianca survived from the protein of dead trolls and rock stew?"

What was he trying to say? Something else was down there? I couldn't think too hard about it. Most of me was trying to keep up with the image of the creature beside me. In the orange light of the late afternoon sun, all mystique vanished. Hearing him speak for long sentences did the same. The short phrases had been threatening commands. In his speech, I heard a slightly nasal rasp, yet his voice boomed. It rumbled through my ears and shook my bones. This thing could invade my dreams to talk to me. It would sacrifice someone who'd devoted decades to him. The evil and harm he wrought was as casual and small a pleasure as brunch.

I said nothing.

Radec pointed to the hill. "Here is my offer. As of this moment, you are a guest of my home. You may enter, but you shall go no deeper than the first level. Your intrepidness, though admirable, has gone too far. You will not pass any further or deeper than the first cavern."

That's not an offer; that's a death sentence.

"Fuck you," I spat the words quickly. Fear cracked my voice on the final syllable.

Radec sighed. "This is a warning, not a threat. You do not want to see the things which lie in places deeper and bleaker than you could imagine. You are good at mining." He pointed to the house. "If you wish for them to be safe and cared for, you will do as I say."

As he referenced the others, my blood ran cold. "Don't you dare threaten them. Tell me what you want."

Radec nodded. "That's better."

I shook my head. "Explain what the hell you want. We've exhausted the veins in that first cavern already. There's barely anything left in the places above where we fought the elemental!"

He smiled. The sunset glinted off his fangs. "Ore shall be brought to you. The four of you may continue to walk to work. Upon your arrival, the carts shall be ready and full. Gold. Copper. Iron. Even some diamonds."

What's the catch?

I didn't ask the question, but I didn't need to. He read it in my expression. "You doubt me. Let me be clear, Jack." In one step, he closed the space between us and placed a large hand on my shoulder.

This, I felt. It was uncomfortably warm. It felt like he'd burn my shoulder if his hand stayed there too long.

"You," he said, "are Acanth's savior."

I blinked several times. "What?"

He took my other shoulder and turned me around so I faced the village. "This place is in decline. It stagnated to the point of rot. Until you arrived. You've already done some fine work. The smith gains new contracts. The pub's patrons drink with mirth rather than commiseration. Even the civic workers appreciate you. What will happen when you start bringing fresh gold and riches to them? That leaves aside your reputation from battle. Imagine how they will see you. Sweet Jack. Kind Jack. True Jack. Valiant Jack. Already, two have joined your bed. How many more? All you need to do is take my offer. Accept what I deposit at the frontmost tunnel every day, and never go deeper."

For a moment, whether by his magic or my strange dream state, I saw a prospering Acanth. The buildings built up taller and larger. It expanded to have a hotel, a bank, a bakery, and so much more. Fran, Gretchen, Karma, and everyone would see me as their hero. I would be able to save this town from all its struggles. The house would grow. More people would come. And everyone would know that it was all because of me.

No fucking way I'll believe such obvious bullshit.

"Why," I asked, "did you come to me? Why not talk to all four of us if you had this offer?"

Radec didn't move. Didn't respond. The subtle motions of breathing or blinking vanished. His hand grew hotter on my shoulder. "Be careful, Jack. You do not understand of what you speak. This is not about Acanth or Antrum. This is about me talking to you. The three in that house are broken. One is an alcoholic; another emotionally disconnected; and the last incapable of being honest with herself. I do not trust them to see my offer clearly. Nor anyone in this dead village. You do not work for Acanth, but it can work for you. You cannot get ahead if you limit yourself to the level of those around you."

There, for a moment, I saw my old boss. With superpowers, sure. Glowing, evil. More charismatic. But this was that little prick at the frontmost desk, trying to make the city work for him.

"Fuck you," I said. "I'm not falling for this *Faust* bullshit."

"I see," Radec said. Suddenly, he sighed. The human mannerisms returned. "I didn't want to tell you this, Jack, but your grandfather agreed to work with me."

"Don't fucking lie to me."

"There is no lie. Why do you think there was such a boom during his ownership? We had an agreement. I alchemically altered the stone so that his crews would always and forever reap profits. In exchange, he agreed that none of his workers would dig below a certain point. Unfortunately, one of them did."

Grandpa...

Is that why he left the fortune to Tabby and them in the will? Why he gave me a potion? No, how about why he was a recluse? He'd let this thing convince him to...

No! No!

"It doesn't matter," I yelled. "You tried to kill us so many times! You admitted that you enjoy messing with me for its own sake. The rock elemental. The zombies. I can't trust a word you say, and even if I did? I don't want to be given everything, I want to earn it with these hands!"

Anger and confusion battled within me. I tried not to imagine my grandpa, sitting alone in his room and hoping that this purple bastard wouldn't decide to go against the deal.

The only thing that was certain was that this thing wasn't trustworthy.

Radec nodded. "I found you entertaining. Seeing you squirm in discomfort and struggle to survive gives me pleasure."

I shook my head. "How the fuck can you expect me to trust you, then?"

"I am here," he said. "I lay everything at your feet. Take my offer. Become the savior of Acanth. Do not disturb the parts of these hills that you do not understand. If you do not agree to this, I will kill whichever of the four of you next enters the mine."

I narrowed my eyes. "What's down there?" I asked.

Radec's red eyes bore into me. It felt like he was probing into my mind to learn my thoughts.

"What," I repeated, "is down there? Be honest with me!"

"You already believe that you're a hero." Radec chuckled. A fresh smile filled his face. "My goodness. You have walked onto this site and relied on the talents of those with experience. You have the perfect story, yes. You've even convinced many of the people of this village. But that is all you have and all you are. Now, do the smart thing. Use that story and let me handle the harsh reality."

"Fuck you," I said again. "If you wanted to do a serious deal, the other three would be here. I refuse to make any decision about Antrum without them. And don't insult my grandpa!"

Radec returned to his pseudo-pause state of unearthly stillness. "Very well. Explain to the others, then, that they will die the next time they enter the mine. All because you felt offended on behalf of a dead man. I suggest you start praying that I reconsider when next we meet."

Suddenly, his arm struck out. Claws ripped through my throat. My breaths ceased as blood poured from the wound. I gasped. Blood spurted from my neck and mouth. I couldn't breathe. My lungs burned as it filled my throat.

"Thus far," Radec said. "I have been playful. You have yet to know what happens when I put my mind to something. Be aware of that."

The world faded. My spectral body collapsed to the ground. I didn't feel the dirt. There was no sensation except the pain he'd caused.

This is part of the dream. It's not real.

Even though that was true, that didn't make the pain any less real.

Suddenly, I was back in bed. "Jaaack!" Sunny lay beside me. She was holding my face and staring at me in concerned terror. "You were writhing like you were in pain. It's just a nightmare, okay?"

My head rose and fell in thoughtless nods. It took a moment before I realized that I was covered in sweat, or that I was gasping. I could breathe. There was no pain now.

Sunny was here.

I grabbed her and held her tight. She relied on me. I relied on her. The same with the others. Our daily lives depended on each other in every way. I needed to tell them.

"It was the demon," I said. "We need to talk to the others. Now!"

CHAPTER
THIRTY

We scrambled into our clothes and rushed out of *The Paw*. A quick *thanks* from me and a hug from Sunny was all that Fran got by way of explanation.

"Will explain later. Thanks again, bye!" I yelled over my shoulder.

"Sorry for the mess!" Sunny added.

With each step, I felt more certain of my decision. Was it right? Maybe not, but I knew what I wanted to do.

Please let the other three agree.

We made it back to the house in record time.

As we got close, Eo ran out the front door. With a tear-streaked face, she leaped into Sunny's arms. "I'm so glad you came back! I was worried that you hated us, and I can't stand the thought of losing you again! Please don't leave us! I know it's hard, but I need you, and Tabby needs you, and Antrum needs you! There's no Antrum unless you're here, and I've been freaking out because this reminds me of all those days when I didn't see anybody and Tabby never left, and you were never sober, and it really freaked me out! I like the models, but I can't go back to spending every moment of my life in the loft again! You shouldn't be alone, and I don't want to be alone! Please stay with us!"

Eo gave her impassioned speech in a flurry of breaths, some syllables tripping on others in their rush. Sunny held her, confused and touched.

"I'm not going anywhere," Sunny said.

Meanwhile, Tabby stood in the open doorway. Her eyes flitted between us, to her feet, and back to Sunny. An undercurrent of cold silence ran beneath the scene. Tabby and Sunny kept neutral expressions. The months of emotional and financial strain pulsed between them. For a moment, I feared that we'd lose our team again.

"I'm sorry," Tabby said. "Even if I didn't think the demon was real, I should have respected your fear. That wasn't cool of me to dismiss you."

Yes!

Sunny nodded. "It's not your fault. I'm still mad and freaked out, but it's not your fault."

With that, Tabby took a deep breath. "Okay, we need to talk. Do you two want to shower first, or should it happen now?"

"Radec spoke to me," I said.

Instantly, Eo's feathers bristled, and Tabby's tail struck out. "Dreams," I added. "Or astral projection? Or he went into my imagination? I don't fully get it, but he showed up, and I talked to him. Let's go inside, and I'll explain everything."

The four of us moved to the kitchen, which had somehow become our de facto meeting place. Eo made tea and toast for Sunny and I, who took it as our overdue lunch. Most of it went cold as I explained everything. They demanded more information. Every word, facial expression, change of pitch. Everything I knew about Radec became part of the conversation. There was nothing too minor.

When I finished, I turned to Eo and asked, "Do you think there's a chance that he's telling the truth about something else deeper in the mine?"

"Yes," Eo said. Her lack of hesitation caught me off guard. "He's right. Bianca needed to eat something. There must have been some underground vegetation or, likely in addition to such, living creatures that we've yet to encounter."

"What could be down there?" Tabby asked.

"Whatever it is," Sunny said. "Can't be worse than a demon."

"Exactly!" I clapped my hands. The more I talked about my time with Radec, the more I considered something. It was a deranged thought, but I clung to it. "We talked about Radec hiding down there. Escaped the hells, all that stuff. What if he's not just hiding? What if he's stuck there?"

"Explain," Eo and Tabby demanded in unison.

"Alright, here, I have some questions. The guy's been here for centuries. We can't touch him down there because of weird multidimensional jurisdiction issues or whatever, but what would happen if this full-on demon started

305

walking around the village? What happens if he leaves the mine and is seen by non-humans?"

"It'd be a major incident," Tabby said. "It wouldn't matter what anyone thought. Literal portals would open to take him by any means necessary."

"I thought so!" I clapped again. "So, in a sense, he's trapped down there. Why else would he come to me instead of anyone else? Why not talk to all of us if there was literally anything worthwhile about his offer?"

"Get to the poooint!" Sunny said.

"He is," Eo said. "We know the laws of the land, we know that Radec can't go on a rampage in this world without consequences. Radec knew that it'd be a risk to communicate with the rest of us for that alone."

"I think that he's bluffing," I said. "He's not that tough. He's had to deal with threats from above and below. Or maybe not threats. Work? He's tired! I think Radec is tired and a coward. What if he didn't help Bianca not because he didn't care, but because he was scared that we'd kill him?"

The more I spoke, the more desperate and unhinged my voice sounded. It was crazy. I'd basically argued that we should get Palpatine now that we'd handled Darth Vader. Crazy though it was, I believed it.

We can kill this thing.

"Radec said that you interfered with his schedule," Eo said. "Maybe he was in the middle of dealing with something. I think that there's some good reason to believe your theory about other monsters in the deep. He's trying to rule his little slice of the dark, but we keep taking his attention. The resurrected goblins. The elemental. That takes energy. Maybe he's stressed and weakened."

"He wants us to think he's got his shit together," Sunny said. "But he's scared and making it up as he goes."

"Improvising." Tabby nodded. "Good chance of that, but I don't think that we should call him scared. A frightened demon is still a demon. It's a serious threat."

"Yeah," I agreed. "A serious threat that's insulted us, taken our mine hostage, and now lies at the most vulnerable it will ever be."

Silence pervaded the room. Glances flew between them. None of fear. Uncertainty, of course, just as I knew I'd feel if I let myself think about the situation. The looks between the three grew steadier.

"I want to fight this thing," I said. "I know that that's not fair, but I think we can—"

"I'm in!" Sunny yelled.

I did a double-take. I'd expected her to be the hardest to convince.

She continued, "I have let that thing terrify me for fucking years! Now, he's some little bitch that tried to make a bad deal with Jack? No! Fuuuck that. You guys know what I thought when I got my first drink at *The Paw* earlier? 'This tastes like shiiit!' It was hard to swallow. I felt like I was stuck there. I'm scared of that thing, for sure, but I'm more scared of going back to how things were before."

"Ditto." Eo pointed at Sunny and gave a decisive nod. "I believe that I summed up my thoughts a few minutes ago.

I'm ready to take care of this thing. Just no monkey missiles."

We looked at Tabby. She had her arms crossed.

"I hate to be the one to say this," she said, "but we need to be aware that there's a chance that we're wrong. Plus, once we deal with this thing, there are more monsters below. Those are some serious threats."

I grinned. *'Once we deal with it.'* Even her posture radiated confidence. Arms folded under her chest, hips cocked to the side, and tail slinking back and forth.

"Tabby," I said. "Will you fight with us?"

"Of course I will. Let's do this quick. Maybe we can catch it off guard."

The four of us practically jumped into our gear. Eo gave us her precious stamina potions to remove any fatigue from the previous battle—and make sure that Sunny was fully sober. There were no scrolls left. Eo had exhausted a lot of her magic. This would be a straightforward fight.

Hopefully.

Sunny and Eo ran out the door first. While I was in the back with Tabby, I leaned toward her and asked, "Is this a bad idea?"

"Maybe. All I know is that I can't live with that thing so close to us."

Together, we marched to Antrum. Unlike the morning, we had confidence and purpose. Sunny almost broke into a run, each step seeming to bring her a new level of righteous fury.

Alright, I thought, *final boss time.*

Once more, we walked into the quarry. We entered the tunnel.

Suddenly, there was a sound of hissing air. I didn't need to look back to know what was happening. Fog. There was a new barrier at the mine entrance. Unlike the first time, however, we were trapped inside.

Looks like we're not sneaking up on him.

CHAPTER
THIRTY-ONE

"So," Tabby said, "this is what it feels like from the other side of the barrier."

"Less talk," Sunny said. "Fight only. Kill Radec. No problem."

She gripped her battle hammer like a drowning person clinging to a life raft. Our nerves were building up. I thought she wanted to convince herself as she said it. But she was right.

"Radec's trying to freak us out," I said. "He's just a melodramatic asshole. We can do this!"

I marched at the head of the party, picking up speed into a jog. Eo kept pace with me. From the sound of footsteps, the other two followed behind.

"He's waiting," Eo said.

We entered the opening into the first cavern. I asked, "How can you—"

Suddenly, a mine cart shot through the air at me. Eo struck her hands out and yelled. A blast of hurricane force wind knocked it off course as I dove to the ground. It grazed my sleeve and embedded itself into the wall with a deafening crunch of metal and crack of stone. Pebbles trickled down as a spider web of cracks spread over the wall.

Holy shit!

My heart felt like it was going to jump out of my throat. "Thanks, Eo."

"You idiots," Radec's calm voice sounded from all around us. "You had a chance."

The four of us moved further into the cavern. Soon, we were surrounded by open space. We held formation with our backs to each other, so there was no angle for a surprise attack. Eyes and ears tuned to every possible. We knew this cavern as well as the estate.

The call is coming from inside the house, I thought bitterly.

"Show yourself!" Tabby yelled.

A stone hurled from above. Sunny crushed it to pieces with her hammer.

"I suppose," his voice echoed from all sides, "that this is my lesson."

A jagged piece of metal, torn from a cart, rushed at me. I knocked it to the ground with my ax. That strike alone might have killed me if I hadn't leveled up so much.

"Where are you, Radec!" I demanded.

"I gave you a chance," he snarled.

More rocks and bits of metal flew at us. We blocked them. Sunny and I rushed back and forth, the best suited for it.

"Can he teleport?" I asked.

"I think he's just fast," Eo said.

A boulder as large as my head flew straight at me.

"Duck!" I yelled.

Everyone hit the dirt as the deadly stone flew overhead. My gaze flew back to see a massive purple blur rushing me. I tried to raise my ax, but there wasn't enough time. Radec gripped the handle just below the blade and kicked. His heel planted itself beneath my ribs. My body folded around the foot. I thought I was going to break in half. Instead, he knocked me back as if I were nothing. As I recoiled, Radec tore the ax from my grasp and threw it far behind him. I collided into Sunny, knocking us both to the ground.

Radec didn't hesitate. He opened his hands to show claws at their tips.

He slashed toward Eo. She dove back to dodge. Tabby lashed out with her sword. It was a feint. Radec sidestepped Tabby. His elbow slammed into her face. Cartilage crunched and blood spewed. Tabby staggered back.

During the attack, Eo threw two kunai. One sunk into Radec's chest while the other bit into his cheek. He sneered. His jaw unhinged to reveal a cavern of fangs that bared itself at Eo. Suddenly, a hellish shriek blasted from his maw. Instantly, Eo wailed in agony, collapsed, and clutched her ears. Blood dripped through her fingers.

Sunny, back on her feet, pounced. "Diiie!"

Radec spun to her with a smirk. He ducked, and his body coiled under her with the boneless slither of a snake. He lunged under her and struck his fist up to her tail. His fingers grasped it, yanked back to destroy her balance, swung her over his head, and smashed her onto the stone. She left blood and teeth on the floor.

"No!" I sprinted.

Radec barely seemed to notice me. He blocked my first punch without effort. My second connected with his face. The hard impact of knuckle on cheek knocked him back. He withdrew, stunned. The same realization occurred to us both: I could hurt him.

In that moment of hesitation, Tabby's short sword slashed across his back. Black blood sprayed from the wound. He howled.

Two more kunai sailed through the air. One lodged in his veiny neck. The other in his chest. I threw another punch.

Radec jumped. His bleeding mass launched to the ceiling of the cavern. The deadly claws sank into the stone and scurried into the crag where goblins had once hid in an ambush.

"Face us, coward!" I yelled.

The words almost made me hurl. That kick made everything hurt. My insides felt pureed. A painful cough tore up through my esophagus. Blood spurted between my lips and flooded my chin.

"Cheeeap shot," Sunny grumbled as she pulled herself from the floor. The stone had indented beneath her.

"Hypocrite," Radec replied from his hidden spot. "For how many battles have you relied on your only magic user? In each fight, you hide behind the owl. Always, you rely upon her. No longer."

Tabby rushed to Eo's side and helped her to her feet. Eo was shaken, but she kept a brave face. "I can't hear," Eo said. "I can't hear," over and over, eyes flitting around with more kunai at the ready.

Another stone flew from a crag. I pulled Sunny back and onto her feet, blinking at the geyser of debris on impact. More stones rained down. Without my ax, I couldn't block them. Eo floundered, Tabby struggled to protect her.

The more we dodged, the more we clumped together. Sunny, the only one with a weapon to handle this, moved faster and faster. She became Thor with a gymnast's baton. We crouched low so she had space to swing and spin. Pebbles and debris rained onto us as smashes and cracks filled the air. *Crash! Crash! Boom!* Sunny knocked them aside or shattered them.

"Four against one, and still you cannot win!" Radec yelled.

Sunny didn't retort. She was too focused, too tired.

He's wearing her down!

Suddenly, a violet blur fell onto one of the cart tracks. Both hands struck out and grabbed the metal lines of the track. With a roar, Radec ripped long jagged chunks from the line. They tore out, broken and gnarled metal at both ends like jagged spears.

"Oh fuuuck!" Sunny said. The word came out a pant, heavy with exhaustion.

Radec rushed at us. Like a demonic Zeus with lightning bolts, he cast the spears at us one after another.

Adrenaline took over. Nothing existed except the impending chance of death. Sunny's hammer arced downward. She wouldn't be able to deflect both. Even if she could, Radec sprinted right behind.

I have to do something!

Sparks flew. The too-near clang of steel on steel rattled my brain as Sunny knocked the first aside. The second spear sang toward her heart. I rushed in front of it. My hands closed around it.

The jagged metal bit into my palms and fingers. The force of momentum threatened to either slice through me or knock me off my feet. Blood seeped from my palms as the metal pierced muscle.

Suddenly, Sunny's hammer flashed in front of me and knocked the weapon away. Unfortunately, Radec followed right behind.

"Dive!" I screamed as I dove to the left.

Sunny rolled to the right, hauling Eo with her. Tabby stayed, sword ready.

Radec's claws fell toward her. She hissed. Her body became a leaf on the wind, weaving around his impossible speed with her usual, impossible fluidity. He had too much momentum. Radec's massive body moved onward. Tabby's sword flashed up and slashed a fresh wound across his back.

The demon snarled and whirled on her. He didn't run. The fire of unknown hells burned as he turned, planted his feet, and prepared to launch himself at Tabby. We needed to keep him down here. If he kept wearing us out and chipping away at us, we couldn't make it.

But that didn't make it a fair fight.

Dammit! What do we do?

I ignored the overwhelming pain in my hands. It felt like my palms were going to split open. Nearby, the bit of the track lay bent and sharp as hell. One section had been dulled by the impact of Sunny's hammer. I grabbed it and ran.

Meanwhile, Tabby struggled to keep away from Radec's attacks. Fangs, claws, and knuckles rained down upon her. She drifted under blows and deflected claws. I'd never seen her move so fast, but there was no way she'd be able to keep it up.

"Radec!" I screamed.

Sure, try the most obvious distraction in the world.

Radec paid me no mind. He continued his assault. His face contorted into impatient fury. With a stomp, his jaw unhinged as it had earlier. Terror propelled me forward as Tabby lifted her sword in vain.

At the first awful note of the sonic attack, there was a blast of wind.

"Go back to Hell!" Sunny careened through the air. The steel head of her battle hammer crashed into Radec's side. His awful shriek went mute as his entire body bent around the hammer. Ribs cracked and tendons ripped in an awful symphony.

I looked at Eo. She was pale as snow and unconscious on the ground. The dual spells must have pushed her to her limit.

Radec almost staggered back, but the demon caught himself. His foot stamped into the stone to steady himself. His hand came down, grabbed Sunny's wrist as it clutched the hammer, and pulled her to him. His great forehead crashed against hers with a blast of thunder. Sunny's head snapped back on her neck as he tossed her across the cavern.

As he did, I attacked. I drove the metal point into his side as Tabby stabbed into his abdomen. Black blood rushed over our hands and down our wrists.

"Go back to hell!" we echoed Sunny's sentiment.

We'd both attacked, but Radec looked at me. I had never known hate like what looked at me in that moment. This was a prideful creature who believed himself incapable of being killed. A coward who disguised his fear as cunning. All his life, he had arranged the world so that he would survive, and this hypocrite didn't even notice the ways he stacked the game in his favor.

He hated me for existing in his presence without his permission. Despite the blood that ran from him and all the damage we'd done, that look frightened me more than anything I'd experienced.

Don't overthink it!

Instinct saved me. I released the weapon and ducked back as his claws tore through my coveralls. Tabby pulled her sword free and stabbed again into his thigh. Radec didn't try to dodge. Instead, he leaned into her strike and drove his fist just below her eye. She tumbled across the stone like a ragdoll.

While he attacked Tabby, I noticed something: Eo's kunai was still stuck in his side. I jumped onto his back. Wrapped my arm around his massive neck and squeezed as tightly as I could. Radec tried to gasp. His throat constricted beneath my bicep. My own strength would have shocked me if I'd thought about it. The cords of tendon and muscle bent under my strength. Radec floundered, stunned and shocked at what this mere mortal could do to him. He didn't even notice as I pulled the kunai from his side.

He drove his claws into my forearm. I grunted through the blinding agony and stabbed the kunai into his eye.

Radec tried to howl, but not even a gasp escaped. His claws hacked my arm open. I stabbed him in the face again and again. His mouth gasped and sputtered, but he couldn't breathe. Soon, he tripped on a bit of stone. We fell together.

Tabby's sword, still buried in his thigh, hit first. Radec's cry of pain died in his throat. He twisted away from the sword to fall on his back. At the last moment, I pushed myself off him. We hit the ground side by side.

Both of us lay still for an instant, gasping for breath. My sight ebbed and flowed. My minced arm hung limp. I didn't know how long I could stay awake. With all my effort, I pushed up. Memory and instinct guided my movements. Not even that. Desperation. Need.

My good hand found the hilt of Tabby's sword and ripped it free of Radec's thigh. Radec hissed and sprung toward me.

I plunged the sword between his ribs. My entire body fell into the attack as if I were trying to tackle him. The blade slid clean through.

Suddenly, two things happened. Radec's body transformed into a million burning embers that flashed bright and burned into nothing like Hell's snowflakes. At the same time, the adrenaline surge hit harder than ever.

My heart slammed against my ribcage. I thought it'd burst out of me *Alien* style. All my muscles went taut as electric adrenaline fired through every vein.

"Ah!" I screamed and leaped to my feet. Aside from the echoes of my primal roar, the cavern was silent. Eo's eyes began to flutter open. Sunny had begun to push herself up on shaky limbs. Tabby groaned.

I felt like a god.

Too bad it was only a feeling. I was still bleeding out. How much had already drained from my arm and hands? My last thought before my body crumpled to the floor was *Hooray for our side.*

CHAPTER
THIRTY-TWO

The fight lasted only a few minutes, but the recovery took several days.

Eo had managed to stabilize me while Tabby staggered into town for medical attention. The sight of Tabby, with her broken face and battered limbs, had sent half the village into a frenzy. We'd been so eager to rush into the mine that we hadn't thought to tell anyone about our insane plan. The village came together to take care of us. Gretchen sent her magic cart to fetch us and carry us to the small local hospital.

The processes of healing, even with magic, were long and complicated. Did I even wake up in the first few days? There were flashes, moments of voices and faces. Bits of light. Clumps of speech, but they were disjointed and rare. I had no awareness then, save for scrambled thoughts.

Radec appeared in all my nightmares. Moments from the attack played on shuffle. Each time, it felt as if I were still there. The terror of being about to die, about to lose the three people who'd become my life, remained just as strong every time. I expected that it would last for a long time.

The more I saw it, the more it bothered me. After all his drama, he was just a cocky asshole. The bastard had believed that he could take care of us alone. Had he used up his magic? Why not summon another elemental or zombies? Was he magically exhausted? Was he just so angry that he wanted it to be more personal?

I didn't know. I probably never would.

At least he's gone now. We won. We sent him back to his rotten home.

The victory felt strange. Maybe because our recovery was so intensive.

Sunny had been confined to her bed. Her skull had been cracked and several of her bones broken. It took several potions and stitches before they were certain that there was no brain damage.

Eo was in the best shape, overall. Frail, but awake. They helped her regain her hearing. If I hadn't known her, I might have guessed that she was okay. She slept a lot, though. She'd depleted her magical energy, and she was too weak to eat solid foods for two days.

Tabby had required the most spells. Her nose had needed magical reconstruction. They gave her a normal anesthetic before the surgery.

Meanwhile, I recovered in a hospital bed. They gave me salves and potions and an IV. Blood transfusions weren't an option, because of my non-magical nature.

Maybe that level up saved me. I had no idea.

The four of us were kept in the same room. So long as one of us was awake, we were checking on the others. Well, as much as we could. There were few moments of daylight when we didn't have a visitor.

Every person in Acanth stopped by to see us. A few came multiple times. Fran spent almost all her free time with us. Gretchen pleaded for us to all recover and get back to business. Store-owners left gifts of their wares. At one point, Karma stopped in to give us flowers. Among the hazy memories of the first days, I heard her say, "Thank you. I'm sorry."

Eo got the go-ahead to leave the hospital and return to the house, but she refused. Tabby received her discharge second. Likewise, she refused. The two of them waited with us. Eo stayed glued to Sunny's side, apologizing over and over for using her as a weapon again. Sunny praised her for saving us. They hugged often.

Finally, the day came for us to leave. "Good morning to our conquering heroes!" Fran hip-checked our door open and walked in with a tray of three coffees and a tea. "Today is the big day. You can rejoin the living."

"Too soon," Eo said. "That wording feels weird after the necromancer."

"Alright." Fran shrugged and put a coffee in my hands. Her attention to detail amazed me as I saw her tray. Mine was black. Tabby's was light with milk. Sunny's had an almond color from a pinch of cream and a lot of sugar.

"Thanks," I said. "*The Paw* was the first place I was going to visit."

"I was looking forward to it too," Tabby said.

"Good to know." Fran looked at Sunny. "A few of my regulars wonder if your time off has made you soft at pool."

"Oooh?" Sunny's left eyebrow rocketed toward the ceiling. "Tell them to see me at the table tonight. You three come, too. We're not spending a penny on food or drink tonight."

"You won't do that, anyway," Fran said. Next, she clapped her hands. Two people with aprons with *The Paw* logo rolled carts into the room. Each of us got a platter with tons of cut fruit and yogurt. "On behalf of the regulars," Fran explained. "They've also paid for your groceries, lunch, dinner—"

"What?" Tabby asked.

"Yeah," I said. "What?"

Eo pointed at us. "What they said."

Fran and her employees looked surprised. "You must have noticed. Acanth loves you. The four of you defeated a necromancer and a demon on the same day! You're heroes to the people of Acanth!"

"We have noticed the visitors," Eo said. "We appreciate the well-wishes."

"You've seen nothing yet." Fran shook her head. A bright grin lifted the corners of her lips. "Well, anyway, I'll leave you to it. If you want a second cup, please stop by."

All four of us looked confused at her. The wagging tail made it obvious that she was hiding something. One of her employees rolled her eyes when she saw the tail.

"Okaaay?" Sunny said.

With that, Fran and her employees left.

I didn't say anything. The coffee smelled too good, and the food was too pretty. "Any idea what that was about?" Tabby asked as she lapped at her coffee.

Eo shrugged.

Guess we'll find out.

Soon, the four of us were back in regular clothes. Someone had gone to the house to get them for us. After days in old-fashioned gowns, it felt good to be in jeans and a tee. Both Eo's and Sunny's were video game related, as usual. Eo's showed the Shinra Corporation logo, while Sunny's had a cartoon barrel with a 'DK' stamped onto them.

Caffeinated, the four of us left the hospital.

Immediately, people swarmed us. Fran and Gretchen applauded as regulars from the Paw showered us with cheers. "Antrum is open!" someone yelled.

"It's staying open!" someone else shouted.

"We have demon slayers in town!"

The four of us had no idea what to do. The physical close-ness and audio overload made Eo look ready to crawl out of her skin. Sunny smirked and basked in the attention. Tabby focused on the people she knew best and returned the hugs.

I had no idea what to do as two cow women rushed up,

grabbed my wrists, sandwiched me between them, and planted big sloppy kisses on my cheeks.

I must have blushed like a tomato. Tabby smirked and caught my eye. My arms were captive between two valleys of cleavage, so I couldn't shrug. A head tilt communicated my feelings on the situation.

Soon, the crowd cleared and gave us some space.

A bunny woman whom I knew to be a tailor approached with bundles of fabric in her hands.

"It's not much," she said. "Consider this a gift from me."

She passed a pressed square of the green fabric into each of our hands. It was thin but durable. I unfolded it to find that it was a cloak.

Ha, I really am an adventurer now.

"It has our names!" Eo yelled. Her feet bounced excitedly as she looked at the stitched letters on the back. I turned mine around, and instantly, my mood soured. It said "Jackal."

Sunny burst out laughing. "That's too good!"

The tailor was confused. "Sunny was the only one awake when I came in. I wanted some measurements to go by. She told me that you'd prefer that. I admit that I was a little surprised. You give a friendlier vibe, but to each their own."

My lips set in a line. "Well," I said. "It's an Antrum thing."

We tried to move, but the crowd had grown. A few people emptied from the civic center. People who had been doing their daily tasks looked over. When someone yelled, "They're awake!" others came to join.

We practically floated on the crowd into *The Paw* for a second round of coffee. The people offered everything. Did we want breakfast? Booze? More than anything, they demanded to know about our experiences.

"What did it look like?"

"Which one of you killed it?"

"Is it true that there was a necromancer?"

Sunny became the lead storyteller. She leapt onto the pool table and used a pool stick to act as her hammer. Eo cast some small spells of light and minor sound effects. Tabby kept near, correcting the most egregious exaggerations.

Meanwhile, I stayed by the bar. As much as I enjoyed the sight, I didn't have the energy. It was bizarre. There wasn't a feeling of victory. I was too relieved to be alive to be overwhelmed. Still, I loved it.

A few people stopped by to talk to me. They asked how I came to Acanth. Where did I learn to mine? What weapon did I prefer? Was Sunny just as energetic at home?

With the bombastic theater show in the corner, I had some casual conversations. We shot the breeze. They kept looking over to Sunny's performance. "Go watch," I said. "This is one of the few times she'll do this sober."

"Good point," one of them said, the goat woman, Hilda. "Hope you're coming back tonight. We hope to have a toast for you guys."

"Wouldn't miss it," I said.

The crowd exhausted me, so I snuck back to the edge of the bar. Just as I was about to order one, Fran pushed a fresh coffee toward me. "How does it feel to be a non-story?" she said.

"What do you mean?" I asked.

"Nobody cares about the human man, anymore. You're the guy who works Antrum. Everyone here knows your face from seeing you in town every day. There isn't even any gossip about you anymore. You're a member of Acanth now. It comes at a price, of course. We expect you to stay."

I laughed. "No place I'd rather be."

EPILOGUE

"Remember," Eo said as she tightened the headlamp on my helmet. "If there is any sign of trouble whatsoever, rush back or call for help. This is merely a pre-emptive scouting mission to ensure that there is no immediate danger to Acanth Village."

"Okay," I nodded. We were in the slanted corridor. All of us were too curious—worried?—about what lay beneath. Had Radec been full of shit when he talked about other creatures? Maybe. If so, we wanted to check on the tunnel beyond that bottom cavern beyond where we'd fought Bianca.

Sunny and Eo had chosen to stay here, in the last section of electric light. Eo couldn't handle being in the place where she'd killed Bianca. Sunny decided to stay with her. Tabby and I agreed that this was purely a reconnoiter mission. Go in, check, and leave.

I looked at Sunny. She shrugged, "I neeeed to know what's down here, but there's no way in hell that I'm going back down there now."

"Alright," Tabby said. She tapped my arm. "Let's do this."

So, the two of us began a new descent. At first, we said nothing. It surprised me how little fear I felt. Maybe it was the headlamp. Maybe the level up. I felt like I had a decent chance of taking down anything that approached us.

When we got back to the cavern where we'd nearly burned to death, I whistled. The floor and ceiling had large patches of black soot. "I don't remember so many scorch marks," I said.

"We didn't have a lot of time to pay attention to small details," Tabby said. It seemed bigger without a fiery spirit, but of course it did. With a few more steps, our goal came into view. A tunnel opening. For the first time, I noticed its shape. It was a clean, large rectangle, like a doorway.

"Hey Jack," Tabby said. "What are we?"

Um, what?

"That's, uh, kind of a big question. I mean, I get it. Ever since what happened with Bianca, I've been thinking about it too. What does it mean to be alive, human or animal person? There are a lot of—"

"No," she said. "You and me. What are we? What is..." she gestured to the space between us, "this?"

Oh.

"I see," I nodded. "Honestly, I'm not sure either. Whatever it is, for what it's worth, I like it."

"Me too, don't get me wrong. You're good around the house. Amazing in bed. I really appreciate you."

I stopped. "This feels like a break-up."

"No!" Tabby's ears and tail struck up. "It's not. Um, can we keep walking? I don't want to stay down here too long."

"Okay. What is it you're trying to say?"

Tabby searched for words. Her hands moved in front of her, opening and closing as if she were trying to get the words from the air. "Well, I don't just appreciate you, Jack. It's a bit more than that." Her tail went wild, curling back and forth. Her pupils were wide. "I know that you care about Antrum and us. That's awesome. It's important to me that you work as a part of the Antrum Mine and Estate. And all Acanth! Of course. Don't get me wrong. Why are you smiling like that?"

I shook my head. "I'm sorry. You're just adorable."

She blushed almost as red as her hair. I stopped her at the head of the tunnel and took her hand. "Tabby, I have no idea what we are, but I'm enjoying the hell out of it. I don't just appreciate and respect you. I want you."

Despite the light of my headlamp, her pupils widened. "I want you too."

We found ourselves in each other's arms before we knew it. It felt natural. My hand fit perfectly in the small of her back. Her arms slid around me. Our lips made contact, relishing in the shared warmth. We pulled each other close, trying to feel the other's warmth through our gear. We settled with her forehead against my shoulder. "I don't know," she said, "how to manage us doing this while working together."

"Me neither," I said. "But if you're up for it, I want to enjoy whatever we have for however long it lasts."

She raised her head. A warm smile softened her features. Warm tears of happiness welled in her eyes. I kissed just beneath her eyelid. "Now," I said, "we need to refocus or I won't be able to think about anything other than fucking you against the rocks."

"No sex in the mine." She chuckled. "I'm drawing a line there."

"Fair," I said.

With that, we went further. At some point, our hands found their way together. Our fingers laced together as we marched.

I have no idea what I'm doing, but I love it.

Sadly, we didn't have much time to relish the moment. We moved down the tunnel. It was just like the entrance, unnaturally smooth. After several seconds, it went down.

Stairs.

"What the hell?" I asked.

"I don't like this," Tabby said.

Well, we've already gone this far. Might as well take a note from Alice: once you enter the rabbit hole you may as well go all the way to the bottom.

Down we went. The staircase, perhaps unsurprisingly, was long. At the bottom, we found a door with a latch instead of a handle. It was massive. The two of us decided to press on with a shrug. I grabbed the latch and both of us pushed with our shoulders.

The great door swung open. Shafts of crystalline light pierced the crack of the door and soon drowned my head-lamp. Tabby and I found ourselves on a lip of a cave wall, overlooking the largest cavern I had ever seen.

"What is this?" Tabby asked.

In front of and below us was a thriving society. Light danced from crystals all around. Gold, onyx, diamond, ruby. Every precious stone glinted in a beautiful rainbow. On the outside were countless stalactites and stalagmites. On many of these, mirrors were fixed, reflecting and redirecting the light.

Below us, in a great egg-shaped bowl, was a city. At least the same size as Acanth with more buildings. Buildings of stone, some with mushroom gardens and statues, filled the space. Many of the buildings had mirrors atop them of all shapes and sizes, directed every which way to spread the light into a technicolor daytime. In the center was a tall, rectangular building topped with a square with four open sides. Instead of a clock, though, it was open. A great ball of warm light like a miniature sun shone there, casting its light to the gems and mirrors.

"Binoculars?" I said.

"In the pack," Tabby pulled the backpack that Eo had made us bring off her shoulders. From inside, she gave me a pair of binoculars. I looked down to the city streets.

Below, there was a bazaar. Vendors set up pavilions with wooden stands and canopy roofs. What struck me most were the people. They had scales dotted around their body like tattoos. Large eyes with vertical slits. Black nails. Wings were folded on their backs.

"Here be dragonfolk," I said numbly.

"That's impossible." Tabby stole the binoculars from me.

Good thing, too. My legs felt weak. I stepped back and leaned against the doorway. They weren't dragons, in the same way that Tabby wasn't a cat. Dragon people. An entire society of them, under the village of Acanth.

"Holy shit..." Tabby said. "What is this?"

"I don't know," I said.

"How long have they been here?"

"I don't know."

"Did they know Radec?"

"I don't know."

I pushed off the doorway and looked at the other side of our large door. It matched the rest of the cavern wall. "Hey Tabby. When this is closed, there'd be no way to know that it was a door. These guys might not know that there's a way out."

"Huh..." Tabby said. Her movements were stiff.

What the fuck do we even do now?

"So," I said with a cracking voice. "What do you want to do?"

333

"Well," Tabby nodded. "I plan to go to *The Paw*, get so drunk I forget this, and deal with it another day."

"I like that plan."

We closed the door and made our retreat as quickly as we could without breaking into a run. When we got to Sunny and Eo, we gave the short version, pushed on, and promised to deal with it later.

For once, we just wanted to relax. After everything, that seemed fair. Eo didn't like the idea, but Sunny was itching to get back into her element.

The four of us arrived at the Paw in the early afternoon. Fran beamed to see us. "Couldn't wait?" she asked.

"That's right," Tabby said. "I need wine."

"Beer," Sunny and I said together.

"Club soda," Eo requested.

The four of us moved to the bar. As Fran prepared the drinks, she said, "By the way, Jack and Sunny, I understood the circumstances, but try not to make such a mess next time."

"Mess?" I asked.

"Oooh shit," Sunny muttered.

Fran nodded toward the side hall and said her next words with casual bluntness. "The room."

Oh.

"Room?" Tabby repeated. Her ears began to lift in suspicion. "What happened, Fran?"

Our bartender hesitated. Her gold eyes looked over the group of us. She tried to assess our relationships to each other in real time.

"It's nooot a big deal," Sunny said. "Jack and I fucked."

"You two did what?!" Tabby asked.

"Oh pleeease," Sunny said. "At least I got a soundproofed room. I didn't hog the only dick in town for myself and wake up my roommates with 'stretching routines.'"

"I...That's..." Her cheeks went bright red. "Fran, wine!"

Eo stood. "I'm gonna play darts."

"Weeell," Sunny nudged my shoulder. There was no regret or judgment in her eyes. "Say something."

I looked around. Fran kept a professional countenance but clearly wanted the gossip. Tabby was confused and frustrated, but unsure what to say.

I'm gonna be here for a while.

"Well," I said, "I'm still figuring things out, but I'm happy to call Antrum my home, and you three my crazy family."

"*Step*-family?" Sunny raised her eyebrows with a cheeky grin.

"Very funny." I gave Sunny a wink and then called to the bar, "Fran, we're gonna need shots!"

To be continued...

Want to read my upcoming story in fully-edited chapters

before anyone else? Check out my Patreon! https://www.
patreon.com/kirkmason

**Free ways to support my writing career, allowing me to
continue writing these books:** It would mean the world
to me if you picked one. I put them in order of importance.

Consider giving me an honest review.

Post about this book in the harem Facebook groups,
Discord servers, and Reddit subreddits.

Join my Discord server: https://discord.gg/jVeUnX4Juf

∫

About the Author

Thank you so much for reading my story! It was written by a regular guy in his thirties, paying rent by tapping on a keyboard. When I'm not writing, I enjoy watching tv shows like Firefly, Steins Gate, and The Witcher. I jog to keep fit, and then ruin it at night by drinking Guinness. I fell in love with the harem genre for the way it lets men be men, leaving behind the worries and responsibilities of their life to experience something crazy and out of this world. But then again, sometimes it's enough just to chill out on the farm with your harem—because real life can be hectic, and you need to get a little cozy. Whatever the story, a review can make or break its success, especially at the beginning of its launch. That's why I'm asking you, if you enjoyed it, to leave an honest review. And please try to avoid mentioning spoilers.

Want to report a typo, or just need to reach me? kirkmason-books@gmail.com

Why not post a review of my book in one of these wonderful groups?

https://www.facebook.com/groups/haremlit https://www.facebook.com/groups/HaremGamelit https://www.facebook.com/groups/dukesofharem https://www.facebook.com/groups/221378869062151 https://www. https://www. https://www.

Made in the USA
Monee, IL
12 January 2024

51638259R00199